Untouchable

IVY SMOAK

To my Facebook group - the Ivy Smoaksters.

I couldn't do this without your encouragement and love.

This one's for you!

CHAPTER 1

Friday

The Untouchables. That's what everyone called the Hunter and Caldwell brothers. At least, it was Kennedy's nickname for them. And since she was the only one that talked to me at my new school, I took her word for it.

The nickname probably came from the fact that they were exorbitantly wealthy. Old wealth. The kind that wasn't flaunted around. But you could tell by the way they carried themselves. I watched the four of them walk past my locker.

Or maybe the name just referred to the fact that they were so beautiful it was almost hard to look at them. James and Robert Hunter were classically tall, dark, and handsome. Mason and Matthew Caldwell were also tall and handsome, but their hair was lighter. It almost looked like it was spun from gold. The same gold as the Rolex watches hidden beneath the sleeves of their blazers.

No matter the reason for their nickname, it was an ironic one. Because I'd only been going to this school for a week and I already wanted to touch them.

The sound of a camera flash made me stop gawking and turn my attention to Kennedy.

"What are you reading, Brooklyn?" she asked without looking up from the display on her camera. She was leaning against the locker beside mine, not at all phased by the Greek gods walking by. Maybe after a year I'd learn how to ignore them too. But right now I was finding it hard not to stare.

I glanced down at the book in my hand. "Jane Eyre." I slid it into my backpack along with the rest of the books I'd need over the weekend.

"How depressing. You should read something a little more upbeat, don't you think?"

I laughed, but it came out sad and forced. I couldn't remember the last time I'd really laughed. But Kennedy was right. I'd had to restart the book a few times already because my mind was having a hard time focusing on the words. Not because it was boring, but because it was hard to be consumed by someone else's pain when my own was so acute. "It's for our English class."

She looked up from her camera. "Then just read the CliffsNotes."

I stared at her. She was kidding, right? The only reason she was here was because she had a scholarship. And the only reason I was here was because my uncle was a janitor at the school and apparently family got legacy preference at prestigious academies like this. I was still on a GPA restriction though. We were lucky to be in the best high school in New York City. And even though I didn't love this school or most of the snobs in it, I wasn't prepared to start over. Again. So I wasn't going to risk not reading for an assignment just because Jane Eyre was depressing.

"I can't. And I know you won't risk a failing grade either. I doubt the public schools around here give you cameras like that for class. Or even have photography classes period."

Kennedy laughed. "I know, right? When I take pictures on our street I'm more worried about getting arrested for possessing such an expensive camera than I am of getting robbed."

"You should be worried about the latter too." I'd only been in the city for a few weeks, but I was very aware of how unsafe it was. Sirens kept me awake at night. Not that I'd have been able to sleep anyway.

"Honestly, I don't think Mr. Thompson would even care. If I lost it he'd just give me a slap on the wrist and a brand new one. The benefits of Empire High." She stepped back and lifted the camera to her face. "This time smile!"

I shook my head. "I have to get home and make something for my uncle to eat tonight while I'm at work. Or else he'll get takeout again."

She snapped another picture anyway. "And what's wrong with takeout? My mom and I eat takeout whenever her shifts run late."

"It's not good for you."

"You're starting to fit into this school pretty quickly." She hiked up her skirt the way the popular girls did. "Cheese curls?" She flipped her hair. "What on earth is a curl of cheese? I only eat locally sourced salmon that my personal chef prepares for me on a silver platter."

I laughed for real this time. "Cut it out." And she wondered why everyone else at this school treated her like a social pariah. Not that I blamed her. She had too much charisma to stay silent like I did. It was one of the reasons why we'd become fast friends. Kennedy oozed confidence and strength. And I needed that. I needed her. Because most days I was finding it hard to even breathe.

Kennedy flipped her hair again. "But like…I've never touched a knife before so how am I supposed to like cut anything? I pay people to do that for me."

"I'm sure they know how to use knives."

"I'm not so sure. But you can ask the queen bee herself." Kennedy pulled her skirt back into place as Isabella walked down the hall toward us with her catty friends.

"I can't wait for the party tonight," Isabella said loudly enough for us to hear. Probably to rub in the fact that we were not invited. Hell, I hadn't even heard about it until this second. Nor did I care. I never had the luxury of attending parties at my old school because I worked all weekend. It would be the same here.

Isabella's heels clicked down the hallway. She was a senior at Empire High and she had all the notoriety of the Untouchables. But unlike them, she wasn't respected. She was feared. At least by me.

I concentrated on zipping up my backpack, waiting for the incessant clicking to disappear. I'd only had one interaction with Isabella. Barely. She'd caught me staring at the Untouchables during lunch. I really needed to break that bad habit before it got me in more trouble than just a sneer from her.

The clicking of her heels finally stopped. Unfortunately, she stopped right in front of us. I looked up from my backpack.

"There's a hole in your shoe," Isabella said to me. Or more accurately, she said it through me. That's how it felt when she spoke. That she wasn't really talking to you at all. Just at you. Her friends giggled.

I glanced down at my sneakers, even though I already knew what she was talking about. There was a hole in the side of my Keds where the fabric was ripping away from the rubber soles. I had enough money saved to buy new ones. But my mother had bought these for me for my birthday a few years ago. And any excuse to be closer to her was one I'd take.

"Don't listen to her," Kennedy said. "She's just jealous that her legs only look good when she wears sky-high heels and yours look amazing in sneakers."

Isabella snickered. "I'd look like a million bucks in cheap kicks. But this school is a little too classy for such things, don't you think?"

I tried to stand up a little straighter, channeling Kennedy's energy. But I had nothing to say to Isabella. All I could focus on was the fact that my shoes weren't cheap. To me, 50 dollars was hours and hours of work. To her it was probably a fraction of an allowance. If rich people even got an allowance. She probably just had a credit card with no limit.

"You should just throw those ratty things out," she said. "They're hideous anyway. Trust me, I'm doing you a favor by mentioning it, darling."

My mother used to call me darling. But not in *that* way. My mother's voice was full of love and warmth. God, I missed her. I felt tears welling in my eyes.

"Well don't cry about it," she said with a laugh that dripped with disdain.

She didn't understand. How could someone like that understand? She had everything. All I had was a memory of my mother's love that was growing more distant by the second, an uncle I barely knew that had taken me in, and a pair of beat-up sneakers that I clung to because I didn't have anything else. But still I stood there. I stood there and took her cruelty because I didn't want her to see me run away and cry.

Kennedy's camera flashed.

"Taking pictures of me for your project?" Isabella asked. "How quaint."

"No, I'd never include someone with such a hideous soul in my project," Kennedy said. "I just wanted to capture an image of you being intolerably you."

Isabella rolled her eyes.

"Come on," Kennedy said and pulled on my arm.

I closed my locker and pulled my backpack over one shoulder. I heard Isabella and her friends' laughter echoing around in my head as we pushed out the ornate wooden front doors of the school. Normally I loved when summer drew to a close and fall began. But the change of season was harder to detect in New York. Everything was concrete. There was certainly a chill in the air this afternoon, but I was pretty sure only I could feel it.

"You know, one day I'm going to show Isabella this picture," Kennedy said. "She'll look back at this interaction and be ashamed of herself. One day she'll regret being a bitch for no reason other than to be cruel."

Maybe. But probably not. I looked over my shoulder, hoping she wouldn't follow us outside and continue torturing me. Empire High was nestled between two skyscrapers. By being in such close proximity to those buildings, you'd think my new high school would be easy to overlook. But it wasn't. If anything it stood out even more with its old charm. The endlessly high set of stairs up to the entrance had been killing the muscles in my thighs all week. The entranceway was adorned with thick marble columns on either side of the doors. The letters branding the prestigious Empire High academy shone in the sunlight, and I was pretty sure they were real bronze. It looked more like a castle than a school. And whenever I walked up the steps I felt just as out of place as if I was walking toward a castle.

"Just wait," Kennedy said. "She'll see. One day you and I are going to be rich and we can serve her a big slice of humble pie. Because we won't be ass faces like her when we have enough money to fill a tub with."

I didn't respond. I used to want to be rich one day. Back when I was living in Delaware with my mom and we were barely scraping by. I thought money could have fixed everything. But when my mom got sick, all I could focus on was time. And not having enough of it. For so long that had been at the forefront of my mind. And I still felt it. A ticking time bomb waiting to explode. But hadn't it already exploded when I'd buried my mother? When I'd moved here? When I started going to this school where I so blatantly didn't belong? But still I felt the ticking. Like the next bad thing was about to happen. Another explosion when I was barely holding on from the first one.

I watched the Untouchables drive off in James' Benz. Despite Kennedy's nickname for the four of them, everyone at this school knew that they weren't the

Untouchables. That title belonged to me. And the other scholarship students like Kennedy. We were untouchable. Because we didn't belong here in their world. We never would.

CHAPTER 2

Friday

"You ready to go?" Kennedy asked from the kitchen.

I jumped, hitting the top of my head on a shelf in my closet. *Ow.* I was still getting used to the fact that she had a key to my uncle's apartment. Not that I was mad about it. Her mom and my uncle were close because they'd been neighbors forever. And if it wasn't for their friendship, I never would have been invited into Kennedy's circle of one. Now two.

She walked into my bedroom eating one of the vegetarian burritos I'd made for my uncle. "When are you going to decorate?" she asked after another huge bite.

Despite her declaration of love for junk food, she didn't seem to mind my cooking. "I don't have anything to decorate with." It wasn't exactly true. I had tons of pictures. But most of them were of my mom and me. Right now I could barely think about her without crying. If I had to see her smiling face every day? I shook away the thought and finished pulling my hair into a ponytail.

"I mean like posters and stuff, not fancy vases or anything. It looks like a guest room instead of your room. You gotta settle in."

"I'm settled."

"You still have boxes packed." She nudged one with her foot. "I'll print out some of the photos I've been taking for you. I mean it's no wonder you don't smile much. Reading Jane Eyre and having walls in such a basic beige color? I'd be sad too."

I gave her the best smile I could. Because we both knew it wasn't the color of my walls or the book I was reading that made it hard for me to smile. And I loved her for not bringing up my mother. "You ready to go?" I asked.

"Yup." She was still staring down at one of the boxes. "Do you want me to help you unpack when we get back?"

My first thought was to say no. But it was Friday night. Didn't normal teenagers hang out with their friends on Friday nights? For just a few hours maybe I could forget. "That would be great."

"Awesome." She tucked her arm in mine and guided me out of my small bedroom.

"Thanks for getting me this job by the way," I said. Kennedy worked for a catering company and had hooked me up with the gig. My uncle insisted that I didn't need to work. But I'd shown up unexpectedly on his doorstep a few weeks ago and I didn't want to put him out more than I already had. So I was going to help pay the rent whether he wanted me to or not.

"Don't thank me yet. It's basically an extension of school. Walking around with trays handing out appetizers I can't pronounce to the city's elite. Plus there aren't any tips. But I swear it's better than waitressing. Waitressing in New York is awful because everyone waitresses here. From aspiring actors to writers and everything in between.

UNTOUCHABLES

The turnover is insane. Before I got this job I'd worked at a dozen restaurants. I hate being expendable."

"Trust me, you're not expendable." I, for one, wouldn't know what to do without her.

She squeezed my arm as we made our way outside. The air was definitely growing chillier by the day. We huddled together and wound our way through the crowded sidewalks. We barely knew each other but I was already comfortable with our bouts of silence. I felt closer to her than I had to any of my friends back in Delaware. Maybe because instead of being there when things got hard, they just stared at me like they pitied me. And Kennedy knew what loss felt like. My uncle had told me she'd lost her dad when she was little.

"Are you going to tell me about the sneakers?" Kennedy asked. "Because I saw some more shoes in one of your unpacked boxes. Without the holes."

"My mom gave them to me." I kept my voice even. I'd already gotten emotional once today and I needed to strengthen my resolve.

"Well, I think they're cute."

"Thanks." It was the perfect opportunity for her to ask more questions, but none came. I was pretty sure her mother had given her the low down and told her she wasn't allowed to ask. But if I was going to talk about it with anyone, it would be Kennedy. "I miss her," I added.

"I think remembering is better than missing."

I'd heard "I'm sorry" more times than I could count. But never that. Only someone else who lost a person so significant could understand. "What do you remember about your dad?" I asked.

"Who knew your uncle was so gossipy?" she said with a laugh. "He's always so quiet." She looked up at the sky. "My dad and I liked to watch the clouds together on the roof of the apartment building. And he always smelled like cigars. I love the smell of cigars even though I hate smoke. I smile so hard whenever I smell them. Do you remember your dad at all?"

"No. I never knew him. My mom said he left us as soon as he found out about me."

"What a dick. Well, your uncle is the complete opposite. He's the kindest man I know, even if he is a little gossip. You're lucky."

I didn't feel lucky. I barely knew him at all. But he'd let me live with him when I had nowhere else to go. That was kindness if I ever saw it. I needed to make more of an effort to get to know him. I added it to my endless mental list of ways to not be a nuisance to him. "So what's the party we're catering tonight?"

"Some old rich guy's birthday I think. Who cares. In three hours we get to have a girls' night."

We stopped outside a hotel I'd never heard of. I went to walk inside, but Kennedy tightened her grip on my arm.

"We have to go around back," she said.

I laughed, but stopped when I saw her face. "Are you serious? Like…the servants' entrance?"

"No. Like the staff entrance. What era are you living in, the early 20th century? Come on, I'll show you." She pulled me past the hotel and down a dingy side street. The unseen side of the hotel looked practically run down. A rusty door stood ajar, allowing a cool breeze into the unairconditioned staff entrance.

I glanced back at the main street. There were women in floor-length gowns and men in tuxes walking toward the hotel. I was wearing holey sneakers and a black apron and I was about to enter through a door that looked like it was from a horror movie. I was used to being poor. That wasn't new to me. But I'd never been surrounded by people so ridiculously wealthy. I'd never felt so out of place in my life. This city. These people.

"I promise it's not that bad," Kennedy said when she caught me staring. "They treat us like we're invisible. All they see is the delectable appetizers we're dishing out."

Invisible. We were definitely the untouchable ones. But with Kennedy by my side, I didn't even mind. I'd rather be untouchable with someone like her than clad in a fancy gown with horrible people like Isabella. At least I wouldn't have to deal with seeing her again until Monday.

"And the best part is that there's usually leftovers that they divvy up at the end. Your taste buds are about to explode. And technically it's not takeout. So it's Brooklyn approved."

Fancy food didn't necessarily correspond with healthy food. I could imagine butter slathered on everything so it would taste better. My chest hurt just thinking about it. Or maybe it hurt because I wanted to go home. Not back to the tiny apartment with my uncle. Home home. The home I no longer had.

CHAPTER 3

Friday

Back home I'd worked every day at a diner down the street from my house. It was small and quaint and hadn't prepared me at all for this. I gripped the tray tighter in my hands, staring at the way the other waitstaff held the trays expertly with one hand. Surely they couldn't balance all that with…nope they were doing it. Perfectly.

I moved my hand to the base of the tray and held it up, trying to emulate the waitstaff that were actually qualified for this job. The tray I was attempting to balance was piled high with wild mushroom tarts. It was heavy and awkward, but at least I didn't have to carry champagne around like a magician. There was a 100 percent chance that I would have spilled the flutes on the floor. Or all over someone's fancy gown.

"Ready for the time of your life?" Kennedy asked with a grin. "Just kidding, it's the worst. Let's do the damn thing." She pushed through the double doors out of the kitchen and into the ballroom, looking every bit the part of the waitstaff supreme.

I quickly followed so that I wouldn't have to try to open the door. "Wild mushroom tart?" I asked everyone I passed. I kept my head down, trying to remain the invisible human I'd become. It was easy. I thrived at invisibility.

After several minutes, my biceps were already aching from the tray. The only reprieve was that my tray got lighter as I got rid of more tarts. I opened my mouth to say "wild mushroom tart" for what felt like the hundredth time, but swallowed down my words. Because I was staring at the back of Matthew Caldwell in a fitted tux that clung to his muscles like it was made for his body. He didn't have to turn around for me to know it was him. The golden hair. The broad shoulders. It didn't hurt that his older brother, Mason, and the Hunter brothers were standing next to him, also ignoring me and my stinky tarts, thank God. Besides, I'd had time to study the back of his head in our entrepreneurial studies class. I'd memorized it better than any of the lessons.

My stomach clenched when he laughed. All the Untouchables were handsome. But there was something about Matthew that made my eyes always gravitate to him. He was why I found myself staring at their group at lunch. And in the hall. And after school. A bad habit that was already getting me in trouble with girls like Isabella. Which was ridiculous. It's not like any of them were looking back at me. Even when I was offering them free little tarts. I'd never be a threat. Just an invisible observer of perfection.

Matthew started to turn his head.

Shit. I practically ran in the opposite direction and almost smacked my tray into Kennedy's face.

"Jesus, what are you doing, Brooklyn? You almost bulldozed me and my spanakopita triangles."

I somehow mustered the balance to pull her and my tray away from the boys I was avoiding. "The Untouchables are here," I whisper screamed.

The expression on her face morphed from annoyed to mortified. "Oh God, really? Well, that's awkward." She peered over my shoulder and sighed. "At least Isabella and her posse aren't…" her voice trailed off. "No, they're here too."

I turned around to see that Isabella had appeared. She was flirting shamelessly with James, the older of the Hunter brothers. In school he always looked handsome in the required uniform blazer and tie. But when he was in a tux? I swallowed hard. What teenager owned a tux, let alone wore one so well? *Matthew, that's who.*

I was about to turn my attention back to the Untouchable that I could never not stare at when James looked up from the champagne flute in his hand. A champagne flute that I was vaguely aware he was too young to hold. When he caught my gaze, I felt locked in place. Not because he was James Hunter. Or because he was drinking underage and I'd caught him red-handed. Or because he smiled. *At me.* But because I felt this overwhelming sadness roll off of him and onto me. His smile didn't reach his eyes. It was as fake as the one I forced onto my face at school.

It was a crime for someone so beautiful to be so sad. Maybe it was because his rumored girlfriend, Rachel, wasn't at the party with him? Or that Isabella was unabashedly marking her territory on him when he wasn't single? He downed the rest of the champagne and grabbed another glass. Or maybe I wasn't the only one standing in this ballroom feeling lost. And depressed. And barely holding on.

James downed another glass and I turned away. The last thing I ever thought was that the Untouchables were relatable. They were the gods of Empire High. They weren't like me. *Right?* "What do we do?" I asked.

Kennedy shrugged. "We keep being invisible. It's not like they'll deign to speak to us here when they don't at school. Besides, they probably don't even recognize us."

She was right. We were just as invisible in the halls of our high school. And James' smile hadn't been one of recognition, just politeness. Very sad politeness. There was just one problem. "Well…Isabella spoke to us today."

"Yeah, just to be a bitch. But she wouldn't do that here in front of all these people."

"Are you sure about that?" Because I certainly wasn't. I didn't think Isabella's bitchiness was a switch she could just turn on and off. It was just her. I looked down at my Keds with the hole in the side. The butterflies I felt when I had seen Matthew died and rolled over in my stomach.

"Positive. That would be admitting that she even knows us. Which is probably mortifying for her." She must have seen the look on my face, because she added, "offload the rest of those tarts on me and take a breather in the back. I'll join you in a sec."

I slid my tarts onto her tray and made a beeline for the kitchen. My reaction to seeing them was ridiculous. Everything Kennedy said made sense. Regardless, I was suddenly finding it hard to breathe. I leaned against a wall in the kitchen and tried to force myself to stop freaking out.

"Spill it," Kennedy said.

I jumped. How did she always sneak up on me like that? I was starting to think she was a ninja. "Spill what?" I was trying very hard not to spill anything tonight.

"What is it with you and the Untouchables? Please don't tell me you want to be one of them. You're way too nice."

"You don't know whether they're nice or not."

She raised both her eyebrows. "I've been walking around Empire High for a year and they've never said one word to me."

"Well, have you said one word to them?"

She laughed. "Touché. But seriously, what gives?"

I leaned my head back on the wall. How could I tell her that I walked around completely numb? That it only went away when seeing Matthew made my stomach erupt with butterflies? That the feeling was the only thing that was keeping me afloat? I knew how it sounded. Pathetic. "I'm fine with being an outsider if I have you," I said. "But what's the harm in staring at them? They're so beautiful."

"Nothing's wrong with staring at perfection. But getting caught up in it? Wanting it? Guys like that will never end up with girls like us, Brooklyn. That's not how things work."

"James is dating Rachel. You said she goes to a public school."

"Yeah…he's dating her *now*. But everyone in that room out there knows that he's going to marry Isabella."

I hadn't known that. And I didn't believe it for a second. But then I pictured James' sad smile. Life didn't always turn out the way you wanted it to. I knew that better than anyone.

"Don't tell me you were hoping James would marry you?" Kennedy said with a laugh.

"No." I could never be with someone who was as sad as me. It's not like I could save him when I needed saving myself. We'd just end up drowning together.

"Oh God. You want to marry one of the other ones, don't you?"

"I never said that." I pushed off the wall. Marriage? Now that was ridiculous. My life wasn't a fairytale. I didn't grow up dreaming of my wedding. I grew up thinking I had to fend for myself. That men like my father lurked around every corner. I couldn't even say that Matthew was nothing like my father, because I'd never met either of them.

I started filling up my tray with more tarts. Kennedy followed me back out in the ballroom, keeping close to me as we flitted through the guests.

"Is it Mason then?" she asked. "I wouldn't mind waking up to that perfect specimen every day either."

I laughed. "I'm not dreaming about marrying any of them, trust me." But I glanced over at Mason. The Caldwells' distinguishing feature was their broad shoulders, which made them the perfect Empire High football stars that they were. High school royalty with championship game wins under their thousand dollar belts. Not that they needed the wins to be the Untouchables. Mason, the older brother, had the female student body practically begging for one night with him. Even though I hadn't been at school long, I could see that before Kennedy had told me. He was promiscuous. Devastatingly handsome. And horribly sad. After seeing James' smile, it was like the façade around the Untouchables had cracked. They were more like me than I thought possible. And I could see the sadness in Mason's eyes just like I'd seen it in James'. Did people see my sadness when they looked at me too?

Old wealth probably carried responsibilities I could never imagine. Is that why the two eldest brothers looked tired? Because they carried the weight of the world on their shoulders? That was something I could relate to. But mine wasn't the same burden. The weight I carried had nothing to do with familial obligations. For years mine had been time. Two weeks ago, I'd run out of it. And now? My burden felt like it was living. Living without the only person that would ever love me.

Kennedy did a very fancy turn considering the fact that she was balancing a tray, and found her way next to me again. "Is it Robert? If he put a ring on your finger, he'd make it his mission for you to laugh every day. It's him, right? More laughter is exactly what you need. And he's so dreamy."

"I laugh enough." I didn't. I glanced at Robert out of the corner of my eye. The Hunters' distinguishing feature was their dark eyes. Robert, the younger brother, was a total goofball. He was always smiling and cracking jokes, never aimed at me...which I was eternally grateful for. His dark eyes shimmered with life. But now that I was finding chinks in all their armor, I had a feeling that Robert was hiding behind his sense of humor. I could understand that. I was hiding in plain sight.

Robert and more laughter definitely wasn't what I needed. No, what I needed was for my mom not to be six feet under and for my new bestie to drop this subject.

But I couldn't help it that my eyes gravitated to Matthew Caldwell. *Matt*. His smile did reach his eyes. It was genuine and warm, even if it was never directed at me. And he walked in a way that made me think he didn't carry a single burden. He was more reserved than Rob. More mysterious. I couldn't read him at all. But he just seemed so…carefree.

"Bingo."

I looked over at Kennedy. Her tray was empty and her hand was on her hip. "You're in love with Matthew."

I opened my mouth to protest.

"Don't even with me, Brooklyn. Besides, I already knew it. You drool whenever you see him in school."

"I don't drool."

"Got you." She pointed her index finger at me. "You basically just admitted it."

I laughed. "I didn't admit anything."

The lights started to dim and the guests made their way to their tables.

Kennedy grabbed my arm and pulled me back to the kitchen. "We have to help with dinner, but don't think for a second that we're dropping this. I need all the deets."

To me it was officially dropped. I tried to focus on what color name card went with what entrée. Table three was my responsibility. Lucky number three. All I had to do was get through serving dinner and dessert and I could go home.

I looked at the image of the tables on the seating chart and made my way out of the kitchen. *Lucky number three my ass.* James and Robert were at the table I was supposed to be serving. Along with Isabella and a few adult couples, probably their parents. I kept my head down as I pushed the cart over to their table.

A blue name card meant fish. Red - steak. Green - vegetarian. I placed a vegetarian entrée down in front of Isabella.

"Oh, darling." She laughed. "Well isn't this tragic."

I forced myself to look at her. She looked blissfully happy despite her comment. She glanced down at my shoes and I could feel my face turning red.

"You're the new kid, right?" Robert asked.

Oh God. They had noticed me at school. They'd probably seen me staring. I suddenly wished I truly was invisible. I nodded.

"I'm Rob. This is my brother, James. And apparently you've already met the troll." He gestured toward Isabella who looked increasingly more furious with each word that fell out of his mouth.

One of the older women at the table cleared her throat. "Robert, that's enough. Stop talking to the help and eat your food."

Rob rolled his eyes.

And I laughed. A real one. The kind of laugh I had before I lost everything.

"What are you laughing at?" Isabella snapped. "Do your job."

She was an awful human. But she was right. I was just standing there awkwardly talking to the guests like I belonged. And I definitely did not. I grabbed another entrée and walked behind Isabella's chair just as she pushed it back to stand.

Maybe if my arms weren't so tired from holding a tray for an hour I could have held on to the plate. But my arms were tired. The food fell onto my shirt as everything dropped, the expensive glass shattering on the floor. It was worse than the champagne spill I'd envisioned in my head earlier. So much freaking worse. *Shit.*

Everyone in the ballroom was staring at me. Every single pair of eyeballs condemning me.

"Clean it up," Isabella said.

I had been standing there like an idiot. I knelt down, hating that I had to listen to her. It was her fault. She'd hit me with her chair on purpose, I knew she had.

It looked like Rob was about to get up and help me.

"She doesn't need assistance, Rob," said Isabella. "She's smart enough to figure it out. Right, darling? Isn't that the only reason you're at our school? Because you were smart enough to earn yourself a scholarship? You're not one of us."

I heard a few snickers behind me. I could feel the tears burning in the corners of my eyes, threatening to escape. She was wrong and for some reason that stung even more. I wasn't at their school because of a scholarship. I was there because my uncle literally cleaned up after them all day, like she was expecting me to do right now. That made me fit in even less. If Isabella knew the truth, she'd be more vicious. She'd crucify me. I wasn't ashamed of what my uncle did. But I was terrified of Isabella's wrath.

I started picking up the food and broken shards of glass. My hands were shaking. I wasn't sure if it was because I was embarrassed or angry. All I could see were her stupid high heels standing beside the mess. She was looking down at me in all her glory. I shoved some of the glass onto the cart and one of the pieces sliced the side of my hand. *Ow.*

"Brooklyn, are you okay?" Kennedy knelt down beside me, ignoring the devil glaring over us. She grabbed my hand. "Jesus. Go take care of the cut. I'll clean this up."

I could never repay her for letting me escape this moment. For putting herself in the spotlight when I knew she wanted to blend in at this stupid party just as much as me.

"Seriously, go. I got this."

"Thank you." I grabbed my hand and stood up.

"Looks like you'll definitely have to replace your shoes now," sneered Isabella.

I looked down. Some of the juice from the steak had gotten onto my Keds. I rushed past Isabella without looking back. If I didn't get some cold water on them, they'd stain.

All I could hear was her vicious laughter in my head as I pushed into the first bathroom I found.

I kicked off my left shoe, turned on the faucet, and plunged my shoe under the water. I started to scrub it with soap, but the stain wasn't coming off. The tears I had been holding back before finally spilled out. I scrubbed the fabric harder. But now the blood from my hand was mixing with the water, creating more of a mess. The sink looked like a crime scene.

"You're bleeding."

I felt the little hairs on the back of my neck rise. My hand stopped scrubbing the fabric. I knew that voice from class. I'd recognize it anywhere. I looked up into the mirror in front of me. Matthew Caldwell's face was reflected back beside my own.

"Am I in the men's room?" *Oh God, why were those the first words I'd ever spoken to him?* I lifted up my shoe like I was about to put the soaking wet bloody mess back onto my foot and run away. What had I been thinking? Now I'd have to walk around with one shoe.

"You can buy new shoes," he said, ignoring my question about which restroom I was in. "You can't buy a new hand." He walked up next to me, waved his hand under the automatic soap dispenser, and then stared at my reflection as he slowly took my hand in his. It was like he was asking my permission. I stayed completely still.

He dipped my hand back under the running faucet and started gently washing the cut.

I didn't flinch from the pain of the water entering the wound. All I could feel was the warmth of his hands. And how rough his palms were. Probably from football. A chill ran down the back of my spine as the pad of his thumb traced the cut.

"Isabella's a disease," he said. "Don't let her crawl under your skin or she'll stay there."

I thought maybe he'd already been in here. That he hadn't seen what had just happened in the ballroom. But that apparently wasn't the case. Had he followed me in here?

I removed my eyes from his reflection in the mirror and looked up at him. We locked eyes for one moment. A few seconds that stretched for eternity. His eyes swirled with the same warmth that I'd felt from his hands. It was hard to stare at perfection. Matthew Caldwell was so beautiful it almost hurt to look at him. And on top of that, he had everything I didn't. Money. A family. And unlike the rest of the Untouchables, he seemed genuinely happy. He was everything I could never be. And for some reason, he

was everything I wanted. Which was ridiculous. Just thinking it was a complete and utter waste of time.

I turned away.

He turned off the water, grabbed a paper towel, and
wrapped it around my hand.

"Thank you," I said, keeping my eyes on the paper
towel.

I saw him shove his hands into his pockets. "I'll see
you around school, Brooklyn," he said and made his way
to the door.

It felt like my heart stopped beating. He knew my
name?

The door closed behind him with a thud. I waited a
beat before grabbing my soggy shoe and walking out of
the bathroom. I looked up at the sign on the door. It was a
women's restroom. Which meant Matthew Caldwell had
followed me in here to make sure I was okay. Maybe I
wasn't as invisible as I thought.

CHAPTER 4

Friday

"Hey, kiddo," my uncle said as Kennedy and I walked into the apartment. He was doing a crossword puzzle at the kitchen table and didn't look up. He was five years older than my mother, but he looked more like he was in his sixties than his forties. The extra weight didn't help. My eyes gravitated to the buttons of his shirt that looked like they were ready to pop off. But I was going to help him shed the weight. I'd have him healthy in no time.

"Hey...Jim." I knew he probably wanted me to call him Uncle Jim. I kept trying to force it out. But I'd only met him a handful of times when I was little. Uncle felt too familiar. And I wasn't familiar with him at all. Despite that, I kind of loved that he called me kiddo. I remembered him calling me that ages ago. It made me feel a little less like I was sinking.

"Hi, Uncle Jim!" Kennedy said and bound into the apartment like she belonged there more than me.

Jim looked up at her and smiled as she gave him a big hug and a kiss on the cheek. I would have found it weird that she was so much closer to him than me, but she'd known him all her life. I'd practically just met the man.

"How was work?" he asked.

"The usual first day jitters for this one," Kennedy said and nodded her head in my direction.

Jim's eyes focused on me for the first time, taking in my shirt stained pink with steak juice and my soaking wet shoe. "Are you okay?" he asked.

Maybe he hadn't been looking at my disheveled outfit at all. Maybe he had been staring at my face. He seemed to know me. He could sense my moods. He could tell when I was hurting just like my mom always could. And I found myself wishing I knew him too. I was tearing up again for no reason at all. I blinked fast, removing any trace of tears. "I'm fine. Those trays were freaking heavy."

He smiled. "You should see if they need some extra hands in the kitchen instead. Those burritos you made me sure were delicious."

"Really?"

He nodded.

I was more relieved than happy. The first couple weeks here he'd been resisting my attempts at changing up his diet. He seemed to finally be accepting the fact that I wasn't backing down. He turned his head and started coughing into the crook of his arm.

"Are you sure you don't want me to pick up some cold medicine for your cough?" I asked. I was pretty sure I was pestering him into annoyance. He was used to being on his own, and it felt like every word out of my mouth was filled with overconcern. I couldn't help it. I needed him to be healthy. He was all I had left and I wasn't going to lose him too.

"It's just a cold," he said. "I'll be fine."

"This should make you feel better," Kennedy said. "We brought home those little cheesecake desserts you like so much!" She placed the box down on the table.

I wanted to scold Kennedy. I was finally helping my uncle make healthier eating choices. The last thing he needed was to reintroduce sugar into his diet.

Before I could say anything, he'd already bitten into one of the miniature cakes.

"Better?" Kennedy asked.

"Nothing like cheesecake to fix a cough," he said with a laugh. "Don't look at me like that, kiddo, it's a miniature dessert." He slid the box back toward Kennedy. "You two can eat the rest."

I smiled.

"It's like living with a mini dictator," he grumbled, but he was smiling too. "I'll leave you two to it. You can put your shoes by the door, kiddo, and I'll get them fixed up for you."

"Oh. You don't have to do that. I was just going to scrub them a bit more."

"If there's one thing I know, it's how to mend things. Leave 'em by the door."

"Thank you." I had no idea what he was planning on doing with them. I honestly wasn't sure if anything could be done. So there was no downside in letting him try. I kicked them off at the door and followed Kennedy into my room.

"Okay, we're going to unpack all your crap." She started to open up one of my cardboard boxes. "And while we do that, you're going to tell me everything you love about Matthew Caldwell."

"I don't *love* anything about him."

"Fine. What do you *like* about him?" She pulled out some of my clothes and started putting them in the wrong drawers.

I followed her around fixing everything she was messing up. "He just seems so…happy."

Kennedy laughed as she tossed an unfolded shirt into my underwear drawer. She was terrible at this. "Happy? That's all you got? What about those muscles? And his gorgeous smile?"

"Yeah, those things too." I wasn't sure Kennedy would understand the fact that I was more interested in the Untouchables' inner traits than outer ones. A nice smile could only get you so far in life. My mother had a beautiful smile. And she'd died single at the age of 36 without a penny to her name.

But she was kind and funny and so charismatic. She was the greatest person I ever knew. And she always said she had everything she ever needed. Me. I would have loved her even if she looked like a monster.

"So you look at him like a love-sick puppy because he's happy? There are plenty of happy people at our school." She took a break from ruining my closet's organization to eat some of the mini cakes.

I started rearranging the things she'd hung up. "And carefree."

"That's basically the same thing."

I pulled out a stack of pictures. The top one was a selfie my mom had taken of the two of us. We were sitting in her hospital bed. She still had so much optimism. So much life left to live. I placed the pictures down on my nightstand.

She'd want me to be living my life. Making new friends. Calling my uncle *uncle*. Trying to start over. Today was the first step I'd really taken in any of it. "He's also really nice," I said.

"How on earth do you know if he's nice?" Kennedy said through a mouth full of food.

"He followed me into the restroom after I cut my hand."

"He did what?"

"I thought maybe I had walked into the men's room and that he'd already been in there. I was focused on getting the stain out of my shoe. And then he was just…there."

Kennedy plopped down on the edge of my bed and stared at me. "Continue!" she almost screamed.

"He washed my hand."

"Weird."

"No, it was really…nice."

"There you go with the *nice* again. God I hate that word," Kennedy said. "Give me more details now or I'll kill you in your sleep!"

I started laughing because I knew she was kidding. At least, I was pretty sure she was kidding.

"Is everything okay in there girls?" Jim said from outside the door.

"Great!" Kennedy yelled. "Go away, we're having a top secret discussion!"

I laughed and sat down next to her.

"Are you sure?" Jim asked.

"Oh my God, Uncle Jim!" Kennedy yelled at the door. "We need a minute alone!"

He laughed and I heard his footsteps walking away from the door.

"So after he erotically bathed you…"

"My hand. He washed my hand. But his hands were so warm and soothing."

Kennedy giggled and flopped backward onto the bed. "It's a classic Cinderella story. He's your prince. You're going to live happily ever after surrounded by wealth and luxury and so many housekeepers."

I swallowed hard. Happily ever after? A happily ever after would have involved my mother.

"What's with the look? I was just messing around."

"Nothing." I stood up and started unpacking more stuff.

"But what happened after he raped your hand?" She knew just what to say to make my smile return.

"Stop saying weird things or Jim will come busting in here to save me."

Kennedy rolled her eyes. "It's so weird that you call your uncle Jim instead of Uncle Jim. I realize that's confusing now that I said it."

I laughed. "I think he prefers it." I didn't know that. I'd never asked.

"Whatever you say. Back to Matthew, stop changing the subject. So after the hand thing…"

"He gave me a paper towel and said Isabella was a disease. To not let her get to me. And then he said, 'See you around school, Brooklyn,' and walked out the door."

Kennedy put her hands to her chest. "Wow, he knew your name? And he stalked you into the ladies' room. That's big."

"It's not that big of a deal that he knew my name. We have a class together."

"Yeah, where you said Mr. Hill calls everyone by their last names. He knew your *first* name. And he's all like carefree and happy and shit."

I laughed.

"Do you think he'll talk to you in class on Monday? Stupid question. Of course he will. He's your knight in shining armor."

If that was true, I'd met him three weeks too late. I'd already lost the one thing I needed help saving.

"These pictures are really cute." Kennedy lifted the stack of photos off my nightstand. "Do you have any pushpins? We need to put these all over your walls."

"Let me ask Jim."

She shook her head like whenever I called him Jim it physically pained her.

I walked back to the kitchen.

"Having fun?" Jim asked without looking up from his crossword puzzle.

"Mhm."

"Kennedy's a good kid. I'm glad you two are hitting it off."

I didn't know what to say to that. He and her mother had basically set us up. It's not like anyone else had even said hello to me at school. Well, except Matthew. I shook the thought away. "Do you have any pushpins?"

"Top drawer, left side of the sink."

I opened up the drawer and pulled out the container of pins. I was about to go back to my room, but stopped. There was something nagging me about what Isabella had said tonight. "Did you know the other kids at school thought I was a scholarship student?" I asked.

Jim looked up from his puzzle. "Well, that might be because the only people at Empire High that know otherwise are Kennedy and the principal. And I asked him to record your paperwork that way so no one else would find out."

"What? Why?"

"A new school is hard enough as it is, kiddo. I didn't want word to get out and to make it any harder on you."

"You didn't have to do that, Jim."

He shrugged his shoulders.

I wasn't embarrassed that he was a janitor there. Not in the slightest. I hadn't been avoiding him at school. But we barely ever ran into each other anyway. Almost like… "Have you been avoiding me at school?"

"It'll be easier on you if the other students don't know."

I opened my lips and then closed them. I'd had that same thought when Isabella was towering over me earlier tonight. He was right. I hated that he was right, but he was. He was protecting me. For the first time since moving here, I felt loved. Really for the first time since my mother's last breath. Maybe I should have told him it wasn't necessary. That I could handle the other kids just fine. But I didn't know how to handle Isabella. So instead I found myself saying thank you.

He looked back down at his crossword puzzle.

Do it, Brooklyn. Freaking say it. "I really appreciate it, Uncle Jim." It wasn't so hard to call him uncle. Especially now. And it sounded better. He was family. My only family. He treated me that way and I needed to make sure he knew how much I appreciated it.

I saw him smile, his eyes still glued on the page in front of him, but he didn't say anything.

I walked back into my room.

"That was sweet," Kennedy said.

"Were you eavesdropping?"

"The walls are thin. Besides, it's a good thing I was. I didn't realize the scholarship thing was a secret. I could have blabbed it to the whole school by mistake."

"Good thing I'm the only one you talk to."

She laughed and grabbed the pushpins from me. "Now let's finish getting you settled in. Because this is your new home. Let's make it feel like it."

***

"Goodnight," Kennedy said.

"Goodnight." But I knew I wouldn't be sleeping. Most nights I just stared at the ceiling counting down the minutes until I could wake up. The sirens outside were too loud. The honking even louder. Everything was just too loud here.

My chest felt full as I stared into the darkness. It was possible that it was because of the cholesterol in my bloodstream from all the dessert I'd consumed. But I was pretty sure it was because I knew my uncle loved me. That maybe he wasn't so put out by me being here. That I wasn't the burden I thought I was.

The Untouchables weren't so untouchable after all. Matthew was kind. His heart was as golden as his hair. I smiled up at the ceiling. It was possible my second week of school would be drastically different than my first. I could picture myself sitting at the Untouchables' table.

Not that I needed anything to change. Because I had a best friend that cared. Kennedy had spent hours with me tonight decorating my room. She was right. This was my new home. And it was starting to feel like it.

I listened to her breathing slow. I'd been wanting to ask her a question for a while now. I didn't really need a response. I knew the answer. But asking it would make me feel better. Just like asking my uncle about the scholarship student thing had made me feel closer to him. Although, this question had the potential to backfire in my face.

"Did your mom tell you to be nice to me?" I whispered when I thought she was fast asleep.

My question was greeted with silence. I breathed a little easier. It was better this way. Me never hearing her say it out loud.

"Yes," Kennedy finally said, breaking the silence.

I swallowed hard. I'd already known it. But I wished I'd never asked. What if she ditched me now that I knew? The jig was up. She didn't have to pretend anymore.

"But she didn't have to. I could tell you needed a friend." There was a long pause. "I needed one too."

I let my tears fall down the sides of my face and into my hair. For the first time since moving here, I didn't feel so alone.

CHAPTER 5

Monday

I pulled my backpack over one shoulder and hurried out into the kitchen. I probably would have taken ages picking out an outfit to wear today if I had a choice. But I only had one uniform skirt and blazer. I had taken a while putting on mascara and lip gloss though. Matthew Caldwell had noticed me on Friday night. I wanted to make sure that wasn't a one-time thing.

I stopped at the front door when I saw my Keds on the floor. At least, I thought they were my Keds. But the stains were completely gone. So was the hole in the side. I lifted them up and ran my finger along the stitching where the hole had been a few days ago. *Good as new.*

There was no note from my uncle. Just my shoes sitting there. I smiled even harder as I kicked off my other shoes and slid on my Keds. I went across the hall and knocked on Kennedy's door.

She answered, balancing a plate of food in her hand. "You look hot," she said and shoved some eggs into her mouth. "You're also twenty minutes early. What gives?"

I shrugged. "Just got ready fast."

"Nothing to do with Matthew?"

How could she already read me so well?

"Is that Brooklyn?" Kennedy's mom called from somewhere in their apartment.

"Hi, Mrs. Alcaraz!" I invited myself into Kennedy's apartment and walked over to her mother in the kitchen.

"Mi amor, are you hungry?" She gave me a swift kiss on the cheek at the same time she flipped an omelet.

"No, I'm good. Thank you though."

"Sí sí." She turned her attention back to her daughter when Kennedy set her plate down on the counter. "Kennedy, you need to finish your breakfast. It's the most important meal of the day."

"I'm full. Besides, we have to get to school early because Brooklyn has a crush on this boy and she wants to make sure she gets to see him before classes start."

Wow. Just the truth then? I thought she might make up a fake project or something as our reason to hurry to school. But I wasn't mad. Honestly, if my mom was here, I would have told her the truth too.

"A boy?" Mrs. Alcaraz asked. "That attends your school?"

The way she said it made me feel uneasy. I understood her skepticism. But she hadn't met Matthew. He wasn't like the rest of the students at Empire High.

"Don't worry, Mama," Kennedy said. "I won't let her get mixed up with the wrong crowd."

Mrs. Alcaraz laughed. "I was more worried about her heart. But only she can protect that." She winked at me. "Have a good day, mis niñas. Don't get into any trouble."

"Nunca!" Kennedy yelled over her shoulder as she grabbed my arm and pulled me to the door.

"What does nunca mean?" I asked as we made our way outside.

"Never."

"Are you fluent in Spanish?" I only ever heard her use a few Spanish words when she was around her mother. I knew Kennedy's father was white from the pictures I'd seen around the house. Kennedy had all her mother's beauty, but her skin was a little lighter. Looking at her you'd just think she was tan.

"No, not really. But I've picked up on the important things. Like nunca," she said with a laugh. "It's really the most important word. I tend to use it a lot."

I laughed as she tucked her arm in mine. We walked down the sidewalk, avoiding the homeless man standing on the corner and licking a slice of pizza.

"I see that you decided to get new sneakers," she said. "I was really hoping you wouldn't give in. If you like your old ones then you should just wear them."

"I didn't buy new ones. My uncle fixed them." What kind of money did she think I had lying around? And I loved my Keds. I wouldn't let one jerk tell me what I could and couldn't wear. Even if said jerk was intimidating. And awful. And a little scary.

"Really?" Kennedy stared down at my shoes as we approached the school. "Wow, they look almost perfect. Go Uncle Jim. First the gossip thing. Now he's a cobbler? I don't know him nearly as well as I thought. He's really pulling out all the stops for you."

I smiled. He was certainly surprising me. When I moved here, I had convinced myself I was a nuisance. That he didn't want me. But now? Maybe he had been just as lonely as I was.

"They're not here yet," Kennedy said and pointed to the spot that the Untouchables' Benz was always parked. There weren't assigned parking spots. But everyone at the school seemed to know not to park there. Which was pretty impressive since most of the students drove to school or were chauffeured by a driver. It was a little silly that this prestigious school was located in the heart of the city when most of the kids that attended it lived in fancy mansions on the outskirts of Manhattan. Some were even from Jersey.

"Come on," Kennedy said and dragged me up the steps toward the front doors. "You can't just wait around for him to show up. You'll seem desperate."

I was a little desperate, but I allowed her to steer me away from their parking spot. All weekend I'd had trouble focusing on my homework. I was even worse at my job. Luckily I hadn't dropped any more trays on my second day of work or I probably would have been fired.

But how could I not think about those few minutes in the bathroom with Matthew? The way he stared at my reflection in the mirror. The way he touched me. He made me feel alive again. He made me want to keep living.

We stopped at Kennedy's locker first. Then mine. Still no sign of the Untouchables and it was almost time for homeroom. Fortunately there was no sign of Isabella either. Maybe the stick up her butt had finally killed her.

Kennedy snapped a picture of me staring at the clock in the hall. "No worries, you'll see him at lunch instead. We should probably get to class so we're not late."

UNTOUCHABLES

It was funny when Kennedy said stuff that made it seem like she cared about doing well in school. Because usually everything out of her mouth claimed the opposite.

I was jealous that she was in the same homeroom as Matthew. I was on the complete opposite side of the alphabet and therefore all the way at the other end of the hall. "Maybe he'll say hi to you in class," I said.

"Doubtful." She was staring at her camera screen. "I'm not the one he has the hots for. Plus he's never spoken to me and we had the same homeroom all of last year too. But I'll let you know if he does." She nudged my shoulder and went off toward her class.

The bell was about to ring any minute, but I still waited a few more seconds before closing my locker. I just wanted one taste. *Look*. I meant look. But the front doors of the school stayed closed. I started to walk to class. *Guess I have to wait until lunch.*

As soon as I thought it, I heard Matt's voice. I turned around. The Untouchables, minus Mason, had just walked into the school. Matt and Rob seemed to be arguing about something, but I was too far away to hear them. James was completely silent. His eyes were bloodshot and his tie and blazer were askew. I thought about the champagne he had been downing at the party on Friday. Was he drunk? He started laughing. I wasn't sure about what. But the other two didn't find it funny.

Matt started to pull James toward the men's room and said something I couldn't hear.

"Fuck off, Matt," Rob said, his voice rising. "I said I've got it covered."

"Is this covered to you?" Matt gestured to James. "He's going to get expelled if anyone sees him like this. If this is covered, you're doing a shitty job."

James started laughing.

"Shut the hell up, James," Matt said.

It looked like Rob was about to take a swing, but then he shook his head. I'd never seen him look defeated before. He was always laughing and making jokes.

"I can handle him," Matt said. "You gotta get to class."

"So do you," Rob said.

"I haven't been late yet. You have. Come on, get to class."

It looked like Rob was about to protest again, but Matt pulled James toward the bathroom to end the discussion.

Whatever was going on, I knew I wasn't supposed to see it. They were late for a reason. And the halls were empty except for them and me. I turned away before they saw me watching.

***

The bell rang, signaling the end of English. Kennedy and I both started to pack up our backpacks.

She zippered hers shut and turned to me. "Matthew strolled in late to homeroom and got yelled at by Mr. Lewis. And before you ask, no, he didn't say hi to me."

I nodded but didn't say anything. Even though I had walked away quickly this morning, my class was at the other end of the hall. They definitely saw me. They'd know that I'd overheard. Although I had no idea exactly *what* I had overheard. I still felt guilty though. Eavesdropping wasn't very becoming. And I didn't usually do it. I just had a hard time not staring at them. And listening to them, apparently.

"Hey, you okay?" Kennedy asked as we both stood up from our desks. "You barely took any notes today."

"Yeah." I shook my head. "Sorry, I was daydreaming."

She laughed. "Shamelessly daydreaming about Matthew? Don't worry, you can borrow my notes."

I had been daydreaming about Matthew all weekend. But my daydreams weren't as fun today. I was lost in thought about what I'd seen in the hall. But I didn't know what to say to Kennedy. "How much do you know about James?"

"Don't tell me you already want to hop in bed with another one of them?"

"No," I said with a laugh. "I just noticed at the party on Friday that he was drinking champagne. Underage."

She laughed. "What high school student hasn't had a drink?"

Me. I hadn't. I'd never been to a party back at my old school because I was always working. And my mom hadn't kept alcohol in the house, not that I'd wanted to try it. "Right."

"Why do you care about James' drinking habits?"

Because it looked like he showed up drunk to school today. And by the way Matt and Rob were acting, it wasn't the first time. Instead of saying it, I kept my mouth closed. It wasn't my business. And the last thing I wanted to do was spread a rumor about something that might not even be true. I knew what it was like for people to talk about me behind my back. I'd never do that to someone else. "No reason," I said. "Just thought it was unfair that they got champagne and we didn't."

Kennedy laughed. "Next weekend we can slip some in the kitchen."

I nodded even though I had no intention of doing that. Taking leftovers that the owners gave us was one thing. Drinking champagne while on the job? Nope. Not happening. Nunca.

"See you at lunch!" she said. "And have fun in gym, weirdo."

She knew how much I loved gym. I didn't have time to do any after school sports because I had to study. Gym was the one class I got to give my heart a good workout. It was quickly becoming my favorite one.

"Have fun in photography!" I called after her.

She waved her hand and disappeared into her class-room.

CHAPTER 6

Monday

After my second mile I collapsed on the bleachers to catch my breath. There was no better feeling in the world than a great workout. I leaned back and closed my eyes, relishing the heat of the sun on my skin.

We were allowed to choose between basketball and prepping for our mile run today. It was an easy choice. No one would have picked me to be on their basketball team anyway. I was the awkward new girl that no one wanted around. But running was for a team of one. That's where I excelled.

My breathing started to slow. I could probably fit in at least two more miles. My goal was to run a mile in under 7 minutes. I was only one of a handful of people that had chosen this option, so I was probably going to crush everyone in a few weeks when they did the official timing.

"You're getting faster."

I opened my eyes and looked behind me to see if whoever had spoken was talking to me. Even if it was doubtful. But there was a boy sitting on the bleachers a few rows above me staring directly at me. I'd noticed him before. He usually elected to run too, but I'd never actually seen him do anything but sit on the bleachers. The PE teacher never came out here to check on us because he was refereeing whatever was going on in the gym. So I didn't really blame him for not trying.

I shrugged my shoulders. "A little. If you're keeping time for me then I guess I can stop trying to figure out how to use this thing." I lifted up the stopwatch Coach Carter had given me.

Bleacher Boy laughed and slid down the few rows to join me. "Not much else to do out here."

"Hmm. Well, you could run. Like you're supposed to."

"Supposed to." He shook his head. "Supposed to isn't very fun. Besides, this class is an easy A. I can sit here for the whole semester and I'd still get an A. I did it last year."

He looked too fit to just sit around lazily all the time. Not as fit as the football players, but still in good shape. "You sat right here on the bleachers all semester?"

"Whenever running was an option. And the other option wasn't tennis or something else outside where Coach Carter could see me sitting here." He propped his feet up on the seats below us.

"You don't look like you just sit around all day."

"Are you checking me out, newb?"

I laughed. "No." It came out more defensive than I meant it to. Which made me sound guilty. He was good looking. But I hadn't been checking him out. I was already obsessed with one student that was out of my league. Two seemed like overkill.

"It's okay if you were. I can't help it that I was blessed with such great genes." He flashed me a cocky smile.

"You're incorrigible."

"No, my name's Felix." He held out his hand.

I laughed. "Brooklyn."

"Brooklyn Sanders. Yeah, I know. Coach Carter calls attendance every day."

Right. But I hadn't known his name. I was always distracted worrying that I would miss the teacher calling my name and totally embarrass myself. I hated saying "here." It was the worst part of this class. Why didn't Coach Carter just learn our names?

"Also, you're on everyone's radar. Scholarship students always get a lot of flak. But you're also on the top of Isabella's shit list. Double red flag."

"How do you know I'm on Isabella's shit list?"

He shrugged. "Heard about the party on Friday night."

Oh God. Hearing about it was probably worse than witnessing it. Maybe. They were probably just equally bad. "Then why are you talking to me?"

"Because I don't care about Isabella. Or how much money you have. I'm deeper than that, newb." He lightly nudged me with his elbow.

I smiled. Felix was only the third person to be nice to me at this school. The fact that he was doing it even though he knew Isabella would give him hell? Even nicer. And I wasn't at all opposed to having another friend here. Besides, I found it incredibly easy to talk to him. "Deeper, huh?"

"Yeah. The deepest. I'll show you with a question. Wait for it…What's your favorite color?"

I laughed. "That's not deep. And I need to get back to running." I stood up.

"Fine. If you insist." He stood up too.

"Are you actually getting off your butt to run a mile?"

"Well, apparently I have to in order to learn your favorite color." He followed me onto the track.

Instead of sprinting ahead like a show-off, he set his pace with me. I was right. He definitely didn't just sit around all the time, because he wasn't out of breath at all.

"Do you play sports?" I asked.

"You can't ask me a question before you answer the one I asked first."

I thought about my home back in Delaware. When my mother was healthy she was always in the kitchen singing while she cooked. Some of my favorite memories were in that kitchen. The walls were bright yellow like the sun. "Yellow."

"Good to know. And no, I don't play organized sports. I'm not an asshole."

I laughed. "What does being an ass have to do with organized sports?"

"Favoritism. Elitists. Literally slapping other guys on the ass. Not my thing."

I'd never thought about it that way.

"Don't tell me you're on the volleyball team or something. I didn't mean to insult you."

"No. Organized sports aren't my thing either." Maybe they would have been in a different life. But I didn't have enough time.

"Well, we're on a running team of two now. So if you ever feel like you're missing out on the ass slapping of organized sports, you're welcome to slap mine anytime." He winked at me.

I started laughing so hard I had to stop running. "No," I said through another fit of laughter.

He ran backward so he could still look at me. "Had to ask. See you at lunch, newb." He waved and ran toward the gym where Coach Carter was calling us back inside.

***

Kennedy plopped her tray down next to mine and took a bite of her apple.

My eyes were glued to the Untouchables' empty table. They had been late to school. And now late to lunch too. I bit the inside of my lip. What the hell was going on?

"What's up with you?" Kennedy asked. "I thought you'd be all excited for lunch so you could stalk Matthew."

"I'm not stalking him." Part of me wanted to tell her about what I'd seen this morning. But it wasn't my business.

"So you aren't going to march up to their table and sit with them? It's the perfect time. You can just sit there and they'll have to join you when they come."

I laughed. "No." *Definitely not.*

"Suit yourself," she said with a shrug. "I'm actually a little relieved. I thought you were going to ditch me."

"Nunca."

Kennedy laughed and took another bite of her apple. "Nunca."

I tried to focus on Kennedy instead of the empty table. "How was photography?"

"Great, I got to develop some prints." She pulled out a picture from her backpack and handed it to me. It was one she took of us Friday night, smiling in my room. It was strange seeing myself so happy when I felt so completely not. I tried to hand it back to her.

"It's yours," she said.

"I can keep it?"

"Yeah. I thought you needed some pictures of me in your room."

I laughed. "Thanks, Kennedy." I was determined to be that happy girl in the picture. Having evidence that I could be was going to be a great reminder.

"Did you break your mile time yet?" she asked.

"No, not yet." I glanced at the Untouchables empty table again. No sign of any of them. "Do you know Felix?"

Kennedy dropped her apple on her plate. "Yes. Why? Do *you* know him?"

"He's in my gym class. He talked to me today."

She raised both her eyebrows. "To like...sell you something?"

"Um...no? He was just being nice."

Kennedy leaned forward. "He's a drug dealer, Brooklyn. Drug dealers aren't just nice for the sake of being nice. He's trying to get you to buy from him."

A drug dealer? I laughed. *No way.* "I think you have the wrong Felix. I didn't get his last name, but it's not the guy you're thinking of. He didn't try to sell me anything."

"That's the whole point. He befriends you and makes you think he's all sweet and then asks you to buy stuff. It's his play." She lifted her apple back up and took a bite that I could only describe as violent. "Trust me. Felix is bad news."

"Bad news?" Felix asked as he sat down next to Kennedy. "I'm hurt. I thought we were friends."

"In your dreams," Kennedy said.

He flashed her that same cocky smile he'd flashed me earlier.

"Brooklyn is not a customer, so take your antics somewhere else."

"Ouch." Felix touched his chest. "That hurts. I'm just being cordial. Can't a guy come say hello?"

"Not when he's you."

"Psh, you love me." He picked up one of her sweet potato fries and ate it.

"You have it backward. I hate you."

I didn't know Kennedy that well, but by the expression on her face, it didn't look like she actually hated him. She looked more annoyed than anything. Or maybe flustered?

"Great picture of you guys," Felix said and nodded toward the one Kennedy had just given to me.

"Thanks," I said.

"Weren't you just leaving?" Kennedy said at the same time.

Why was she being so mean? I glanced over at the Untouchables' table. Still no sign of them.

Felix laughed. "So tell me," he said and leaned forward, trying to get my attention. "How did a girl like you end up in a shitty place like this?"

I laughed, trying to ignore the table that was calling to me. "You mean the nicest school in the city?" *Because my mom died. Because my uncle works here.* But I didn't want to talk to him about my mom. And my uncle didn't want anyone to know he worked here. "Like you said during gym. I have a scholarship."

"Obviously, but I meant the fact that you're not a lo-cal. You're clearly not from New York."

I wasn't sure whether to be offended or take it as a compliment. I wasn't a New Yorker. And I was glad I wasn't. Before I could think of what to say, I noticed movement out of the corner of my eye. Mason, James, and Rob were all seated there now, but Matt was still missing. James didn't look anything like he had this morning. I was pretty sure he was even wearing a freshly pressed uniform, because the one he had on earlier had looked disheveled.

"I'm sorry, what was your question?" I asked.

"Where are you from?"

"She's from a small town in Delaware," Kennedy said. "And she knows better than to get mixed up in whatever the hell you're doing. So scram."

Felix laughed. "I'm just talking to you guys. I'd never sell anything to someone like Brooklyn." He winked at me.

Again, I didn't know whether to be offended or not. But his statement seemed to confirm that Kennedy was right. Felix was a drug dealer. She was probably right about all of it. He was trying to befriend me so I'd buy from him. He should have been talking to the rich kids here, not me. I didn't have money for drugs, not that I'd ever take them. "Kennedy's right, I don't do drugs."

"Great." He glanced at her and then back at me. "Be-cause I'm not trying to sell either of you anything. I swear."

"I find that hard to believe," Kennedy said.

He shrugged. "Believe me or not, I have more than enough clients. I didn't come over here to sell you pot. I was actually inviting you to a party at my house on Friday night."

Kennedy laughed. "No thanks."

"Newb?" he looked at me.

"God, you already have a nickname for her and everything?" Kennedy rolled her eyes.

"What Kennedy meant to say is thank you, but we're working," I said. "I'm sorry." I was apologizing more for her behavior than anything.

He smiled. "It'll go pretty late, so swing by after. Kennedy knows where I live. Catch you girls later." He tapped twice on the table, stood up, and walked away.

"What the heck was that?" I asked. "You didn't have to be so mean." I felt the hairs rise on the back of my neck, the same way they had when Matthew had walked into the bathroom Friday night. I glanced at his table out of the corner of my eye. But he still wasn't there.

"Me? You kept looking at the Untouchables' table the whole time he was talking to you. That was just as rude."

"You kept telling Felix to leave," I said without acknowledging her comment. I knew I kept glancing at the Untouchables' table. I was practically addicted to looking at them. But this wasn't about me. Something was up with her. "Why?"

Kennedy shook her head. "Stop talking."

"Really, what did he do to you? Please don't tell me you used to be addicted to crack or something."

Even though I said it as a joke, Kennedy started to shake her head even more frantically.

"You weren't, were you? A crack addict?"

"Sh! He'll hear you."

I glanced over at Felix. He was across the cafeteria now. "You can tell me. You know that, Kennedy. What did he do to you?"

"Stop talking," she mouthed silently at me this time.

"Sometimes one taste is all it takes," Matthew said and sat down next to me. "Your friend is just looking out for you."

It felt like all the air left my lungs. Oh my God, that's why she was shaking her head. I silently cursed myself for not realizing she was trying to tell me Matthew was behind me. And I had no idea what I had just been saying. Hopefully it wasn't something embarrassing. But I was pretty sure I had been talking about crack. "Hi, Matthew," I said. My voice came out all weird and high.

He smiled. "You can call me Matt."

"Matt." I was pretty sure I was melting under his gaze. I'd been waiting to talk to him all day, and that was all I could muster to say? I'd watched him a lot at lunch, but I never realized how comically big he was for the little seats attached to the table. He barely fit, which made so many parts of him a fraction of an inch away from touching me. Or was he just leaning in closer to me? My heart started beating fast. We'd been this close once before, but not in public. Not when we were surrounded by other students that I was pretty sure he knew didn't want me around.

"I'd recommend staying away from Felix too," he said. "You don't want to get mixed up in that."

I nodded. "Nunca."

He laughed. "Never. That's good to know."

I hadn't even realized I'd said it out loud. Kennedy laughed too.

Matt looked over at her. "Mr. Lewis is kind of an ass huh?" he said.

Her face flushed. "Definitely. You were only a few minutes late. It wasn't a big deal."

He smiled at her and then looked back down at me. Or rather…my hand. "How's the cut?" He'd lowered his voice, but I knew Kennedy could hear. Still, it felt intimate, even though we were in the crowded cafeteria.

"Better. Thanks to you."

He reached out and ran his index finger along my Band-Aid. As if only seeing it for himself would reassure him.

Yup, I was definitely melting. I'd thought about this moment a lot. But it was never like this. He'd invited me into his world in my dreams. There was something nice about the fact that he'd come over and sat in mine. We both knew I didn't belong in his.

And he didn't seem as untouchable over here. Or maybe it was because he was touching me.

"And your shoe?" he asked.

"All better too."

"Close call."

If only he knew.

He leaned a little closer to me, his thigh brushing against mine. I thought his hands were warm. The rest of him was scorching. It felt like I could barely breathe.

"About what you overheard this morning…" he said.

I shook my head. "I really didn't hear anything. I was on my way to class. I just saw you guys and it looked like you were fighting. It's none of my business anyway."

He licked his bottom lip as he listened to me. If that was the way he concentrated, I wanted to be his new study partner. Maybe he'd let me lick his lips for him. His smile grew, like he knew I was staring.

I forced my eyes back up to his. For a moment everything disappeared. It was just us alone in that bathroom again. My heart started beating even faster as he stared at me intently.

"Just don't tell anyone, okay?" he said. "We're taking care of it."

I nodded even though I didn't know what exactly I was agreeing to. But I trusted him. It was hard not to believe everything that fell out of such a perfect mouth.

He cleared his throat. "Sorry, I shouldn't have even mentioned it. That's not why I came over. I was thinking," he said and leaned in even closer. "Maybe we could go…"

"Matthew," Isabella said, cutting him off. She put her hand on his arm. I watched as her fingernails dug into the fabric of his blazer. "We need to have a word."

"I'm in the middle of something, Wizzy." He shrugged her off.

The expression on her face made it look like she was going to slap him. I wasn't sure if it was because he'd called her Wizzy or that he had shrugged her off. Probably both. But I was way more curious about why that was her nickname.

She didn't slap him, but she didn't back down either. "Now. It's about that *extracurricular* we talked about the other day. You know the one. I wanted to see if we should tell our friends all about it." I was pretty sure she tried to smile sweetly at him, but it looked like she was about to bite his neck and suck his blood.

Matt lowered his eyebrows. "Yeah. No." He shook his head and turned back to me. "I'll see you in class, okay, Brooklyn?"

Isabella pulled him away before I had a chance to respond.

The ticking I always heard in my head stopped. *Boom.* No wonder Isabella hated me. *Extracurriculars my ass.* I swallowed hard. Were they dating?

"You got asked out twice in one day," Kennedy said without looking up at me. "I think that's a new record." She pushed around her sweet potato fries with a fork.

What was up with her? "Felix asked us both to come. And Matt didn't get to finish his sentence. But I don't think he was asking me out." *He ran off with Isabella the second he got a chance.*

"Of course he was. Stupid Isabella just cut him off."

"Maybe." But I had a sinking feeling in my stomach. "I guess I'll find out in class."

Kennedy continued to absentmindedly push her food around her plate.

"Do you want to talk about what happened with Felix?" I asked.

The bell rang, signaling the end of lunch.

"Saved by the bell," she mumbled and got up so fast I didn't get a chance to say goodbye. But she hadn't said goodbye either.

I sat there for a moment longer. My new friend Felix was a drug dealer. Kennedy was mad at me. And Matt was probably dating Isabella. Could this day get any worse?

CHAPTER 7

Monday

It was finally time for my last class of the day. Entrepreneurial studies. Better known to me as my class with Matt, because I was much better at studying him than the assignments. I sat down in my usual seat, which was always directly behind Matt. It was the only time I could stare shamelessly at him. And even though my stomach was twisted in knots from my shitty day, I was still excited to see him. Talk to him. That would be a first in this room. But I wasn't going to pretend that nothing happened at lunch like I was pretending I hadn't seen anything this morning. I needed to know if he was seeing Isabella. The thought made my stomach churn even more.

Matt and Rob came in right before the bell rang.

I smiled up at Matt and he…didn't even glance in my direction as he sat down in front of me.

I opened my mouth and then closed it. That was harsh. Was he seriously going to act like Friday night hadn't happened? Like he hadn't just sat with me at lunch? What the hell?

I pressed my lips together. He was probably just focused on getting to his seat in time. *Right?*

Mr. Hill was writing something on the board.

I took his moment of distraction to lean forward. "Matt?" I whispered.

He didn't turn around. He didn't move at all. It was like he hadn't even heard me. I touched my throat, like maybe there was something defective in my vocal cords.

The girl that sat to my left snickered. I recognized her from Isabella's posse. I was pretty sure her name was Charlotte.

"In your poor girl dreams," Charlotte said with a laugh. She didn't even bother to whisper. A few other students laughed too.

Matt didn't laugh. But he also didn't come to my rescue like he had on Friday night. He just…didn't acknowledge that anything had happened at all. For some reason, that stung even more.

I didn't feel like I was going crazy though. Because Rob turned to him and gave him a strange look, like he was trying to figure him out too.

"You're here," Charlotte said and put her hand on my desk. "The Caldwells are here." She lifted her hand above my head. "So why are you even attempting to speak to him?"

"Because we're friends," I said, more to the back of Matt's head than to her. And despite the fact that I believed it, the words came out as more of a question than a statement. Because right now I could really use a friend. And Matt? He was ignoring me like what Charlotte was saying was true.

Matt ran his fingers through his golden hair instead of agreeing with me. But I noticed the way his shoulders were moving up and down a little faster like he was breathing hard. Was he holding back laughter?

He's trying not to laugh at me. The realization hit me like a ton of bricks. *He actually agrees with her.*

Rob looked at him and then turned around. "How about you just leave her alone, Charlotte?" he said. "You're acting like anyone here actually likes you when all you are is Isabella's minion."

She glared at Rob. "This is between me, her, and Matt. It has nothing to do with you."

"It does if you…"

"Nope." Charlotte popped the "p" in nope. "She's a loser. No one would be friends with her, including you, Rob. So don't even pretend to be her knight in shining armor when we both know she'll never deserve one."

More students started laughing. I could feel the tears prickling the corners of my eyes.

She turned her attention back to me. "How about you go back to whatever public school you came from?" she said. "Nobody, and I mean *nobody*, wants you here."

The pencil in Matt's hand snapped in half.

"Isn't that right, Matt?" Charlotte said. "Don't you wish she'd just…disappear?"

The way she said it made me swallow hard. What did she mean by that? I wanted to think it meant nothing. But I was pretty sure people as rich as her had the means to make people disappear without a trace.

"Poof. Gone." She snapped her fingers.

"Shut the hell up, Charlotte," Matt finally said. His words were like ice and I felt frozen in place. But he didn't turn around to look at me or her. He just kept looking straight ahead at the board.

"What…it's true," Charlotte said. "He'll never go out with you, Brook or whatever your name is. He'll never even speak to you again. I'm positively sure of it."

"Brooklyn. My name is Brooklyn." I wasn't sure why that was the only thing I'd decided to defend. Like suddenly the only thing I knew for sure was my name.

"Class has started, Miss Sanders," our teacher said and tapped his chalk against the board. "How about you turn to page 27 of your book like everyone else has and read the section about innovation aloud?"

Charlotte snickered.

I felt my face turning red. Was Mr. Hill really calling me out for talking? All I'd said was my name and Charlotte had been antagonizing me for the first few minutes of class. Kennedy had told me that there were rumors about Mr. Hill hating scholarship students. That he sucked up to the rich kids so they'd invest in one of his crazy entrepreneurship ideas or something like that. I'd initially thought about dropping the class, but then it was the only one I had with Matt. And Mr. Hill had seemed okay until…this moment.

"Now, Miss Sanders. Or would you like to spend the remainder of class in the principal's office?"

I opened up to the page he'd written on the board and started reading.

Mr. Hill tapped his chalk against the board again. "I said the section about innovation. You're three paragraphs too high. Pay attention."

It seemed like everyone was laughing at me now. Matt's shoulders were still moving like he was holding back laughter. But my eyes landed on the broken pencil on his desk and suddenly it didn't seem like he was laughing. He seemed…angry. The rage was rolling off his shoulders. I could feel it.

I wanted to stop staring. Because the only person he had to be mad at was himself. Despite what Charlotte thought, I didn't need a knight in shining armor. All I needed was a friend, and he'd failed pretty hard in that department.

"Last warning, Miss Sanders."

Screw me. I'd been staring at Matt instead of reading. I started again three paragraphs down. With all the giggling around me I kept stumbling over my words, making their mockery significantly worse. I kept waiting for Mr. Hill to tell me I could stop reading out loud. But the reprieve never came. He made me recite page after page until the bell rang.

Thank God. My throat was on fire. I wasn't sure I'd ever talked so much in my life. And my ears were ringing with the students' laughter. I was barely holding back my tears.

"Next time don't talk during my class, Miss Sanders," Mr. Hill said. "You're all dismissed."

I wasn't at all surprised when Matt stood up and walked toward the door without saying a word to me. But he turned his head at the last second and glanced at me. I'd recognize the look on his face anywhere. Pity. It's how everyone looked at me after my mom died. But he didn't know anything about my mom. He actually didn't know a single thing about me. And I didn't need his pity. I didn't need anything from him. Not in this classroom. Not ever.

"Later, Brook," Charlotte said and followed Matt out of the classroom.

"Brooklyn," I croaked. "My name is Brooklyn," I corrected again, not that anyone was listening to me. Charlotte was right. I didn't fit in here. It was one thing for the other students to hate me. It was another for my teacher to pick on me too. I rushed out of the classroom.

I gathered my things from my locker and shoved them into my backpack. Fuck entrepreneurial studies. Fuck Matt. And fuck Empire High. I was done with this school. I didn't have any intention of coming back. I was going home.

I heard the click of Kennedy's camera but ignored it.

"Why are you emptying out your locker?" she asked.

I didn't respond.

She leaned against the adjacent locker. "Cold shoulder, huh? I get it," she said with a sigh. "I owe you an apology for earlier. It's just…freshman year I thought Felix liked me. And for like five minutes I maybe sorta liked him back because…it's hard not to like the guy. It turned out he just wanted to sell me pot though. I guess I'm still a little bitter about it." She grabbed my hand to stop me from shoving more stuff into my backpack. "Seriously, Brooklyn, what are you doing? I said I was sorry."

"I can't do this anymore." The tears I'd been holding back for the past hour were seconds away from spilling over.

"Can't do what? What happened?"

I shook my head and the dam burst. Tears cascaded down my cheeks.

Kennedy closed my locker before I could pack anything else up and pulled me to the restroom. I thought she was going to ask me a million questions. Instead she just hugged me.

She hugged me while I cried. And cried. And cried some more.

I was an idiot. Because instead of appreciating that someone had my back, I was just sad that Matt hadn't followed me into yet another bathroom to see if I was okay. I cried even harder.

Everything Charlotte had said was true. Matthew Caldwell was a god at this high school. And all I'd ever be to someone like him was a joke. Clearly.

"Do you want to talk about it?" Kennedy asked as she rubbed her hand up and down my back.

"There's not much to talk about." I sniffed and pulled away from her embrace. "Matt didn't talk to me in class. Not even a hello. And he just sat there while Isabella's underling, Charlotte, berated me for five minutes. I don't know what happened. Matt just pretended I didn't exist. And then Mr. Hill yelled at me for talking during class and I had to read out loud for an hour."

Kennedy cringed. "So which one should I kill first…Charlotte, Matt, or Mr. Hill?"

I laughed.

"See, you're better already. Fuck them." She said and pulled me back into a hug. "Who needs any of them?"

"I really just want to go home," I said, ignoring her question. Because the truth was that I needed Matthew

Caldwell. He was the only one here that made it feel like my heart hadn't stopped beating after I buried my mother. And I couldn't let go of the feeling he gave me or else I'd be drowning again. As I stood there crying in the bathroom, I realized it was already too late. I'd been lying to myself the whole time anyway. I was drowning. I'd been drowning for weeks.

"Then let's go home."

She didn't get it. I didn't want to go back to my uncle's apartment. I wanted to go home to Delaware. Where people had known me my whole life and smiled at me when I walked by instead of sneering. I wanted to sit on my mother's grave and tell her about my shitty day. I was too far away from her here. And I didn't know how much longer I could keep going with so much distance between us.

CHAPTER 8

Friday

I pushed my sweaty bangs off my forehead as we started our fourth mile.

"Are you coming tonight?" Felix asked. He didn't seem out of breath even though he still preferred the bleachers. Today he didn't have a choice though because the rest of our gym class was playing frisbee golf outside. Coach Carter had a clear view of the bleachers and the track.

I wanted to go to his party. Despite what Kennedy seemed to think, Felix was a genuinely nice guy. Every day since he'd first talked to me on the bleachers he kept talking to me. Which apparently was a rarity when it came to Empire High. I tried to shove the thoughts of Matt aside. I wasn't sure why one stupid moment in a bathroom had gotten under my skin. Matt was an asshole. Ever since Monday, he'd pretended I didn't exist. Like I was as invisible as I always felt. Each day that went by, it hurt a little less. It wasn't like I even really knew him. Besides, I was used to living in pain. What did one more scar on my heart matter? I just wished he'd never talked to me at all.

Felix on the other hand? I glanced at him out of the corner of my eye. Kind, sweet, handsome. *Drug dealer.* "Who else is invited?" I asked.

He smiled. "That means you're coming."

"I didn't say that. I told you, I have work tonight." But I knew I was smiling back at him. This was only the second time he'd brought up his party to me. I hadn't stopped thinking about it though. And it wasn't just because back home I never had enough time to go to one. Back home no one had ever technically asked me either.

"And I told you that the party will be going till the wee hours of the morning."

I laughed even though all I wanted to know was the exact end time. "You didn't answer my first question." I was starting to think it was just going to be a bunch of other drug dealers. Or drug mules. Or even more sinister individuals.

"If you're worried about Isabella, don't be. I doubt she'd come to a party at my house."

"And why is that?"

"Haven't you figured it out yet?" He got a little closer to me. "I'm not one of them," he whispered and then nodded to the other students in our gym class in the adjacent field playing frisbee golf.

"Not good at frisbee? Tell me about it. Whenever I throw a frisbee it ends up nowhere near where I intended. There's a reason why I chose running today." Even though I chose it every day.

"No, newb. I'm not one of them because I'm not a legacy student. I'm not old wealth. Neither of my parents went here like lots of theirs did. Scholarship students aren't the only outcasts in this dump."

I laughed. This dump? We were literally running on a hundred thousand dollar track. But I got his point. "But they all like you."

"No. They need me. There's a huge difference."

"Why do they need you?" As soon as I said it, I realized it was a dumb question. He sold them drugs.

His smile grew. "Simple supply and demand."

Kennedy thought that Felix was only talking to me to turn me into a customer. But he never brought up his business with me. He probably sensed that I wanted nothing to do with it.

I thought about the Untouchables' conversation I'd overheard on Monday morning. And how disheveled James had looked. Was it possible that he was on drugs? Felix's drugs? I wasn't sure why I cared. But I couldn't get the image of James out of my head. I knew what it was like for a life to be cut short. And it was like James was trying to cut his life short intentionally. Matt had said that he had it taken care of. But I didn't believe a word out of his mouth.

"Why do you sell to them?" I asked and picked up my pace. "You don't need the money."

"Why does anyone here even take drugs?" he countered. "They have everything they could possibly want at their fingertips. It's a rush, newb. An escape. It makes you feel alive."

To take drugs? To sell drugs? I was pretty sure your heart beating was what made you feel alive. But I knew I was a hypocrite. Because I'd told myself that being around Matt had made me feel alive. A rush. A high. And I knew I needed to get him out of my system. My heart beating was enough. I didn't need Matt.

"You know what else makes you feel alive?" he asked. "Parties."

I laughed. "I'll try to come. If I can convince Kennedy." That *if* was key. Because Kennedy had already said no, and I doubted I'd have the courage to go if she wasn't by my side.

Coach Carter blew the whistle to signal the end of class.

"Text me if you need directions or something." Felix pulled a pen out of his pocket and popped the cap off with his teeth. Then he scribbled his phone number onto the back of my hand. I didn't bother to tell him that I didn't have a cell phone. That I couldn't text him even if I wanted to. Which I did. He wasn't an outcast like me. But he said he felt like an outsider. It was possible that he needed my friendship as much as I needed his.

Felix lifted my hand up to his lips. For a second, I thought he was going to kiss it. As if he was a Disney prince. Instead, he blew on the ink.

A chill ran down my spine. I should have known. Princes didn't sell pot.

"And I can make you a promise," he said as he dropped my hand. "Tonight you're going to remember what living feels like."

I knew Felix was bad news. I knew it, but for the first time in my whole life, I didn't care. What was the point of always following the rules? There were no guarantees that I'd have a tomorrow. And I knew that heartbeats weren't enough. My heart was beating and I felt...stuck. Because each time it beat all I could think about was how my mom's had stopped.

I didn't know how Felix was going to make his promise come true. But I wanted him to try. Now I just needed to convince Kennedy to come with me tonight.

***

"No," Kennedy said and plopped her tray down in the hotel's kitchen. We only had a few minutes before our dessert trays would be missed at the party. This was my last chance to convince her.

"But…" I started.

"No. God, I knew you were going to try to get me to go to that stupid party when I saw Felix's number on your hand."

I'd tried to wash it off after I'd memorized every digit. The last thing I wanted was for my uncle to ask me about it. Or Kennedy for that matter. "I just don't understand why you don't want to go."

Kennedy put her hand on her hip. "We hang out with those people all week. Why on earth would you want to go to a party with them?"

"Well, you didn't even let me tell you my very important point."

She just stared at me.

"Isabella's not going to be there."

"I wouldn't be so sure of that. She has a way of showing up when you least expect it. Pretty sure she's a witch."

"Definitely some kind of monster."

Kennedy finally smiled. "I still don't understand why you want to go. Even if Isabella's not there, Matt probably will be. I thought the plan was to avoid him until you graduate?"

That was the plan. Although it was hard when he sat right in front of me in class. Maybe if I sat in front of him it would be easier to forget him. It sure worked for him.

But this had nothing to do with him. I could care less if he was there or not. Felix had promised me that tonight would remind me what living felt like. I needed that. I didn't want to go back to my uncle's apartment and hang out in my bedroom that wasn't even really mine. I wanted one night where I could forget that my life had fallen apart.

I refilled the last of the apple rose puffs onto my tray. "I maybe also have never been invited to a party like this before."

Kennedy laughed.

I finished putting the pastries on my tray.

"Wait, really?" There was the pity again. The look I was used to from everyone but Kennedy. "Why?"

No one wanted the kid whose mom was dying at a party? I don't know. I was kind of a buzzkill. Instead of saying any of that I just shrugged my shoulders. "I was too busy working all the time." And when I wasn't, I was in the hospital.

"Ugh." Kennedy looked up at the ceiling. She took a few slow breaths like whatever she was about to say was going to pain her.

Which made me so freaking excited.

"Fine, we can stop by," she said.

"Really?"

"If you're absolutely positive you don't want to snag a bottle of champagne and have a much better time just the two of us."

"As enticing as that is…I really want to go."

She sighed like tonight was the biggest burden of all time. "But you're paying for the cab up town."

"Done."

"And if you ditch me at this thing I will literally murder you." She started to pile desserts onto her tray too.

"I wouldn't dream of it." Who on earth did she think I'd ditch her for? "I'll be glued to your side all night, I swear. As long as you aren't openly rude to Felix the whole time."

"I'm never rude. Just…honest." She lifted her tray with one hand like a boss. "And we can't stay out too late or my mom will worry. The latest one of these catering events has ever lasted was 1 a.m., so we can't stay out much past that."

I had no idea if my uncle would worry. He hadn't given me a curfew, but I also hadn't given him a reason to give me one. "Deal."

"And…"

"How many ands are there going to be?" I asked.

Kennedy laughed. "Just one more. Promise me you won't smoke weed or something even worse?"

"Yeah, I promise." *Oh, God, is that what Felix meant by reminding me what living feels like?*

"Luckily I brought a change of clothes for both of us. They're in my purse."

UNTOUCHABLES

I had so many questions. But the main one was…how tiny were the clothes if they fit into her purse?

CHAPTER 9

Friday

I stared at the door that had an uncanny resemblance to the ornate front doors of Empire High. Felix said the party was at his house. But this wasn't a house. And I didn't just mean that because he lived in an apartment building. I meant that there was a doorman when we entered the lobby downstairs. There was elevator music. And the thick rug under my feet looked like it cost more than my mother's house. "We must have the wrong address."

Kennedy snapped a picture of me staring. "No, this is it."

"Are you sure?" I ran my fingers down the skirt Kennedy had made me change into. It was way too short. Which made no sense because Kennedy was taller than me. I was pretty sure if she wore this that her ass would be hanging out. Maybe that's why she had forced me into it. She was all long legs and tan skin in her tight dress, despite the fact that she was in the pair of flats she'd worn to work. I was pretty sure I looked the way I felt. I'd settled on the term deflated troll. "We should probably just go home."

"We took the ride all the way up here. You're not backing out on me now." She grabbed my arm and pulled me up to the door. I could hear the music blaring from inside.

"But I thought I'd be wearing my work clothes, not this ridiculous skirt."

"You look hot."

I shook my head. I didn't want to look hot. I just wanted to look like me. Besides, I was a deflated troll, not hot. "And I definitely didn't think Felix's place was so...this." He said he wasn't from old money. This apartment building screamed old money.

"Everyone's apartments at our school look like this. You'll get used to it." Instead of knocking, she opened the door and walked right in, pulling me along with her.

The apartment was huge. And it was as fancy inside as it was out. But where the outside was classically designed the inside had clearly been redone. Everything was modern with sharp lines and cold stone. The foyer had that kind of modern art that looked like a five-year-old made it, but it was probably worth hundreds of thousands of dollars. The only thing that didn't seem fancy was the fact that the floor was shaking from the blaring music. I was pretty sure Felix was literally about to tear down the building with this party.

"Let's go get a drink!" Kennedy shouted over the music and continued to pull me farther into the apartment. It was packed and we had to wind our way through the crowd. And Felix thought *he* didn't fit in. If I threw a party, only he and Kennedy would show up. I'd only been at the party for two minutes and I was thinking my party of three sounded a whole lot better. These things were overrated. I couldn't even talk to Kennedy because it was too loud. She pulled me into the kitchen. It was as big as my uncle's whole apartment.

"Here," Kennedy said and shoved a plastic cup into my hand.

"What is it?"

She shrugged. "Some kind of punch."

Oh. Yum. I loved a good punch. I took a huge sip. It was delicious. At least one thing at this party was good. "Should we try to find Felix?" I asked.

"No need," Kennedy said and nodded behind me.

Before I could turn around, Felix threw his arm around me.

"You made it," he said and smiled down at me, keeping me tucked into his side.

I was pretty sure he'd known all along I would try to come. Even before I did. "Yeah, work ended early."

"My lucky night. You look beautiful, as always."

I could feel my cheeks turning red.

Kennedy snapped a picture of the two of us.

Felix lifted his head. "Sup, Kennedy?"

"Great party," she said, but her tone was laced with insincerity. Her eyes were glued to the display on her camera instead of him.

God, she promised to be nice. I took another sip of my punch.

"Let me show you two around," Felix said.

"I've already been here, remember? Never mind, of course you don't. But you two go ahead. I'm just going to take some pictures." She lifted up her camera.

"Not for blackmailing purposes, I hope," Felix said with a laugh.

"Yeah, I'm not an ass. Unlike some of us." She disappeared into the crowd before I could stop her.

I had promised I'd be glued to her side all night. But she'd taken the first chance she could to unglue herself. "I'm so sorry," I said. "She promised she'd be on her best behavior."

"I don't think it's in Kennedy's nature to be nice. Here, let me refill that for you." He grabbed my cup.

That wasn't true. Kennedy was always nice to me. I thought about last weekend when I'd asked her if her mom had made her hang out with me. She had been forced to be kind to me. But we had quickly become friends. And Kennedy was one of the sweetest people I knew. Felix was a close second. So it was strange that they weren't friends. I needed to ask Kennedy more about what happened between them freshman year. She said she thought Felix had liked her, but that she'd only liked him for about five minutes. How many hard feelings could there still be?

Felix handed me my cup. It was filled to the brim with the delicious punch.

"Thank you." I took another huge sip. "So about that tour…"

He smiled and grabbed my free hand. I was pretty sure the last time a boy had held my hand was in fifth grade. And he'd been dared to do it at recess.

Felix wound me through all the people, showing me the living room, dining room, and every other room you could possibly imagine. Including a movie theater and something he called a jungle room, which from what I could tell was just a room filled with plants. But I wouldn't put it past him if there were some monkeys or something hiding in there. And all of that was just on the first floor, which was crazy because I didn't realize apartments could be two stories.

"You really do look beautiful tonight, newb."

I pushed my bangs off my forehead and laughed. "I'm wearing sneakers with a skirt. I look ridiculous. I was actually standing outside earlier thinking I looked like a deflated troll." What the hell? Why had I just said that out loud? It was like I had completely lost my filter ever since I stepped into Felix's apartment.

His lips dropped to my ear so I could hear him better. "A troll? Not in a million years. You look sexy as hell."

I was pretty sure my throat made a weird squeaking noise, but I couldn't be sure when the music was so loud. Fortunately that meant he hadn't heard it either. No one had ever called me sexy before. Not even the boy in fifth grade that had held my hand for five whole minutes.

Felix had kept his head dipped down, so when I turned to look at him, his lips were only a fraction of an inch away from mine. I'd never been kissed. But I'd also never wanted it more than in that moment. The music seemed to fade away. I stared into Felix's blue eyes. They reminded me of the ocean. God, I could get lost in them.

He stayed completely still, like he knew this moment was precious too. For some reason my mind started racing. If he closed the gap between us, I was almost positive it wouldn't be his first kiss. He was…Felix. He lived in an apartment mansion that looked like a modernist museum. He was popular at school. And his eyes were definitely easy to get lost in, because I was already swimming in them.

It felt like my brain short-circuited as he moved a fraction of an inch closer. I wanted to follow his lead. But if it was my first kiss and his hundredth kiss? It would be inadequate. I'd be inadequate. Because despite what he said, I wasn't beautiful. I was an invisible girl in a world that I'd never belong in.

"So what's on the second story?" I asked. As soon as I said it, I realized that it sounded really forward. "An arcade?" I said, because it was the first thing I could think of when my mind was focused on the fact that his bedroom was probably up there.

"No, that's down a level," he said.

Three floors? "Seriously? I was kidding."

He smiled. "It's just a few games, not a whole arcade."

"Cool. Oh rats, I'm all out of punch," I said and stared into my empty cup. "Could you bring me some more?"

"Are you sure? You've already had two glasses."

"Of course I'm sure. It's punch. I love punch. Did you make this?" I asked and lifted my cup. "It's yummy. Like your eyes." *What?* "Not that I want to eat your eyes. I just meant that your eyes are this really pretty blue and I want to swim in them. God, I'm thirsty. Are you thirsty? It's hot in here."

He laughed. "Okay I'll get you that drink," he said and lifted my empty cup from my hand. "But then you owe me a dance."

"Deal." I had no idea how to dance. But I did feel like dancing. Just thinking about dancing had me moving my shoulders to the beat. The rest of my body seemed to follow.

"Stay right there, okay? I'll be right back."

"You got it, sir." Where the hell else would I go? I saluted him. *Oh God, why did I just salute him?*

He laughed and disappeared into the crowd.

I stood there by myself, swaying to the music. A yawn escaped my lips and my eyelids closed. I was so tired from work that my mind felt all fuzzy. The sleepier I felt, the more I wanted to dance. Or sleep. It was a hard choice. But my throat was so dry that all I really wanted was to have more punch. I leaned against the wall behind me.

"What are you doing here?"

I closed my eyes even tighter. Was I dreaming? I was pretty sure I had just fallen asleep. But I was also pretty sure I was still standing up because my legs were tired. Why was I standing in bed?

"Brooklyn."

The voice sounded real. And it sounded like Matt. I opened my eyes. I blinked because he was way too close. His face only a few inches away from mine. I was definitely dreaming.

"Sorry, what was the question?" I asked even though I was asleep. My body was all warm like when I wore my flannel pajamas. And he was blurry like I still had sleepy in my eyes.

"You told me you'd stay away from Felix." He looked mad. Like he had in class when he yelled at Charlotte. I remembered the sound his pencil made when it snapped in half. He was so strong. And a dick.

"That's not a question," I said. "And I never said that."

"Nunca. Remember?"

"I don't speak Spanish, weirdo. My friend does. Kennedy. She's my best friend. You probably know her because she's been going to the same school as you for a while now. Not that you care about scholarship students. She's here somewhere but she's taking pictures because I think she's mad at me for some reason. How long ago was that? Never mind, I'm just dreaming anyway. Because in real life you aren't speaking to me." I put my hand on his face. The scruff on his jaw line was rough against my palm. "I do remember that. You pretending I don't exist."

His Adam's apple rose and then fell. "How much have you had to drink?"

I moved my fingers to his lips. They were so soft compared to his scruff. "A couple glasses of punch."

"You're drunk."

I laughed. "No. I've only had punch."

"There's alcohol in the punch, Brooklyn."

"Psh. No. Besides, I'm asleep. I dream of you a lot. You actually talk to me in my dreams. It's nice." I moved my fingers to his hair. It was soft too. Maybe it really was spun from gold.

"Let me take you home."

"I don't need a knight in shining armor, Matt. And even if I did, it wouldn't be you. Because you don't speak to me, remember? Why are you even talking to me now? Because your girlfriend's not here?"

"What are you talking about?" He grabbed my hand and removed it from his hair.

I felt the same spark I had in the bathroom as he cradled my hand in his. Like I was a dumb baby that had just stuck my finger in an electrical circuit. But I wasn't a baby.

And he was just a handsome boy, not a super complicated electrical circuit. I pulled my hand away from him. "I'm talking about Isabella."

"Isabella is not my girlfriend."

"But you stopped talking to me after you talked to her at lunch."

He didn't respond.

"So if it's not because of her…why aren't you talking to me anymore?"

"It's complicated."

"Complicated? Really? You know what's complicated? My mom is dead. She's dead and I'm all alone. I'm alone." I sighed. I was getting sleepier by the second.

Matt opened his mouth again and then closed it. "I'm really sorry, Brooklyn. I didn't know."

"Yeah." I shrugged. "Well, like you said. Life is complicated. I don't have any parents. You're kind of dating Isabella and ignoring me. Whatever, whatever. It's life. And I don't care anymore."

"I'm not dating Isabella. I'm not dating anyone."

A Backstreet Boys song that I used to listen to when I was little came on. I used to dance to it in the kitchen with my mom. She'd turn up the radio as high as it would go. The memory made me smile. Now I really wanted to dance. If my tired body would allow it.

"What about your father?" Matt asked.

"Oh he never wanted me." I waved my hand in the air like it meant nothing even though my heart ached. "He left when he found out my mother was pregnant. I don't even know his first name." I reached out and touched Matt's hard bicep. "You're always such a good listener in my dreams. Do you want to dance?"

"I'm going to take you home now, okay?"

"But I really feel like dancing. I love this song." I tried to pull him toward the dancefloor but his hard body was as heavy as it looked.

"No, I'm taking you home."

"But...it's the Backstreet Boys." Was he insane? This was dance music if there was ever dance music.

"Yeah, you're definitely drunk."

"I only had punch," I said.

"And like I literally told you a few minutes ago...there's alcohol in the punch."

I shook my head. "No. I've never had alcohol before."

"Well, tonight's a first then."

Almost a first. I was about to have my first kiss with Felix. I knew it in my bones. My very hot bones. Was it a thousand degrees in here? "It's hot."

"Yeah, that happens when you've had too much to drink."

Matt was insane in the membrane. I didn't drink alcohol. He probably did. And all the Untouchables. Because they pretended to be cool even though I knew their façade was just that - a façade. They were as broken as me. Except him. I squinted my eyes at Matt. "I don't get it," I said.

"Get what?"

"How much one week can change things. I thought you liked me." I reached out to touch his face again, but he caught my hand in his.

"Let's talk about it on the way home."

Matt was such a buzzkill.

"Hey," Felix said. He was standing next to me with the punch I'd requested.

"Oh, thank you." I grabbed it with the hand Matt wasn't holding and took a huge sip. My dry throat felt a million times better.

Matt pulled the cup out of my hand, spilling some onto the ground. "That's enough."

"But…"

"I'm taking you home." He said it more sternly this time.

"Ignore him," I said to Felix. "He's just a dream." I pulled my hand out of Matt's. "Do you want to dance?" I asked Felix.

He lowered his eyebrows slightly.

"Brooklyn, I'm taking you home," Matt said and grabbed my arm.

"Let go of me." I tried to pull away from him, but his grip was firm.

"She said to let her go," Felix said.

"Why? So you can get her even drunker?"

"She asked for a refill. Get your fucking hands off her."

"And you're taking advantage of her," Matt said.

"Me? Seriously? You're the one about to stuff her in a cab to take her *home*. Get out of my house."

"Yeah, no innuendo there, man. She needs to sleep this off."

Oh my God, what was happening? This time when I pulled my arm away from Matt I did it successfully. "Stop pretending that you care about me."

"I do care," Matt said.

"Really? Did you care when Charlotte ripped me apart in class? Or when she said she wished I would disappear? Or when Mr. Hill made me read out loud for an hour? Or the past week when you didn't even glance in my direction even though you sit right in front of me?"

"I told you it was complicated…"

"Don't throw that bullshit excuse at me when I told you my mom just died. Don't…" I let my voice trail off. "Don't you dare." I could feel tears welling in my eyes as the room started to spin. I felt like I was going to be sick. I tried to swallow down the lump in my throat but it wouldn't budge.

Kennedy showed up just in time. Because she was the only person here who actually cared about me. "How much punch did you have?" she asked after giving dirty looks to both Felix and Matt.

"Just two cups."

She shook her head. "Lightweight."

I laughed even though I didn't know what she was talking about. "And I'm having a nightmare. Matt's pretending he's speaking to me and I messed up my first kiss." I looked at Felix.

Felix's eyes grew a little wide.

So easy to get lost in them.

"Yup, just a bad dream," Kennedy said. "Let's get you home, okay?"

I nodded. "Can we have a sleepover again?"

"Absolutely."

I was pretty sure Kennedy kicked Felix's shin as we walked past him. But none of it mattered. Because I was definitely dreaming.

CHAPTER 10

Friday

"That was so much fun," I said as the taxi pulled up outside our apartment building. "Can we do that again next week?"

Kennedy opened the cab door. "I think you'll be singing a different tune tomorrow morning." She stepped out onto the curb and I followed her.

The movement made my stomach feel weird. Or was it my legs that felt off? Like they weighed more than usual. The thought made me laugh, which made Kennedy start laughing too.

"Cut it out, we have to be quiet."

"But my legs are so heavy," I managed to say through my laughter.

She grabbed my arm to steady me on the curb. "Seriously you have to stop laughing or I'm going to keep laughing. I can't believe you only had two cups."

"I love punch!" I yelled.

She put her hand over my mouth. "Oh my God, Brooklyn stop. You're going to get us in so much trouble. We're definitely sleeping at your uncle's instead of my place." She removed her hand from my mouth and gave me a hard stare. "Did you just lick my palm?"

I started laughing again.

"No more punch for you." She pulled me toward our apartment and somehow managed to force me up the seven flights of stairs, despite my protests.

"I really do love punch," I said as we finally made it to our floor.

"You're a closet alcoholic."

"How many times do I have to explain this to people? First Matt, now you." I leaned against the wall outside my uncle's apartment. "I only had punch."

"Which had alcohol in it."

I shook my head. "I don't think so. I've never had alcohol before."

Kennedy shook her head. "Well that explains a lot. You should have told me. I wouldn't have let you have any."

"But I love it!"

"Shhh! I got that. Be quiet for one minute, okay? Hopefully your uncle is already asleep." She pulled out the key from her purse and was just about to turn it when the door opened by itself. Like magic.

Only it wasn't magic. It was my uncle. And he looked…not happy.

He shook his head. "Get in here before you wake up the whole floor." He opened the door wider and Kennedy pulled me inside.

"I'm sorry, Uncle Jim," Kennedy said. "We're just really wound up from an exciting night of work. So we should probably just go to Brooklyn's room to cool off." She started to pull me toward my room.

"Not so fast."

I bumped into Kennedy when she froze.

"Brooklyn, look at me," my uncle said.

I turned around and looked. Really looked. I just wasn't sure what I was supposed to be looking for.

"Have you girls been drinking?" he asked.

"Only punch," I said.

Kennedy elbowed me in the side, which made me start laughing again.

My uncle ran his hand down his face. "Where were you two tonight?"

"At work," Kennedy said.

But at the same time I said, "At Felix's house."

He just stared at us, waiting for our stories to align.

Kennedy sighed. "We went to a classmate's party for a few hours after work. Please don't tell my mom."

"It was my idea," I added. "I forced Kennedy to go with me. I'd never been to a party before and I thought it would be fun. And it was. It really was. But I'm also pretty sure I'm asleep so…"

My uncle started coughing, drowning out my words.

"Are you okay?" I asked. I started to walk over to him but he held up his hand.

He cleared his throat. "You two need to take better care of each other, okay? I know teenagers drink. I'm not an idiot. I prefer if you don't, but if you're going to drink, make sure to have a glass of water between every glass of alcohol. I don't expect to see either of you like this again. Is that clear?"

"I'm sorry," I said. But I was more concerned about his cough than his lecture on underage drinking. I really hoped this was a dream, because his cold was getting worse instead of better. I was getting worried that he had the flu or something.

"I don't want an I'm sorry. I want you to promise me that the two of you will take care of each other. No more getting drunk. No more of this nonsense."

"I promise I'll watch out for her better," Kennedy said.

"Me too," I said. Which sucked because I really did like punch. "My arms are heavy now too."

Kennedy laughed.

"Go to your room," my uncle said, his voice sterner than I had ever heard it. He didn't have to tell us twice. We both ran out of the kitchen.

Once the door was closed behind us, I breathed a sigh of relief. "That was a close one," I said.

"A close one? Brooklyn, we got caught." Kennedy collapsed onto my bed.

"But he wasn't that mad. Besides, it's all just a bad dream."

She shook her head. "Was it also a bad dream that you almost kissed Felix tonight?"

"No, that was a good dream." I lay down beside her. "But I don't know if he was actually going to kiss me. It just seemed like he wanted to."

An uncomfortable silence stretched between us. I was just nodding to sleep when she spoke again.

"Do you like him?" she asked.

"Who?"

"Felix." Her voice was barely a whisper.

"He's nice to me. He understands what it's like to not fit in at school. He doesn't make me feel invisible."

"Yeah." Another long stretch of silence. "He's good at that."

My eyelids were getting heavy now too. "Then why are you so mean to him?"

Kennedy didn't respond. I turned to look at her, but her eyelids were closed. They must have been as heavy as mine.

***

Oh God, I'm definitely not dreaming. I ran out of my room as fast as I could, trying not to leave a trail of vomit. I reached the bathroom just in time as the contents of my stomach came back up and into the toilet. Again. *Fuck my life*. And again. Until nothing was left.

There was a knock on the door. "How are you doing, kiddo?" my uncle asked.

"Bad."

"Can I come in?"

"Mhm." I draped my arm over the toilet seat.

He walked in. To his credit, he didn't look disgusted. He didn't even look upset anymore. He sat down next to me on the bathroom floor, his back against the vanity.

"Do you want to talk about why you drank so much tonight?"

"I thought it was just punch. I swear I didn't know. But for a few minutes, everything felt better. You know?"

He nodded. Somehow in that one nod, I wanted to tell him everything. Like I knew he'd understand.

"My heart didn't hurt anymore." I rested my head on my outstretched arm. "Like I was numb. Happily numb."

"Numb is numb. There's no happily about it. And being numb is no way to live."

I closed my eyes when I felt a tear fall down my cheek. "But I miss her so much that it hurts."

"Me too, kiddo."

I let my tears fall freely.

"You know, you look so much like your mother. I actually caught her many times in this very same position. Right here in this apartment."

Was that why I liked punch so much? Because my mom was secretly an alcoholic? It would explain why there wasn't any liquor in the house.

"Only once because of drinking," my uncle said, like he could read my mind. "But lots of times when she was pregnant with you. She had really bad morning sickness."

"She was here when she was pregnant?"

He nodded. "Your room was hers. Until she left town in her third trimester."

I always thought my mom was all alone during her pregnancy with me. It was us against the world. Apparently my uncle had been part of that us. And for some reason, knowing she had been here in this apartment made me feel closer to her. She had sat right where I was, sprawled out on the bathroom floor. The thought made my tears stop. "Why didn't you two see each other more when I was little?"

"She hated the city. And it was hard for me to get time off of work."

"Why did she hate it here so much?"

"Because your father was here."

My father? I lifted my head. "Do you know who he is?"

My uncle opened his mouth and then closed it again.

"You do." For some reason I thought that secret had died with my mom. I never cared about my father before she died. He hadn't wanted me, so why should I want to know him? But ever since my mom had died, I'd thought about him more. Because maybe, just maybe, I wouldn't feel so alone if I knew he was out there. And maybe after sixteen years he'd changed his mind about wanting me. "Who is he?"

"This is a conversation for another day." He patted my shoulder and started to stand up. "You need to get some more rest."

"You said he *was* in the city. Does that mean he isn't anymore?"

"Kiddo, your mom didn't want you to know him. And I have to respect her wishes. I have to."

My tears had started again. "But he's all I have left. You have to tell me. Don't you see that I'm drowning? I can barely breathe in this city. I'm all alone." I started sobbing harder. "I'm all alone without her."

My uncle knelt down beside me and pulled me into his arms. "You're not alone. I'm here."

He held me even though I smelled like vomit and my tears and snot were staining the shoulder of his shirt.

"I'm here." He ran his hand up and down my back. "You have me."

I hugged him tighter.

He let me cry until I didn't have any tears left. I appreciated him more than I could ever say. I knew he was trying his best here.

After Uncle Jim gave me a glass of water and sent me back to my room, I lay down and looked up at the ceiling. My mom had been here. Right in this room, staring at the same ceiling I was. Had my father been here too? Had he loved her once? Was it possible that he was somewhere in this city wishing he could know me too?

I stared at the ceiling all night. Eventually the sun started filtering into the room. The sound of cars honking increased. Kennedy started to stir.

I'd come to three very important conclusions. One: Alcohol was absolutely not worth those few minutes of numbness. Two: I could never speak to Felix or Matt again after how embarrassing I was last night. Three: Secrets weren't meant to be kept if the only person that wanted them kept was dead.

CHAPTER 11

Monday

Kennedy snapped a picture of me as I pulled some books out of my locker. "You know you can't wear that all day. It's against the dress code."

I was wearing a hoodie with the hood pulled low over my face and a pair of sunglasses. No one was going to notice that I was breaking the dress code because I was invisible here. But I did hate the idea of breaking the rules. The only thing I hated more was the thought of Matt or Felix seeing me this morning. Or worse…trying to talk to me. I was going to hide from them for the rest of my life.

I adjusted my sunglasses. "I'm going to risk it."

"At least you don't have a hangover anymore," Kennedy said as she scrolled through some pictures. "I can't wait to develop these. Check this one out."

I reluctantly pulled off my sunglasses to look at the screen. *What the hell?* It was a picture of me and Matt from the party. The fact that I was staring up at him with stars in my eyes would have been cute if I wasn't running my hand along his jaw line. I grabbed the camera from her. "You took a picture of me touching Matt's face? Why didn't you stop me?"

"I thought it was like…your thing."

"My *thing*? What does that even mean?!"

Kennedy laughed and took the camera back from me. "I don't know. That you like to touch a man's face before you make out with him?"

"Delete that picture."

"Nah."

"Kennedy, please."

"Nunca."

"Give me the camera!" I reached out for it but she lifted it in the air out of my reach. I jumped but she dodged me and I almost ran into...*screw me*. Mr. Hill. Who stopped. Turned. Stared down at me with that look of hatred he always gave me in my entrepreneurial studies class.

"Miss Sanders, are you going to take off that sweatshirt or will you be spending the morning in the principal's office?" he asked.

"I'm going to take it off." My voice was barely a whisper. And for a second I thought he didn't hear me, because he was still standing there staring at me like I was a piece of shit he'd just stepped into. Which was ironic because he seemed like the exact kind of horrible person that would walk a dog, let it poop on the sidewalk, and not pick it up. *Asshole.* I stared back, wondering if he was going to wipe off the bottom of his shoes.

"Now, Miss Sanders, or I'll escort you to the principal's office myself."

I pulled off the rest of my disguise and shoved it into my locker.

Mr. Hill sighed as if I was the most exhausting person in his life. "Don't let me see you breaking the dress code again or I'll issue you detention myself."

"Wow, the rumors about him are true," Kennedy said when Mr. Hill was out of earshot. "He really does hate scholarship students. I mean, look at Isabella." She nodded her head toward Isabella, who Mr. Hill had just passed in the hall. Her collar was popped and too many buttons at the top of her shirt were undone. And it wasn't even one of the standard-issue collared shirts we were required to wear. Hers was practically sheer. Everything about her outfit was clearly against the dress code. But she actually got a friendly wave from Mr. Hill.

"Pretty sure he just hates me," I said and slammed my locker closed.

"Speaking of hating people..." Kennedy was staring daggers at someone behind me.

I looked over my shoulder to see Felix walking over toward us. Unlike her, I didn't hate him. Quite the opposite. Which was why I couldn't speak to him this morning. Or ever. I was mortified about how I had behaved at his party. Kennedy said that if I had drunk a tiny bit more maybe I wouldn't have remembered anything from Friday night. I wished that had happened. But unluckily for me, I remembered every tiny embarrassing detail.

"See you in English," I said and hurried off before Kennedy could even say goodbye.

***

The avoidance had been going great. But I also hadn't had my classes with Felix or Matt yet. Matt ignored me anyway, so that would be easy. But Felix? My class with him was going to start in a minute. Felix and I always ran together. Which meant I was going to have to participate in whatever horrible lesson Coach Carter had planned in order to keep my distance. Hopefully it wasn't even outside. I didn't want to be anywhere near the track.

I waited till the last second before leaving the locker room. I was going to be fine. But the knot growing in my stomach made me feel anything but fine.

I could feel Felix's eyes on me as Coach Carter called attendance. When he told us the choices were dodgeball or practicing the mile, I was almost tempted to face Felix. *Almost.* But I'd rather literally take a ball in the face than face him. I knew it was cowardly. Sometimes it was easier to hide under a rock though. Bravery was overrated when it came to high school.

I walked over to the side of the gym with the other students that were going to play dodgeball. I glanced at Felix out of the corner of my eye. He was leaning against the doorjamb, his hands shoved into the pockets of his gray sweatpants. He smiled when our eyes met and then nodded towards the track, trying to get me to go outside with him.

I shook my head and turned my attention to the two captains that Coach Carter had just called. A new fear settled into my stomach. I was going to be chosen last. I could already picture the other students laughing. I'd successfully avoided this horrible situation until this moment. But all of them laughing at me was somehow better than Felix laughing. Which would absolutely happen if I spoke to him. I cringed, remembering how I was basically yelling at Matt about him screwing up my first kiss with Felix. My first kiss *period*. Felix was going to think I was such a loser.

One by one, the other students' names were called. Well, I was a loser, so I guess Felix's thoughts were fitting.

When only half of us were left, I saw Felix finally move. But he didn't go outside. He started walking toward me. No. *No, no, no.*

"First you made me run, newb. Now you're seriously going to make me play this stupid game in order to talk to you?" He flashed me that smile that I was growing used to being directed at me.

I shook my head. "I just really love dodgeball, it has nothing to do with you."

"Okay." His smile faded.

One of the captains called his name almost immediately.

He ignored the captain for a second. "Are you mad at me because I didn't text you after you left? I wanted to, but I realized too late that I never got your number."

"I don't have a cell phone."

"Felix," the captain called again.

"Can we please just go outside and talk?" Felix asked.

I kept my eyes glued to the captains. Felix would forget about me soon enough. Besides, he was wrong about us being on the wrong side of the popular crowd together. Everyone loved him. He wasn't like me.

Felix raised his hand.

"Yes, Felix?" Coach Carter said.

"Brooklyn and I changed our minds. Can we run instead?"

"Too late for that, your name was called."

Felix cursed under his breath and joined his team. The captain high fived him like he was thrilled he got so lucky with a late pick. Felix whispered something in the guy's ear. And the next time the captain called a name, it was mine. There were still ten people standing here that had to be better at this stupid game than me.

I walked over to the team, keeping my distance from Felix. But he quickly appeared at my side.

"You didn't have to do that," I said. "I can handle getting called last."

"I told him to pick you because we're in the middle of a conversation. Not because I pity you."

"Good, because I don't need your pity."

For the first time Felix wasn't smiling and joking around. He looked frustrated. And annoyed. All of it aimed at me.

"Is this because of what Matt said?" he asked. "Because I swear to you, I didn't realize you were drunk. I would have cut you off if…"

"Can we please not talk about this right now?"

"When are we supposed to talk about it then? You've been avoiding me all day."

I'd only run in the opposite direction of him twice today. Not *all* day. Well, and the whole dodgeball thing. *God, why am I about to play this stupid game if he's talking to me anyway?*

Coach Carter blew his whistle, at least saving me from answering Felix.

But it didn't stop Felix. The game was in full swing. I was trying not to get hit, but all he seemed focused on was talking to me.

"I don't know about you, but I had a really nice time on Friday." He caught a ball perfectly even though he wasn't paying attention.

"You don't have to lie."

"I'm not lying." He used the ball in his hand to block one from hitting me and then launched it across at the other team. It slammed into one of our opponent's chests.

"Nice one, Felix!" someone called.

He seemed annoyed that other people were talking to him and I wasn't. He grabbed my arm and pulled me out of the way of another ball. "For someone who loves dodgeball, you're pretty terrible at it."

I laughed. I couldn't help it.

His smile returned.

And for a second I remembered how nice it was when he'd held my hand on Friday night. And how easy it was to get lost in his eyes. I looked away.

"Is this about that thing you said about your first kiss being interrupted?" he asked. "Because I can fix that right now…"

I wasn't sure if I was more shocked by what he said or horrified that he'd remembered what I'd said. Regardless, I was distracted when the ball flew directly at my face. It hit me right in the nose and I fell backward, landing hard on my ass.

"Jesus, are you okay?" Felix crouched down beside me and cradled the side of my face in his hand.

"Ow." My face felt like it had been squashed. There was someone on the other side that should be a major league pitcher.

A ball hit the back of Felix's head while he was crouched down with me, but he didn't even flinch.

Coach Carter blew his whistle. "Felix, take her to the nurse!" he called then blew his whistle again.

The game restarted around us as Felix helped me to my feet.

"Is my nose broken?" I asked.

"I don't think so." His arm wrapped around me like I needed his assistance walking. I didn't. But I didn't push him away either.

"What the hell, Cupcake?" Felix said to the captain on the other side. "She was five feet in front of you, why'd you throw it like she was a mile away?"

The captain laughed.

"Idiot," Felix said.

"What'd you say to me?" the captain said. "You wanna take this shit outside?"

Coach Carter blew his whistle again. "Nurse. Now. Cool your loins, Joe. There's no cursing in my gymnasium."

Felix mumbled something under his breath as he walked me out of the gym.

"I think I have a concussion," I said.

"I doubt Cupcake is that strong. He was just standing really freaking close to you. That guy is such an ass."

"Cupcake?" I shook my head. "I definitely have a concussion."

"You really never heard Joe's nickname before?"

"How on earth is someone with the name Cupcake not the least popular person at this school?" I asked.

Felix laughed. "Cupcake's father owns Dickson & Son's Sugarcakes and he always brings in samples. He's a jerk, but his cupcakes are good."

"Private school is so much different than public school. Someone with that nickname would have gotten eaten alive at my old high school. Yet, I'm the loser here. Figures. And what the hell is a sugarcake?"

"You're not a loser, Brooklyn."

"I would have gotten chosen last if it wasn't for you. Everyone at this school pretends I'm invisible or ridicules me. They don't even try to get to know me because I don't have money and prestige like they do. And the only reason I ever attend fancy events on the weekends is because I'm catering them. I'm a social pariah."

"Don't forget the fact that you've never been kissed," Felix added as we walked into the nurse's office.

I was pretty sure it was his new mission to mortify me. I could feel my cheeks flushing. "God, please stop reminding me."

He laughed.

"Oh my, your face is beet red," the nurse said and rushed over to me. "What hurts?" She put her hand on my forehead. "Hm, I don't feel a temperature."

I could feel my face turning even redder.

"She got hit in the face with a dodgeball," Felix said. "She mentioned that her nose hurt."

"I've been telling Coach Carter to outlaw that blasted game. You don't know how many times I get students in here with dodgeball injuries." She grabbed an icepack from the freezer. "You're sure nothing else is wrong? Your face is so very red."

Every time she said it, I'm pretty sure I blushed harder. I placed the ice on my nose. Luckily the icepack was big enough to pretty much cover my entire face. "Nope, I'm good otherwise," I said.

"Alright. Sit down for a minute and ice your nose then."

I sat down on the little cot in the corner of her office. The thin mattress sagged as Felix sat down beside me.

"Seriously though," Felix said. "Money doesn't make up for a bad character. It doesn't make up for anything. And I don't think you're a loser. You're kind. And sweet. And funny. And easy to talk to."

I placed my hand down on the cot between us. I was a coward earlier. But when there was an icepack hiding my face, I found it a lot easier to be brave. One of the things that stuck with me the most about Friday night was how comforting it was when Felix held my hand.

"And beautiful." He placed his hand down on top of mine. "You're really beautiful, Brooklyn."

I was glad the ice pack was hiding my eyes, because they were tearing up. He'd called me beautiful on Friday night. I'd forgotten that underneath all the embarrassing things that had happened.

Our fingers intertwined. And for a few minutes we just sat in silence. I was pretty sure they were the best few minutes of my life.

He reached over and pulled the icepack down from my face. "And one day when your nose isn't hurting, I'd really like to kiss you, newb."

I stared into his blue eyes. I wanted to focus on the fact that he wanted to kiss me as badly as I wanted to kiss him, but a question in the back of my mind was suddenly all I could think about.

What if? I didn't know my father. *What if?* I knew I looked nothing like Felix. I mean, Felix was Felix. *What if?* But my mind had already started racing. *What if?* It was possible. It was horribly possible. *What if Felix and I were related?*

I swallowed hard and forced myself to smile before I pulled the icepack back over my face. I needed to talk to my uncle before I accidentally kissed someone who could be my half-brother. Or cousin. Or…nephew? Was that even possible? I was horrified by the fact that Felix could be in any way related to me. But more so by the fact that I wanted for him to be my first kiss without even knowing the truth. *Please God, don't let Felix be related to me.*

CHAPTER 12

Monday

I plopped my lunch tray down in front of Kennedy. "I have a serious problem."

"Me too. Do these look okay in black and white or would color be better?" She slid a few pictures toward me. "I'm thinking color might be better."

I stared down at the pictures of me molesting Matt's face. As in more than one. More than one angle. More than one shot. "What the hell are *these*?"

"You're right. Color would be better. You can keep those in the meantime."

"I asked you to delete that picture. And there's even more?" I lifted them up and sorted through the nightmarish stack of photos. "Why are you doing this to me?"

"Because I think you and Matt make a great couple. Just look at how he's looking at you. He's smitten."

I noticed before that there were stars in my eyes. But I was pretty sure the same stars were reflected in Matt's eyes. I shook my head. It was just in my imagination. He didn't look at me in *that* way. "Matt is ignoring me. And I'm avoiding him. We are not and never will be a couple. Can we focus on my problem for one second instead of whatever the hell this is?" I tossed the photos back at her.

"Mhm. But those are for you." She slid them over to me again.

"I don't want them."

We proceeded to push them back and forth until I noticed Matt walking into the cafeteria.

Shit. I grabbed them and shoved them in my backpack.

"You're welcome," Kennedy said with a big smile.

"I didn't thank you."

"You will eventually." She shoved a huge forkful of spaghetti into her mouth. "How's the whole avoidance plan going?"

"Not great."

"So is that your big problem? How to better avoid Felix and Matt? With Felix I think the running in the opposite direction thing you've got going on is really productive. And it sends a good message. He'll stay away soon enough."

That plan had failed entirely. If anything, I wanted to be closer to Felix than before. Which was seriously freaking me out now. I thought I could figure out a way to convince my uncle to tell me the truth about my father on my own. But the few times I'd mentioned it since Friday night, he'd quickly changed the subject. And now it was all that I could think about. Well, that and kissing Felix. Which just reminded me of the questions about my father. *Ugh. Gross.*

"No, that's not my big problem. My problem is that my uncle mentioned that my father used to live in the city. What if he still does? What if he has other kids? What if one of his other kids goes here? Or his brother or sister's kid? Or something else like that?"

Kennedy shrugged. "It hardly changes anything for you." She took another huge bite.

"Of course it does. What if I'm related to Felix? What if I kiss my half-brother? Or cousin? Or worse?"

Kennedy started choking and spit her spaghetti all over her tray. "Wait, did Felix kiss you?"

"You're missing the point! I could be related to him."

"But did you kiss him?"

"No. I got hit in the face during dodgeball and ended up at the nurse." I gestured to my nose which was still red from the icepack. "Oh…and there's the little fact that I might be related to him! Of course I didn't kiss him!"

Kennedy took a huge breath. "Well that's good. You should probably not ever kiss him then."

"You're not helping."

"That's just my honest opinion. You shouldn't kiss him because you might be related to him." She shrugged and started eating again.

"I was kind of hoping this conversation would lead you to helping me figure out who my father is."

"Why? You said your father didn't want you. So you shouldn't want him in your life either. Period."

I put my elbows on the table and leaned forward as far as I could. "Did you not hear the fact that I could be related to someone in this school?" I whispered. "How am I supposed to live like that?"

"By not kissing Felix."

Kennedy was exasperating today. It was like all she cared about was whether or not I kissed Felix. She was completely missing the bigger picture. "I need your help.

You know my uncle better than I do. Can you try to get the information out of him?"

"I don't know if I know him better than you…"

"You grew up next door to him. You call him Uncle Jim. Your mom and him are basically best friends."

"Fine. I'll see what I can do. But it might take some time."

"Thank you." Hopefully it wouldn't take that much time. I couldn't always get drunk or hit in the face with a ball to avoid kissing Felix. And I was afraid I'd have to if I was going to be able to resist him.

Kennedy twirled some spaghetti on her fork. "What if you really are related to Felix? Wouldn't that be hilarious?"

"No. Clearly I don't find it hilarious. What's up with you today?"

She shrugged. "Nothing. I'm having an excellent day."

"Okay, weirdo."

She made a kissy face. "Love you back, weirdo."

***

Matt was incredibly easy to avoid. As usual, he didn't glance at me as he sat down at the desk in front of mine. I eavesdropped on his conversation with Rob. They were talking about the football game on Friday. Apparently, Matt got a touchdown and everyone loved him. Yadda yadda.

I knew Matt would never talk to me in class. He'd made that pretty clear. So why did I still stare at the back of his perfect head when he was such a jerk? Unlike the rest of the student body, I no longer viewed him as a god.

Gods didn't ice people out of their lives so blatantly. And then pretend to care at parties. He was as flawed as the rest of the Untouchables. And I no longer wanted to touch.

I stared at my blank notebook page instead. Maybe I was putting too much weight on the whole not knowing my dad thing. I mean, what were the odds that I was actually related to Felix? Pretty slim. My mother and I weren't well off. I doubt she mingled with anyone rich enough to have kids or nephews in this school. Besides, my uncle would have told me if I was about to do something terrible. *Right?* He wouldn't just let me run around kissing my brother. Absolutely not. But I also hadn't told my uncle about Felix… I was going to have to tell my uncle that I liked someone. That could get the truth out of him.

"It's finally time to start our group projects," Mr. Hill said. "From concept to business plan, you and your group will come up with a new, innovative business keeping in mind the things we've been studying in class. And it's worth a quarter of your grade, so you need to take it very seriously."

Whispers broke out throughout the classroom as students started picking their group members. I melted into my seat, invisible as always. It was like gym all over again. But I didn't run the risk of being picked last. I ran the risk of not being picked at all. Hopefully I'd just be allowed to do the project alone. I looked around the room. There were an uneven number of kids in the class, which would leave one student out of a duo. *Perfect.*

Mr. Hill cleared his throat. "Before you get too excited, I already picked the groups."

Everyone in the class groaned except for me. But I should have. Being the outcast forced to work alone was one thing. I could handle that. But being randomly put into Matt's group? That could not happen. And just the thought of it happening had my stomach twisting in knots.

I took a deep breath. The odds of being forced into a group with Matt were slim. But then Mr. Hill started calling out the groups. And it wasn't two people in each, it was three. Which raised the odds significantly…

"Mr. Caldwell, Mr. Hunter, and…Miss Sanders."

"Screw me," I said. Out. Loud. I immediately slapped my hand over my mouth, wanting desperately to go back to being invisible.

Rob laughed and turned around in his seat to face me. "What…we're not *that* bad to be teamed up with, Sanders." He flashed me a smile with his perfectly white straight teeth.

I swallowed hard.

Matt just stared ahead like he hadn't been called at all. How were we supposed to work on a group project if he wasn't speaking to me?

Charlotte raised her hand.

"Yes, Miss King?" Mr. Hill said.

"Brooklyn is having such a very hard time adjusting to our school. I think that it would really benefit her to be in my group. I can help her so much."

Gag. Why was she trying to get me in her group? To torture me to death?

"Can I trade Missy for her?"

"Hey," Missy said and gave her a dirty look.

Mr. Hill placed his attendance sheet down on his desk. "Although I agree with you that Miss Sanders is not adjusting well, the groups are set in stone."

"But…"

"Stone." I'd never heard him so stern with anyone but me.

Charlotte made a huffing noise and crossed her arms over her chest.

It was easy to ignore the fact that Mr. Hill thought I didn't belong here. And that Charlotte was somehow trying to ruin my life in a new and odd way. Because all I could focus on was the fact that I was in Matt's group. I was supposed to be avoiding him.

"Now split up into your groups and start brainstorming what your business is going to be."

Chairs squeaked as everyone started moving their desks around. But I didn't have to move. Matt sat right in front of me. Rob to the left of him.

Rob turned around with another easy smile. "I wonder why Charlotte wanted you in her group. I thought she hated you."

I looked over at Charlotte who was staring daggers in our direction. "She probably just wanted to torture me."

Rob laughed and then hit Matt's shoulder. "Turn around, man, we have to start talking about our business."

He was probably as mortified to talk to me as I was to talk to him. I'd molested his face on Friday night. He'd seen me drunk. I wouldn't want to talk to me either.

"One sec," Matt said. He stood up and walked over to Charlotte who was beckoning him over. They started discussing something, but I couldn't hear them over the chatter around me. Neither looked particularly happy.

Matt said he wasn't dating Isabella. Was he dating Charlotte instead? That would explain why he didn't defend me in class when she was berating me. It would explain why she kept looking over here like she wanted to throw me out the window. It would explain everything.

"What's up with them?" I asked Rob.

He looked over his shoulder. "I don't know. Why, are you jealous? I saw that you two were all over each other at that party."

"No." *Oh God.* I could feel my face turning red. "Matt's a jerk. He and Charlotte deserve each other."

Rob laughed. "No one deserves to be with Charlotte. And Matt's not that big of an asshole once you get to know him. He saved you from being teamed up with her, after all."

"Pretty sure the teams were randomly assigned," I said.

"Everyone knows that nothing in Mr. Hill's class is random."

What the hell did that mean? Before I could ask, Rob started talking again.

"So about this project." He rubbed his hands together. "I was thinking we could do something fitness related."

"That would be really great." This project could end up being a breeze. Rob and I were completely on the same page. Plus he seemed fine talking to me, unlike his friend.

He laughed. "I was joking. I thought that would be the last thing you wanted to do."

"Why?"

"I heard Cupcake nailed you in the face with a dodge-ball in gym today."

"Oh." I laughed. I guess everyone did call that kid Cupcake. "I didn't realize there were rumors spreading around about me." *Besides the fact that I don't have a lot of money and am not as cool as a student nicknamed Cupcake.*

"Everyone's always fascinated by the new kid. You also have a tiny little bruise right there." He pointed to the inside of his left eye.

I mirrored him and reached up and touched the spot on my face.

"Other side," he said with a laugh.

I touched the left side of my nose and flinched. *Ow.*

"Sorry about that," Matt said and sat down in his chair facing me. He had a huge smile on his face and was looking directly at me.

Wait, was he talking to me? I looked over my shoulder even though I was in the back of the classroom. *Nope, just me.* Maybe I really did have a concussion.

"I heard about dodgeball," Matt said. "Are you okay?"

Caring? Again? I just stared at him. He stared back like he was acting completely normal. Nothing about this was normal. It was the first time he'd spoken to me in school for weeks. He'd literally never spoken to me in this class before. I figured we'd have to do our project in hotel bathrooms and drunken parties or cut him out entirely.

"It looks like it hurts," he continued, even though I hadn't acknowledged the fact that he was speaking to me.

You know what hurts? You pretending I'm invisible. "No, it doesn't hurt," I lied. I didn't need Matthew Caldwell to fake care about me. *You hurt. You hurt me.*

He lowered his eyebrows slightly like he could read my mind.

"We were just talking about her dodgeball incident," Rob said, breaking the awkward silence. "She wants our project to be fitness related."

Matt smiled and rested his elbows on my desk. "Even after today?"

"Just because I'm not super coordinated like the two of you doesn't mean I don't take fitness seriously. I prefer running."

"I feel the passion," Rob said.

Matt locked eyes with me. "Me too."

They were both acting weird. I grabbed my notebook and wrote down "fitness" at the top. "We could do something health food related if you'd rather," I said without looking up.

"Yeah, yeah, that would be fine," Matt said. "Whatever you want to do is fine with us. I'm glad you got home safely on Friday. I was worried about you."

Worried? Yeah, right. This wasn't supposed to be how today went. I wanted to crawl under my desk. Instead I had to sit there, my heart rate increasing by the second with his eyes on me.

"Maybe next time avoid the punch altogether."

Please don't talk about this. Ever. "Yup." I jotted down the health food idea in my notebook.

"We should probably exchange numbers for the project, don't you think? And that way I can text you if I'm ever worried again."

I forced my eyes not to roll. "I don't think that's necessary."

Rob laughed. "Shot down, buddy. Sanders, you're even cooler than I realized."

"Okay, so no phone number," Matt said. "We're going to have to work on this outside of class though. So I need a way to contact you."

My notebook page was very interesting so I didn't look up. "I think we should just roll with the fitness thing since we're all so passionate about it. We can split up the work for the project and do it independently."

"Double shot down," Rob said with a laugh.

Matt leaned forward even more, his strong forearms dangerously close to my notebook. "I was kind of hoping that we'd work really really dependently. Lots of visits to each other's houses. Late-night study sessions. That kinda thing."

I looked up at him to tell him he was ridiculous. That this project didn't need study sessions because it was a project and not a test. But I swallowed down my words when I looked into his chocolaty brown eyes.

He smiled.

My throat made an awkward squeaking noise.

And the bell rang to save me.

"See you tomorrow, Sanders," Rob said. "We'll hash out the rest of our topic so you never have to hang out with Matt outside of school."

At least Rob understood what I wanted. I quickly shoved my notebook into my backpack and zipped it closed. Before I stood up, I noticed a piece of folded up paper on top of my desk. It hadn't been there a few seconds ago. I picked up the paper and unfolded it.

UNTOUCHABLES

*I'm sorry about the past few weeks. Let me make it up to you.
Meet me in the auditorium in five.*

I looked up to see Matt walking away. He was the last
one leaving the room. I knew it was from him even though
he hadn't signed it. But he didn't realize that actions spoke
louder than words. Being nice to me in one class didn't
make up for weeks of silence. A simple note didn't make
up for it either. It was just further proof that he didn't
want anyone to know he was speaking to me. Forced to be
in a group with the new loser of Empire High was one
thing. Voluntarily hanging out with them? Social suicide.

I pulled my bag over my shoulder and made my way
past Mr. Hill who I swear glared at me. Instead of turning
left toward the auditorium I went right toward my locker.

There was nothing I needed to say to Matt. I didn't
want to play whatever game he was playing. And the more
I thought about it, the more it seemed like I was being set
up for something awful. He had talked to Charlotte before
inviting me to the auditorium. She and Isabella and all the
Untouchables were probably waiting there to make fun of
me. I wouldn't be part of their prank.

Still, I found myself putting the note in my blazer
pocket instead of tossing it in the trash where it belonged.
I hated how nice it felt next to my heart. I hated that even
thinking about Matt still made me feel like I was breathing
easier. And I hated how badly I wanted to run to the auditorium, even though I knew he wasn't sorry.

CHAPTER 13

Monday

"What are you looking at?" Kennedy asked.

We were sitting at my uncle's kitchen table going over our notes about Jane Eyre for our test later this week. But instead of looking at my English notes I was staring at the note from Matt. I quickly turned the page in my notebook, hiding it from sight. "Nothing," I said. "Do you think Edward Rochester ever really loved his first wife?"

"Who is Edward Rochester?" Kennedy asked as she reached for my notebook. I pulled it away.

"Have you not read the book yet? The test is in two days." And I was hoping she had an answer to my question. Could true love be thwarted by an old lesser love? Or infatuation? Or whatever the hell my feelings for Matt were? I mean, Edward's feelings for Jane, not mine for Matt. Jane Eyre had nothing to do with Matt and Felix. I was focused.

"That wasn't even your handwriting," Kennedy said. "Please tell me you got notes from someone who already took this test and aced it."

"I don't know any upperclassmen."

"And here I thought you'd become besties with Isabella."

"Ew. No." I laughed.

"But seriously," Kennedy said. "No secrets between actual besties." Before I could react, she pulled my notebook away from me.

Crap.

I watched her turn the page back and lift up the note. "I'm sorry about the past few weeks. Let me make it up to you. Meet me in the auditorium in five." Kennedy looked up from the note. "Who is this from?"

"Matt. I mean, I don't know. I found it on my desk in class. But I'm pretty sure it was him."

She studied the handwriting. "Yeah it's definitely from Matt. Here, let me read it again." She cleared her throat and switched to a deep voice. "I'm sorry about the past few weeks. Let me make it up to you. Meet me in the auditorium in five."

I grabbed it back from her. "Why are you so sure it's from him?"

"He passes notes in homeroom and I maybe kinda spy a little. It's his handwriting. What do you think he wanted to meet about?"

I shrugged. "Probably something about the group project we've been assigned in Mr. Hill's class."

Kennedy glared at me. "You seriously waited..." she glanced at the clock "...two whole hours after school ended to tell me you've been paired up with Matt for your project? What am I? Spoiled escargot?"

I laughed. "More like rancid foie gras."

"Ha. Ha." She folded her arms across her chest. "When were you planning on telling me?"

"It's not a big deal."

"It's a huge deal. You were trying to avoid him and now you're forced to do a project together just the two of you? It's like a romantic comedy come to life."

"No, it's not. And we're not a pair. Rob's in our group too."

"Even better. He's always hilarious. Romcom for the win!"

"My life is not a romcom. And just because Matt is talking to me in class and randomly wants to meet up with me in the auditorium it doesn't mean anything. He's a jerk."

"No, he's a jock. You're pronouncing that word wrong."

"I mean jerk. Not jock."

Kennedy sighed. "So…what did he want in the auditorium?"

"I don't know. I didn't go."

"You what?! Are you crazy? When an Untouchable asks you to meet up with him, you meet up with him."

"I thought you didn't care about social status."

"I don't. But it's Matthew freaking Caldwell."

"Matthew Caldwell is just a boy like any other boy at our school. There's nothing special about him." Except his golden hair. And perfect smile. And the feeling of his hands on…*stop*. "Why do you keep pushing me toward him anyway? You know I like Felix."

She lifted up the note. "Because this is some star crossed lovers scenario that deserves to be played out." She slapped the note down in front of me. "And Felix is an egotistical liar with a drug problem."

My uncle cleared his throat.

Kennedy and I both froze. I hadn't heard him come in, and I'm pretty sure she hadn't either.

"What's this about a drug problem?" he asked.

"Nothing," Kennedy and I both said at the same time.

He cleared his throat again. "We just talked about honesty in this house. And drinking. I don't want to be standing here in another few weeks talking about drugs instead. Spill it."

"We were talking about Felix Green," Kennedy said. "He's this kid we go to school with and he's really bad news. But Brooklyn's been hanging out with him. I've tried to stop her but she won't listen. He's the one that gave us alcohol at his house Friday night. He's such bad news."

What the hell, Kennedy?

"That's not…" I started, but my uncle cut me off.

"You two best be staying away from him then," my uncle said. "I don't want either of you mixed up with someone like that."

"Kennedy's exaggerating. Felix isn't bad news. At all. He's nice and…"

"I said to stay away from him."

"Why?"

"Because I said so."

He was new to this whole parenting thing. But "because I said so" was not a sufficient answer. Before I could press him, Kennedy cut in.

"Also, is it possible that Brooklyn is related to him? Because we don't know who her father is and I have a hankering suspicion."

"What?" my uncle asked. "No."

"Are you sure they don't have the same dad? Or maybe he's her cousin? Or…uncle? Is that possible? That would be pretty freaky."

"She's not related to Felix," he said. "It's time for you to head home, Kennedy. I need to speak to Brooklyn alone."

Even on Friday night, I hadn't been scared of my uncle's reaction. Maybe it was the booze in my bloodstream that made me unworried. Or maybe it was the fact that he always seemed pretty happy. But today? He looked really pissed.

"Sure thing, Uncle Jim," Kennedy said and gathered her notebooks.

I'd wanted Kennedy to ask my uncle about my father. But not at all like this. What had gotten into her? "Traitor," I mouthed silently at her.

"You're welcome," she mouthed back.

When the door closed behind her I got up from the table. "I'll be in my room."

"Now hold on one minute there, kiddo."

I froze in my tracks.

"Why are you hanging out with kids like Felix? I'm in over my head here. First the drinking. Now the mention of drugs. And dating? You're sixteen years old. You don't need to be dating anyone. You don't need to make the same mistakes your mother did. Are you acting out because of her? I can make an appointment with a therapist. We can get you someone to talk to. Someone that can help you through this."

Every word out of his mouth made me feel smaller and smaller. But the word mistake? That's what hurt the most. I wasn't a mistake. I shook my head. "I don't need professional help. Missing my mom isn't something I can work through. I'm never going to stop missing her."

"I didn't…"

"And she wasn't 16 when she got pregnant with me. She was 19. And she wanted me. I wasn't a mistake. I wasn't." I could feel tears forming in the corners of my eyes. "My mom wanted me."

He cringed at my words. "I meant unplanned. Your mother hadn't planned on getting pregnant when she was a teenager."

Wasn't that the same thing as a mistake? My mom always said I was the greatest thing that had ever happened to her. But when she first found out? Of course I was unplanned. Of course I was a mistake. I had just never thought of it that way. My mother hadn't wanted me. Just like my uncle didn't want me either. I was the unplanned mistake that had shown up on his doorstep with nowhere else to go. "May I be excused now?"

My uncle didn't say anything this time when I retreated to my bedroom. I slammed my door and threw myself down on top of my bed. And I let myself cry. I let myself cry for being stuck here with an uncle that thought I was a mistake. In a city I hated. Without my mom.

I was vaguely aware of the apartment door opening and closing. Maybe my uncle would leave me too. Just like my mom had. There was a lump in my throat that wouldn't go away no matter how much I cried.

***

A knock on my bedroom door made me sit up. My cheeks were tight from my dried tears.

"Can I come in?" my uncle asked.

"Yes." My voice came out croaky.

He walked in with a Duane Reade bag dangling from his hand. "You were unexpected, Brooklyn. But as soon as your mom found out she was pregnant, she knew she wanted you. She always wanted you." He sat down on the edge of my bed. "Don't you ever think otherwise."

I would have started crying again if I had any tears left.

"And about Felix. We can talk about stuff like this. Boys. Whatever." He cleared his throat. "You can talk to me."

"He's not bad news. Besides for Kennedy, he's the only one in the whole school that's nice to me. He even protects me when I stupidly attempt to play dodgeball. If anything he's good news." That might have been a stretch. I was pretty sure he didn't do drugs. But I knew for a fact that he sold them.

My uncle nodded. "You really like him, huh?"

"Yes."

He handed me the bag he'd carried in. "Please just use these. Always use these. There's directions on the box. Just…follow those and you'll be all set."

I glanced in the bag. A large box of condoms stared back at me. I quickly collapsed the top of the plastic bag down so I couldn't see them anymore. "I don't need those."

He was staring at the wall, which apparently was easier than looking at me when he handed me a bag full of condoms. "Hold on to them just in case."

"I really don't…"

"Please. For my sake. And if you have any questions about…"

"I'm good," I said. "My mom already filled me in about the birds and the bees. You have nothing to worry about."

"Nothing to worry about?" He laughed and finally made eye contact with me again. "Do you trust this boy?"

"Yes." I was worried that it came out as more of a question than a definitive answer. Where was this going?

"I want to meet him."

What was he planning on doing? Throwing a box of condoms at him and reprimanding him about drug usage? "Oh…no. I think it's a little soon for all that."

He pressed his lips together. "Right." He looked back at the wall. "Not a problem. Forget I even mentioned it." He looked…embarrassed. I still wasn't very good at reading his emotions. But then it hit me. Maybe I was getting better at reading him than I thought. Because my uncle definitely looked hurt.

And I realized how my answer sounded. Like I was embarrassed of him. Or of where we lived. Or of something. And that wasn't it at all. He asked me if I trusted Felix because he wanted to let him in on our secret. That I wasn't actually a scholarship student. "Actually, maybe it would be good for you to meet him," I said.

"Yeah?"

"I'll let Felix know he needs to meet you. Maybe he can come over for dinner one night this week?"

"Whatever day works for you two works for me. Speaking of dinner, do you want to watch a movie and get takeout from that diner on…"

"You pick the movie and I'll cook us something," I said and slid off the bed. I wasn't embarrassed of my uncle at all. But I was embarrassed that there was a bag filled with condoms on my bed. And the sooner I got out of this room the better.

CHAPTER 14

Tuesday

I caught up with Felix after class. I'd been chickening out from asking him to meet my uncle all day. And I had no idea why. I knew I could trust him. Despite Kennedy's reservations, I knew Felix was a good guy. The worst that could happen? He'd laugh and tell the whole school I was related to the janitor. The best that could happen? Telling him the truth would make us closer. And now that I knew I wasn't related to him, I wanted to be closer to him. He'd promised me a kiss. It was hard not to fantasize about it.

"Hey, I need to ask you something," I said.

He stopped at his locker to pull out a few books. "What a coincidence. I have something to ask you too."

"You do?" I was stalling again and he was giving me the perfect out.

He slammed his locker closed and we started walking toward the cafeteria. "There's a party this Saturday. Come with me."

"Like…as your plus one?"

He laughed. "It's not a fancy thing, newb. Just a get together after the football game. But yeah. I want you to be my plus one." As we entered the cafeteria, he slipped his hand into mine like it was the most natural thing in the world. "I know you're working, but we could go after. I can pick you up."

His hand felt warm and safe. I didn't know why my eyes gravitated toward the Untouchables' table. Or why my heart skipped a beat when I saw Matt glaring in our direction. I turned my attention back to Felix.

"I'll have to ask my uncle. Speaking of which…" Now was my chance. The perfect lead in. "He wants to meet you. Do you maybe want to come over for dinner sometime this week? I make a pretty great vegetarian lasagna." I didn't have to tell him everything right this second. The whole secret non-scholarship student thing could wait. But for some reason he still looked confused. He stopped me before I could get in line for a salad.

"There's a whole lot about everything you just said that I need clarification on," he said. "First…vegetarian lasagna? What's wrong with good old fashioned beef?"

I laughed. "It's bad for your heart. And I'm trying to get my uncle to eat healthier."

"Fair enough. That brings me to my second question. You want me to meet your *uncle*? That's a first. Already introducing each other to extended family?" He laughed.

"He's not…" my voice trailed off. "He's not my extended family. He's my only family. I live with him."

"Shit. I'm sorry. I know you mentioned at the party that you lost your mom. I'm sorry I didn't ask you about her. I just knew it would be…I don't know why I didn't ask. I'm sorry."

I cringed at his third apology. I hated when people said they were sorry. It wasn't like he had killed my mom. He had nothing to be sorry for.

"I just assumed you lived with your dad?"

I shook my head. "No, my dad was never in the picture. It's always just been me and my mom. I mean was. It was me and my mom." I wasn't sure I'd ever get used to referring to her in the past tense.

"I'm sorry."

Why did he keep saying that? "Honestly, I'm not. If he didn't want me then I don't care to know him either. But I should probably clarify that even though I don't know who my father is, my uncle does. And you have nothing to worry about, my uncle told me that we're not related."

Felix just stared at me.

"Like you're not my...secret brother or step-brother or something. Or cousin. None of that. Not that I was thinking you were. But it's good to double-check that kind of thing. Just to be safe."

"Just to be safe." He flashed me a smile. "It sounds like you were worried about that. Which you shouldn't have been. Wouldn't you like being my sister? I think it would be great if we were related. I've always wanted a sibling."

What? Seriously wait...*what?*

Felix started laughing. "You should see your face." He tried to catch his breath.

"What is wrong with you? That's not funny. At all."

"Well, it kinda was."

I slapped his arm. "I thought you were serious for a second. That you wanted me to be your sister instead of..." I let my voice trail off. What were we exactly?

"No, definitely not. It would have been really hard to unlike you, newb."

I felt my cheeks flush.

"I can do dinner Thursday. And I'll ask your uncle about Saturday myself, okay?"

I nodded.

"Save me a seat at your table. I'm going to go get something with tons of beef."

I laughed and his hand slipped out of mine. Felix had only ever sat with me at lunch that one time to ask me to his party. But he probably knew that saving him a seat wasn't really necessary. The only person I ever sat with was Kennedy. Speaking of which…she had been avoiding me all day a lot better than I had avoided Felix and Matt yesterday. I grabbed my salad and sat down across from her.

"Hey," I said.

"Hey." She was staring at the display on her camera instead of at me. "Look, I'm sorry about yesterday. I was just trying to help."

"Trying to help? You were trying to get my uncle to lock me away like Rapunzel."

She slowly swallowed the green beans she'd just put in her mouth and finally looked up at me. "No. I was trying to push you toward Matt instead of Felix. Because…you two make more sense."

"Yeah…no. He's still not speaking to me in public."

She put her chin in her hand. "But he's staring at you."

"He's not staring…" my words died away when I turned around to look at the Untouchables' table. Matt was still staring. Directly at me. I swallowed hard and turned back around. "Random coincidence. But it doesn't matter anyway. Because my uncle calmed down and now he wants to meet Felix."

Kennedy spit water out all over the table. "He what?"

"Geez. Watch it." I grabbed a napkin and started blotting up her mess.

"What do you mean he wants to meet him? Why would Uncle Jim want to meet Felix?"

"Because I told him how much I like him."

"But…that's…that's not…but…"

"Hey," Felix said and sat down next to me. "Thanks for saving me a seat."

Kennedy closed her mouth. And then opened it again. Closed it again. And then a smile spread over her face. "Hey, Felix. So great that you could join us."

"It is?" he asked. "Why do I feel like this is some kind of trick?"

"What?" She laughed but it came out way higher than usual like she was pretending to be someone else. "I was just saying how fun it would be if you ate lunch with us today."

She most definitely hadn't been. I watched as she started eating again without spitting anything anywhere.

"Uh…yeah," Felix said. "I was kinda hoping to make it a normal thing."

Kennedy swallowed the food in her mouth. "Awesome. We can be the three amigos. Amigas? Probably amigas since there's only one boy." She reached across the table and lightly flicked Felix's hand.

"Sure. Are you feeling okay, Kennedy? You're acting all…well…more like you used to freshman year."

"What do you mean?"

"Like…nice to me."

"Psh." She waved her fork in the air.

The other day I would have been worried she'd stab him with it. But she didn't look murderous today.

"When have I ever acted mean toward you? We go way back. We knew each other before Brooklyn even started going here. Before she even moved to this state. We were already a twosome. The first twosome."

"Right." Felix gave me a weird look. "Well, great. I'll even be part of your awesome girl group if that's what you want."

"Definitely. The three of us can hang out all the time. Like…always together all three of us. Speaking of which, what are you guys doing Thursday night? I was thinking we could all hang out."

"Kennedy," I said. "I just told you Felix was going to meet my uncle on Thursday. We're having dinner…"

"Great! What time? I'll be there."

Felix glanced at me again and then back at her. "Actually, Kennedy it was more of a date kinda thing."

"The three amigas classic date night! Plus Uncle Jim. Awesome! Can't wait." She shoved more green beans in her mouth.

I didn't know what I was supposed to say. I was glad that Kennedy was being nice to Felix for a change. I didn't want her to go back to being mean by uninviting her. Not that I'd invited her in the first place. But having her at dinner would make Thursday night less awkward. I was worried my uncle was going to go all Spanish Inquisition on his ass. Or maybe that was what Kennedy was doing in some weird twisted way? Why was she being so overly nice?

"The three of us are going to have so much fun," Kennedy added and gave Felix a big smile.

I shrugged. "Yeah. Dinner Thursday's going to be great."

"Yeah. Great," Felix added. Although neither of us sounded quite as excited as Kennedy.

At least she was speaking to me again. Her weird behavior was better than her avoiding me altogether and berating Felix. So lunch was kinda sorta a win. *I think.*

***

I pulled my notebook for my entrepreneurship class out of my locker and a piece of paper fluttered to the floor. *What the hell?* I bent down and lifted it up.

We really need to talk. I'll be waiting for you in the auditorium after class.

Matt. Again it wasn't signed, but I knew it was him. And again he was pleading with me to meet up in the auditorium. But why not just talk to me in class? Was he too embarrassed to let Rob hear what he had to say to me? Was he worried stupid Charlotte would be jealous? He clearly didn't want a paper trail or he'd sign the notes. And meeting in a dark auditorium away from the scrutiny of the elite pricks in our class? Screw him. I wanted to crumble the paper up and throw it on the ground. Instead, I folded it and shoved it into my pocket. I was such an idiot.

I walked into Mr. Hill's class, trying to ignore the note burning a hole in my pocket. Matt wasn't there yet. He always strolled into class at the last minute looking devastatingly handsome. I tore a blank page out of my notebook, wrote "NO" in big bold letters, and slapped it onto his desk before anyone else entered the classroom. A few minutes later Matt and Rob walked in and I stared at my blank notebook like it was the most interesting thing in the world.

"What the hell is that on your desk, Matt?" Rob asked as he sat down. "Still haven't learned that no means no?" He laughed at his own joke.

Instead of laughing it felt like I couldn't breathe.

I heard Matt lift the paper up off his desk. "It's nothing."

I continued to stare at my notebook, waiting for the sound of him crumpling the paper in his fist. When it didn't come, I looked up. He'd folded the note and was stuffing it into his blazer pocket. The same place I'd put both notes he'd given to me. Why didn't he throw it out?

"We'll be working in our teams today," Mr. Hill said. "I want the topics finalized and handed in by the end of class."

Charlotte raised her hand.

"Yes, Miss King?" Mr. Hill asked.

"Will these projects be completed in class? Like…we won't be working on them at all outside of class, right?"

Mr. Hill shook his head. "These projects are to be treated like homework. The majority of the work will be done on your own time." He turned his attention back to the class. "Which means the sooner you hash out the topics, the sooner I can go back to teaching. Break up in your groups."

"But…" started Charlotte.

"Now, Miss King."

Charlotte sighed and headed over to her group.

"I wonder what's eating her," Rob said and turned around. "Probably no one, that's the problem." He held up his hand for a high-five, but Matt ignored him. "Geez, you're no fun today. What about you, Sanders?" Rob said. "You won't leave me hanging, will you?" He put his hand up in front of me.

"I didn't get your joke," I said.

Rob lowered his hand and leaned forward. "You know…I meant no one was eating her out."

"Oh." I laughed even though I had no idea what he was talking about. "Right."

A smile spread across Rob's face. "You're adorably naïve, Sanders. It means when you stick your tongue in…"

"Shut the fuck up," Matt said.

Rob gave him a sideways glance. "What? I was explaining the dual benefits of oral…"

"I said shut up."

"And someone's not getting any head." He nodded toward Matt.

I laughed. And then I immediately blushed. Because now I understood Rob's joke. And the fact that he'd mentioned Matt's penis didn't help my flushing cheeks either. I cleared my throat. "So we're running on the fitness topic?" I asked. My voice came out weird and high-pitched.

"We said we'd do whatever you want," Rob said.

I didn't like all the pressure being on me. "It's a quarter of our grade. I don't want you blaming me if we fail."

Rob laughed like that was the most entertaining thought in the world. "We never fail, Sanders."

Again, I felt like I was out of the loop on a joke. "Okay…but what do you want to do that's fitness related? Fitness itself isn't a topic."

"We could make a website," Matt said. "With different workouts."

"Oh, like what workouts to get you on the football team," Rob said and gestured to Matt. "And the soccer team," he gestured to himself. "And the…" he moved his hand in my direction. "Whatever you've got going on seems good. The…shy scholarship student hot body workout. Boom. Project done."

I was pretty sure my face couldn't get any redder. Robert Hunter had just called me hot. Kind of. No, he definitely did. Or maybe he was making fun of me. He was always joking around. But he hadn't laughed. I stared down at my notebook, hoping to hide my face. "Okay, well, we have to film workouts then. And design a website to upload them to. And we have to have a way to monetize it so that we're actually creating a business."

"We can charge a monthly fee to access the videos," Matt said. "Mr. Hill will love that it's a recurring revenue stream. It's the business model dream."

"That's good." I jotted it down. There was no need to write down the football, soccer, and hot body workouts. That would be seared into my mind for eternity. "But do either of you know any coding? I definitely don't know how to make a website."

"My brother can help us," Rob said. "He's a computer genius. Pretty sure he can just do most of it for us."

"But…we're supposed to do it ourselves."

"Success is all about delegating, Sanders," Rob said.

"But…"

"How about we all get together at Rob's one night this week and we can ask James for help?" Matt asked.

"I thought we agreed that we could just split up the work," I said.

"You heard Mr. Hill. He expects us to work together outside the classroom. So, what night works best for you?"

Mr. Hill had said that. *Crap.* I started scribbling on the side of my notebook, hoping Matt couldn't see how much he affected me. "Any night but Thursday."

"Why, what are you doing Thursday?"

I placed my pen down and stared right at him. "I have dinner plans."

Matt lowered his eyebrows slightly. "With who?"

I was very aware of the fact that he seemed desperate to know who I was hanging out with, not that it was any of his business. At all. "Felix." I could have added the fact that Kennedy and my uncle would be there too. But for some reason I found myself biting my tongue.

"So a date?" Matt asked. "You have a date with Felix?"

"Yeah…I guess you could call it that." Or a three amigas classic date night if you were asking Kennedy.

His eyebrows lowered even more. "Cancel. We have to work on this."

"We can do it another night," Rob said. "What about…"

"Cancel your plans with Felix." Matt was staring at me so intently it was hard to find words.

So I just shook my head.

"Please, Brooklyn."

I swallowed hard. "Can't we just do it another night?" It was hard to say no outright to him when I couldn't just write it down and slap it on his desk without him looking. How was I supposed to say no to that perfect face? To those eyes that were begging me for…what exactly? What the hell did he want from me?

"No, Thursday is the only night I'm free," Matt said.

"But you just asked me what night was best for me…"

"I forgot that I'm booked the rest of the week. It has to be Thursday. Which means you have to cancel your date." The way he said date made the hairs on the back of my neck stand up.

"Dude, what the hell do you have to do the rest of the nights this week?" Rob asked. "I thought we were just hanging out tonight anyway. Can you come over tonight, Sanders?"

The thought of going to Rob's house tonight made my stomach churn. But I was technically free. I found myself nodding.

"No," Matt said. "It has to be Thursday night. I forgot that I have football practice late every other night this week to prep for the game this weekend. She has to cancel her plans."

"You're being unreasonable," I said.

"*I'm* being unreasonable? I can't change my practice schedule. But you can cancel your plans with Felix." He bit out the name Felix as he glared at me.

What was his problem? I felt like I was shrinking under his gaze. I didn't know what to say. I didn't know how to disagree with him when he was staring at me like he was going to bite my head off.

The bell rang, saving me. I breathed a sigh of relief.

"We'll just do it next week then," Rob said as he stood up. "Later, Sanders."

"Auditorium," Matt whispered as he pulled his backpack over his shoulder. "Five minutes." He walked away without waiting for a response.

"No," I said to the empty classroom. I was beginning to think that Matt had never heard that word before.

CHAPTER 15

Thursday

Two more notes demanding a secret auditorium meeting. Two more instances of whispered words in class when no one was looking. And as if Matt knew I wouldn't come for the fourth day in a row, there was another note staring back at me in my locker. It was placed so perfectly I was pretty sure he hadn't stuffed it through the slats. He'd opened up my locker and put it right where I'd see it. He knew the combination to my lock. He was officially being creepy. And disrespectful.

I lifted up the note and read his words.

Please tell me I'm not too late.

Too late for what? It was the weirdest note yet. And even though it didn't say to meet him in the auditorium at the end of school, he'd said he'd keep waiting in another note. He'd be there. I slammed my locker closed. Enough was enough. I didn't care if this was some weird hazing the new girl thing. Or a prank I didn't understand. I wanted to have a good night with Felix. And I didn't want to spend any more time thinking about these stupid freaking notes.

Felix was supposed to walk home with me and Kennedy today. But neither had stopped by my locker yet. I'd just quickly tell Matt to leave me alone and have a great night.

I opened the heavy wooden door of the auditorium. The lights were off, and when the door closed behind me with a thud, everything was bathed in darkness.

I was mad at Matt for making me come here of all places to talk. Pissed that he kept trying to make me cancel my plans with Felix. Furious that he thought these notes could make up for the fact that he just sat there while Charlotte tore me apart in class last week.

But I was also a tiny bit scared. Maybe a lot a bit scared. I'd never been to the auditorium and my thigh bumped into one of the seats. *Ow.* "Matt?" I whispered.

No answer.

"Matt, this isn't funny." God, this was definitely a hazing thing. Any minute now Isabella would show up and throw red paint on me or something worse. Charlotte's words about making me disappear came back to me. "Matt?" My voice trembled this time.

A floorboard creaked behind me and I turned so quickly I almost ran right into him.

"You came," he said.

I was breathing hard, trying to hold back the scream that had wanted to come out a second ago. "What the hell?" I shoved the note into his chest and ignored the fact that his pecs were so hard that the action hurt my hand. Well, I tried to ignore it. Because I kept my hand there, splayed on his chest. I felt the rise and fall of his breath.

"Brooklyn."

Him saying my name finally brought me back to reality. I pulled my hand away, hating how cold it felt. "You're infuriating. You know, I actually thought you liked me when you followed me into the bathroom at that fancy party. But I get it now. You came to my rescue in the bathroom so no one would see you helping me. Because I was *the help*. I'm not good enough to be seen with in public. Isn't that right?"

"Brooklyn..."

"And the silent treatment in the halls? You only ever talk to me when you *have* to in class. Or when people are too drunk to remember the night. Or when no one else is watching." I threw my arm out, gesturing to the abandoned auditorium.

"Brooklyn..."

"You've made it perfectly clear that I'm beneath you."

His Adam's apple rose and fell at my words and for a second I forgot that I was mad. Because everything about him was so beautiful. And I hated that I could see how beautiful he was when all he could see about me was that I wasn't good enough to be with him. I'd never fit into his life. He was one of the Untouchables. And I was just...untouchable.

"Why are you doing this?" I asked. "What the hell do you want from me?"

He stepped even closer. "I want you to tell me I'm not too late."

"For what?"

"This."

His lips crashed against mine before I had time to realize what was happening. He buried his fingers in my hair, angling my face up to his.

And my body felt alive. Like I was truly breathing for the first time in a month. Like my heart wanted to keep beating again.

His tongue slid between my lips. He tasted like cinnamon. And I wasn't a huge believer in desserts, but I had also never tasted one quite like this. God, I wanted more.

He groaned, and I had never heard such a carnal sound. I felt like I was on fire. And he was consuming me.

One of his hands fell from my hair, his fingertips running down my neck. He pressed his palm in the middle of my chest. Like he wanted to feel my heart beating. Like he wanted to know I was alive too. Like he wanted to see if my heart was feeling the same thing his was.

He pulled back far too soon. "Tell me I wasn't too late."

"For what?" I was panting. Desperate for a redo. My eyes gravitated to his perfect lips.

"To be your first kiss."

Oh my God. Shit. I shoved him away from me. *Damn it!* That kiss wasn't meant for him. I'd already promised it to Felix. *Felix. Shit.* He was probably waiting at my locker for me. God, what was wrong with me? "You're a…a…you're a kiss thief, Matthew Caldwell." Apparently it was easier for me to throw the blame on Matt instead of myself.

"You kissed me back."

I swallowed hard. "I did not."

"You did."

It felt like it was a thousand degrees in the auditorium. I had to get out of here. God, what had I just done? "I did not," I said back as my fingers fumbled around the doorknob in the darkness.

"I'm going to be all your firsts, Brooklyn."

My hand finally made purchase with the doorknob. I flung it open. The bright light of the hallway was blinding.

"Every single one of them," Matt said from behind me.

I ran out of the auditorium as fast as I could. As far away from him as possible. Because I was terrified that he was right. He could take everything he wanted. He was Matthew freaking Caldwell. He never had to ask, he just took and took and took. He'd stolen my first kiss. I wouldn't let him steal anything else.

CHAPTER 16

Thursday

As I hurried back toward my locker, a terrible realization crept into my mind. Worse than the fact that my first kiss had been stolen. Worse because what if…what if…I swallowed hard. God, what if I was related to Matt? I'd only gotten the all-clear about Felix. What if my first kiss had just been stolen by my half-brother? And Matt was right…I'd freaking kissed him back. No. I didn't. Did I?

"Are you okay?" Kennedy asked. She was leaning against my locker. "All ready for our three amigas dinner? I'm excited that we can all walk home together."

"Yeah. No. No, I'm not okay."

"What's wrong?" The smile that seemed permanently affixed to her face the past few days disappeared. "You look really pale, Brooklyn. Are you going to be sick?"

"I just…I…just…he…"

"Hey," Felix said from behind me. I spun around and the guilt I felt from kissing Matt grew tenfold. I'd promised Felix he'd be my first kiss. And not just that…I'd wanted it to be him. *Stupid fucking Matt!*

"Are you okay?" Felix asked. "You look a little pale."

Because Matt literally just sucked all the oxygen out of my body. Stop it. "I'm fine." I did not sound fine. But I needed to immediately or everyone would know what just happened.

And Felix could not know. No one could know. *God, I may have just kissed my brother. And I liked it.* No. *No, I did not like it.*

"Do you need to go to the nurse?" Kennedy asked.

"I'm fine." I took a deep breath. "Really. Let's get going."

"If you're sure?"

"Definitely"

"Okay." Kennedy maneuvered herself between Felix and me. I was so grateful. It was like she could tell I needed a minute to myself. We all started walking. I wasn't sure if the silence was awkward because of me, but it certainly felt that way. I kept my eyes trained straight ahead as I walked past the auditorium. Was Matt still in there?

"Earth to Brooklyn," Kennedy said and lightly nudged me with her elbow.

"What?"

"Your hand," she said like she'd just asked me a hundred times before. "What's in your hand?"

I looked down at my hand. Matt's most recent note was balled up in my fist. "Nothing." We walked by a trashcan on our way out of school. I wanted to toss it. I wanted my mind to tell my heart that the kiss meant nothing. But I found myself quickly smoothing out the note, folding it, and sliding it into my blazer pocket. His words were stuck in my head on repeat. *Please, tell me I'm not too late.*

"So…" Felix said.

God, he knows. He knows what I just did. It felt like my heart was ricocheting against my ribcage. Is this what guilt felt like? A heart attack?

"What's your uncle like?" he asked instead of accusing me of making out with Matt in the auditorium.

"He's so nice," Kennedy said.

Felix laughed. "I meant Brooklyn's uncle. You know…the one I'm meeting."

"Right, I know. But I call him Uncle Jim too. He's always lived down the hall from me. He's like a surrogate uncle I guess you could say. And he's going to love you."

"Okay." Felix sounded more confused than anything. "So what does he do, Brooklyn?"

I'd completely forgotten about the awkward conversation we still needed to have. I pulled my jacket tighter around myself, trying to keep my heart from bursting out onto the dirty city street. The fabric was growing threadbare and it was too cold for the rapidly decreasing temperatures. And too thin to cover up the sound of my rapid heartbeat.

"She hasn't told you?" Kennedy asked. She turned her attention to me and whispered, "You haven't told him?"

Felix cleared his throat. "Told me what?"

That I kissed Matt! No. That he kissed me. Stupid kiss thief.

"Um…" Kennedy looked at me and then back at him. "It's not my place to say. I'm sworn to secrecy."

I knew she was waiting for me to start talking. But I was afraid if I opened my mouth I'd confess everything.

"Is he like in the CIA or something?" Felix asked.

Kennedy didn't respond as we turned down a dingy side street. Well, not just any dingy side street. The street my apartment was on.

They were waiting. Waiting for me. Felix thought he was about to have dinner with a CIA agent and a girl who had never been kissed. I took a deep breath. "Kennedy, could you give us a minute?"

"Yeah." She smiled reassuringly at me. "But just a quick one. I'll meet you guys at Uncle Jim's. I want to change real quick anyway."

There was no such thing as a quick minute. A minute was 60 seconds no matter how you looked at it. And probably 80 heartbeats. Scratch that. My heart was beating at twice that rate.

Kennedy walked out in front of us and I stopped Felix, pulling him out of the way of the passersby.

"Are you sure you're okay?" he asked and grabbed my hand. "You look like you've seen a ghost."

I shook my head. I needed to tell him what I'd just done. I couldn't risk introducing him to my uncle and letting him in on my secret if he had no intention of forgiving me for Matt practically assaulting me. *He didn't assault you.* "I'm sorry. I'm so so sorry."

"Hey." Felix moved a fraction of an inch closer. "What's wrong?"

I tried to swallow down the lump in my throat.

"I know this is kinda awkward," he said and discreetly nodded toward Kennedy. "But she put us in a position where we couldn't exactly say no. And it's fine. After I get your uncle to like me, I'll be able to take you out just the two of us. No three amigas bullshit."

He thought I was being weird about Kennedy. I wasn't even able to process how awkward her overly enthusiastic third-wheeling was because I was stuck in my own threesome from hell. One that included Matt and his stupidly kissable lips.

"Really, it's okay." Felix squeezed my hand. "Let's just have a fun night. I'm excited to meet your uncle and see your home."

Home. For the first time the thought was comforting. And I realized that my uncle's apartment was quickly becoming my home. It was the first thing I'd thought of.

A part of me felt like a traitor. Like believing this was my home was somehow forgetting about my mom and my real home back in Delaware. The one with the foreclosure signs in the windows. The one with the yellow kitchen and the memories of dancing. Laughing. Not being sick.

"I live in a 500 square foot apartment." I said it more to convince myself it wasn't a home. Not Felix. But it was a double-edged sword. It made me feel guilty for making it seem like I didn't love that my uncle had given me a place to call home now. And I think a part of me was hoping it would make Felix leave. As much as he said he didn't fit into the world of Empire High, he did. I'd seen his fancy apartment. I'd seen how different we were. And it would be a hell of a lot easier if Felix decided to leave now rather than me telling him that I'd kissed Matt and him leaving because of that.

"Is that what this is about? Brooklyn, I don't care where you live."

That. That right there was why my first kiss should have been with him. Because he was kind and caring. And he didn't make me feel small. He didn't hide me away in a dark auditorium and leave unsigned notes in my locker. He wasn't ashamed of me. I was the one acting ashamed of myself.

"I really like you," he said.

"I really like you too."

He smiled. "So let me see this awesome 500 square foot apartment."

I laughed. "Okay." He turned to start walking again, but I stopped him. "There's one more thing. Well, two more things." I focused on the fact that his hand felt comforting in mine for a second. "Can you keep a secret?"

"Don't tell me I really am related to you," he said with a laugh.

"No. Nothing like that." I really wished I'd never told him I was worried he was my brother. I wasn't sure the teasing would ever end. I swallowed hard, trying to figure out how to word what I needed to say. "I'm not a scholarship student." God, that felt good to say. "And my uncle isn't in the CIA. His name is Jim Sanders." I waited a beat, hoping that Felix would just figure it out on his own. I'd heard a few faculty members at school call my uncle Mr. Sanders before. But Felix didn't react. "The only reason I go to Empire High is because my uncle is a janitor there."

Felix laughed. But he quickly stopped when he saw I wasn't laughing. "Oh." He cleared his throat. Finally the realization hit him. "Janitor Jimbo is your uncle?"

"What?"

"Janitor Jimbo. The one with the big beer belly?"

I pulled my hand out of his. "Don't call him that."

"I didn't mean anything by it. It's just what everyone calls him."

"I've never heard anyone call him that."

"Brooklyn, literally everyone calls him Janitor Jimbo. It's not a big deal."

"It is to me. Don't call him that."

Felix held up his hands. "I'm sorry. I won't call him that anymore."

"Good."

"Can we just rewind until a minute ago? I meant to say…Jim Sanders is your uncle? Oh, right *Sanders*. I should have put that together faster. Awesome. Now I know his profession and I'll have something to talk to him about because I love fixing stuff too."

It was really hard to be mad at him when he was smiling at me like that. And when he was trying so hard to make peace.

"I'm excited to meet him," he added. "Come on. If we're lucky you can give me a tour of your place before Kennedy gets there.

***

"And that's my bedroom." I nodded toward the open door without walking toward it. The tour had taken all of two minutes.

"I never got to show you my bedroom," Felix said and walked over to the open door. "Aren't you going to finish the tour?"

I had no idea how my uncle would feel about a boy being in my room. But for some reason all I could think about was the fact that there was a huge box of condoms hiding in the top drawer of my nightstand. What if Felix saw them? "I mean…it's just a normal bedroom."

He leaned against the doorjamb. "Come here." He reached his hand out.

I walked over to him, slipping my hand into his.

"Are you nervous to have me here?"

"I feel like this is a trick question." My heart had started beating again, but not because I felt guilty. Felix had nailed it. He made me uneasy. Being alone with him made me uneasy. Him finding out about Matt made me uneasy.

"Not a trick question." His eyes drifted to my lips. "You make me nervous, you know."

"*I* make *you* nervous?"

"Rumor has it that the best way to squash nerves is to distract yourself." He pulled on my hand, drawing me closer. "I can think of a few ways we can distract ourselves right now."

"A few ways?"

"Well, one way in particular. After all, I think I promised you something."

The kiss. The kiss I gave to someone else.

He leaned forward.

"Yay! Group hug!" Kennedy yelled and lunged at us, somehow wiggling between us, creating a Kennedy sandwich. "We should probably get some studying done, don't you think?"

"The only class I have with Brooklyn is PE."

"Awesome. That means you can do pushups while Brooklyn and I go over English notes."

"Kennedy," I said. "I actually need to start making the lasagna. Maybe you two could help with…" my voice trailed off when Kennedy dislodged herself from her attack hug. She was wearing…well, she was wearing barely anything at all. Because a miniskirt, a tight top that revealed her midriff and way too much cleavage, and a pair of heels didn't count as clothing to me. And she'd applied a lot more eye makeup. Like the amount of eye makeup I'd seen some women on the corner down the street wearing.

I was still in my school uniform. Knee socks and Keds included.

"Oh how about a game?" Kennedy asked and looped her arms through either of ours, pulling us away from my bedroom. "Let's play Twister."

I hadn't played Twister since elementary school. "I don't have Twister." Which was a relief. Because if Kennedy bent over she'd be mooning the entire apartment.

"Bummer. Okay, let's do your dumb lasagna thing. Come on, Felix, I can show you how to thinly slice some mushrooms." She pulled Felix away, leaving me alone in the living room.

What the hell? There weren't mushrooms in my vegetarian lasagna. I hurried after them before they could mess anything up.

***

"Oh, I almost forgot." Felix pulled out a bottle of wine from his backpack. "Where are your wine glasses?"

"What are you doing with that?" I asked.

"I grabbed it from my parents' wine rack. I wanted to make a good first impression."

"By bringing a bottle of wine? My uncle is going to kill me. Put it away." I pushed his hand holding the bottle back toward his backpack.

My uncle walked in a few seconds too early. He spotted the wine bottle and my hand on it. I removed my hand like the bottle was on fire.

He cleared his throat. "You must be Felix Green. The young man who's been serving my very underaged niece alcohol."

Kill me now.

"Hi Mr. Sanders," Felix said and lifted up the bottle. "I brought this for you."

"How old are you?"

"Sixteen," he said.

"Sixteen." My uncle took off his coat and hung it on the hook by the door. "That's five years too young for that."

"It's just for you," Felix said. "I wasn't planning on having a drop, sir."

A bomb slowly ticking down to zero. I waited for an explosion. But instead, my uncle smiled.

"Right answer." He took the bottle from Felix. "It smells great in here, kiddo," he said to me. "What are we having?"

"Vegetarian lasagna."

"Sounds good." He uncorked the bottle and poured himself a glass. "Will you be joining us for dinner, Kennedy?"

She was currently adjusting her shirt to cover herself a little more. "Mhm."

He grabbed four plates and set the table just in time for the timer on the oven to go off.

"So, Mr. Sanders," Felix said as they took the seats across from each other.

"Please, call me Jim."

Felix smiled. "Jim. How long have you been working at Empire High?"

"Ever since I graduated from high school. What do your parents do?"

"My mom is an art dealer. And my father manages the business."

"I'd like to meet them."

"They're in France right now for some art gala. I can arrange something when they're back in town."

"Are you living alone?"

"We have a staff. I'm not a good cook like Brooklyn," he said and put his hand on my knee underneath the table. "I'm pretty sure I'd starve if I was left to my own devices."

My uncle's rapid-fire interrogation continued as I silently chewed my lasagna. My very delicious, mushroom-free lasagna. I was pretty sure I learned more about Felix in that thirty minutes than he'd ever offered to me. He didn't have any siblings. He used to go to public school when he was little. He'd lived in a small apartment on the wrong side of town like this at one point. He was pretty much a C student. He didn't participate in any extracurriculars. At least, not ones he was willing to share with my uncle.

"I was actually wondering if Brooklyn could come to a party with me on Saturday night?" Felix asked. "I know she has work, so I was hoping it was alright if I took her after? I'd have her back here no later than 1."

"Will there be alcohol at this party?"

"I won't drink. And I'll make sure she doesn't either."

My uncle pushed his plate aside. "No later than 1 you say?"

Felix nodded and squeezed my knee beneath the table. I smiled over at him. There was something so comforting about the way he kept his hand there all throughout dinner.

"Uncle Jim," Kennedy said. "There's nothing to worry about. I'll be there too."

She would?

"Oh. In that case, it's a definite yes. That makes me feel better."

Kennedy beamed at him.

"Of course," Felix said. "She's definitely invited to come too." His phone buzzed in his pocket and he pulled it out. "My driver just pulled up. I have to get going." He smiled at me. "Thank you so much for dinner. Who knew vegetarian lasagna could be as good as normal lasagna?"

I laughed and pushed my chair back.

"It's okay," Kennedy said. "I'll walk him out. I need to get home and study anyway."

We usually did our homework together. But I was okay with being alone tonight. I needed a second to breathe. I thought about how easy it was to breathe in Matt's exhales. *Stop.*

"Goodnight," Felix said. He leaned down and hugged me, his breath warm in my ear. "I promise we can have some alone time on Saturday. You look beautiful tonight, by the way."

I felt my cheeks flush. "You too. Goodnight," I lamely said back as he and Kennedy left the apartment. *Did I just tell him he looked beautiful too?*

My uncle was quiet as I cleared the dishes from the table. And while I started scrubbing the plates. I looked behind me and he was doing his nightly crossword puzzle.

"What did you think of Felix?" I asked as I wiped my hands dry on a towel.

"I'm glad he has a driver," he said while he filled out another word. "I don't want you in a car with him if he's behind the wheel. Do you understand?" He looked up at me and I had never seen him look so serious.

I shook my head. "Why?"

"I remembered what Kennedy said about him having a drug problem."

"Uncle Jim…"

"I looked at his school records. He's gotten in trouble several times for getting high on school premises with that Hunter kid."

I remembered James Hunter coming into school looking like death. The dark circles under his eyes. The way he downed champagne at that party. The awkward conversation I'd had with Matt about him handling it. That there was nothing to worry about. "Which Hunter brother?" It was a strange question to ask. I should have been defending Felix. But for some reason my mind always ended up wandering back to the Untouchables.

"The older one, I think. James was the name in the write-ups. Look, I trust you, kiddo. I do. That's the only reason I'm letting you go to that party Saturday night. But I don't trust him. He came here with a bottle of wine, for Christ's sakes. He's clearly been left to his own devices for far too long. A staff isn't the same as having parents." He coughed into his shoulder.

"Felix never smokes around me. He's never offered me drugs. All I've really heard are rumors. I've never seen it."

"That doesn't make it untrue."

"I get that. But…" my voice trailed off. "I don't know why any of it matters if you trust me."

"Just promise me you won't smoke."

"I won't."

"And I don't just mean cigarettes. I mean anything he tries to give you. Promise me that." He looked so serious. Like his life depended on my answer.

"I promise."

"Okay." He lifted his pen back up for his crossword puzzle. "Other than that, he seems like a good enough kid. Just make sure you have a few of those things I gave you on you at all times. Just in case."

I was pretty sure my face was redder than it had ever been. Thank God he hadn't brought up the condoms when Felix was here. I had wanted to ask if Matt was my half-brother. But now that my uncle had basically just mentioned sex, I didn't know how to bring Matt up without sounding weird. And honestly, it didn't matter. I'd never tell a soul that he kissed me. And our kiss was certainly a one-time thing. If we were related? It was best if I never knew.

"I'm going to go do some homework."

"Alright, kiddo." He didn't look back up.

I went to my room, sat on the edge of my bed, and pulled out the note that was tucked into my blazer pocket. *Please, tell me I'm not too late.*

My fingertips touched my lips, remembering how being kissed felt. Like my whole body was on fire. And the sound of Matt groaning? I swallowed hard and dropped my fingers from my lips.

My mom had once sat in this same bedroom when she was pregnant with me. And even though she wanted me, I knew I was a mistake. A mistake she probably brooded over. I didn't need any time to brood over what happened today. That kiss was a mistake. And I would never. Ever. Kiss Matthew Caldwell again.

CHAPTER 17

Saturday

My elbow hit one of the walls of the bathroom stall and I cursed under my breath. I doubted Kennedy would let me leave here in my catering attire. So I'd brought a change of clothes to ensure she wouldn't dress me again. I didn't want to repeat anything that had happened at the last party.

Tonight would be different though. I was wearing a comfortable sundress instead of a slutty miniskirt. And I was going to stay clear of punch, even if it was delicious. I was not going to get drunk again. Or make a fool of myself. I remembered touching Matt's face like he was make-believe. I had picture evidence to prove it.

I pulled on my brown riding boots and shoved my other clothes into my backpack. When I walked out of the bathroom stall Kennedy was applying lipstick.

She smacked her lips together before turning to me. "You ready?"

As ready as I'd ever be to face another party. My first one had been such a disaster that my stomach had been upset all day just thinking about it. I nodded my head.

"This is going to be so much fun. The three amigas at it again!"

We made our way out the back entrance of the hotel and toward the main street. "Are you sure you're okay with all this?" I asked. "You've been acting really weird ever since I told you I liked Felix."

"Psh. What? No." She laughed. "I mean yes, I'm sure I'm okay. We're going to have so much fun tonight. Oh, I almost forgot." She pulled out her camera and held it out in front of us. "Smile!" She pressed her cheek against mine and snapped the picture.

A car pulled up in front of us. The door opened and Felix leaned out. "Hey." He was all smiles and his energy was contagious. All my worries about the party suddenly vanished. What was the worst that could happen when he was by my side?

"Hey!" Kennedy said. She climbed in before me, sliding into the middle seat next to Felix.

I sat down next to her and shut the door behind me.

"How was work?" Felix asked.

"Great," Kennedy said. "Neither of us dropped anything and we didn't run into anyone from school. So it was a win."

He laughed.

"I need another picture." She held out the camera and I moved closer.

"Don't be shy," Kennedy said to Felix. "You have to get closer to be in the frame. Here." She threw her free arm around his shoulders, pulling him in. "The three amigas!" she shouted.

Was she already drunk?

Felix leaned forward so he could see me around Kennedy. "I like your dress," he said. "And the boots."

I smiled. "Thank you."

"Excited for the party?"

"I'm excited to finish the tour of your place," I said.

"My place?"

"Yeah, I never saw the second floor." What am I talking about? Why did I keep asking to see his bedroom? I'd had him standing right outside mine and I hadn't invited him in. Why on earth did I keep trying to get into his?

"The party isn't at my apartment," Felix said.

Wait, what? "Oh. Where is it?"

"The Caldwell's."

I swallowed hard. Yesterday after class Matt had leaned over and whispered in my ear, "See you in the auditorium again." I hadn't gone. Of course I hadn't gone. But he thought I would. He thought I liked our kiss. My stomach churned.

"That should be interesting," Kennedy said.

I hadn't told Kennedy about my kiss with Matt. I hadn't told anyone about that kiss. I wasn't exactly fond of gossiping about incest. Did Kennedy somehow know I may have kissed my brother? *What is my life?*

"Why should this be interesting?" Felix asked.

Kennedy looked at me and I gave her my best death stare. She laughed and turned back to Felix. "You didn't seem to get along very well with Matt at the last party. I'm surprised he invited you tonight."

He shrugged. "We'd all been drinking. It wasn't a big deal. It's old news. Besides, Mason invited me, not Matt."

"But certainly Matt's going to be there," Kennedy said.

"Probably. But it's a big house. I doubt we'll run into Matt anyway. And even if we do…like I said, it's old news."

"If you say so," Kennedy said slowly.

My stomach was already upset. And now I was really overheated. I felt like I was sweating as hard as I did on my runs.

Kennedy gave me an encouraging smile. "You know what would be fun? If we ditched the party and went like miniature golfing or something."

"I don't think they have any mini golf near here," Felix said.

"I'm pretty sure they have it at Coney Island." She leaned forward like she was about to reroute the driver.

"That's like an hour out of town," Felix said. "Come on, the party will be fun. And I promised I'd be there."

I nudged Kennedy, letting her know it was okay. It was so nice that she had my back again. And I realized I was feeling a little guilty for not telling her about Matt. She'd help me through this. And even though I wanted to bury the secret a hundred miles underground, I knew that wasn't possible. I was a brother kisser. I was probably going to wind up in jail.

"And we're already here," Felix said and gestured out the window. There were fancy cars parked all along the circular driveway. But I barely saw them because all I could see was the house. No, not house. It was a freaking museum, or hotel, or something from a movie set. A super mega gargantuan behemoth stone mansion. It had gargoyles and everything. There were even bushes cut to look like gargoyles. It was kind of spooky. I wouldn't be surprised if we had crossed a moat a mile back that I somehow missed. A moat filled with blood.

The car pulled to a stop in front of the big black doors. We climbed out of the car and up the stone steps out front. Was it colder on the outskirts of the city or was it just me? I folded my arms across my chest.

I was expecting a total transformation when I walked inside like when I'd gone to Felix's place. Felix's parents had made everything inside modern. But the inside of the Caldwell mansion was as gothic as the outside. Dark marble floors. Dark red wallpaper. Black and white pictures on the walls in what were probably pure gold frames. The only thing that didn't match was the modern music drifting into the foyer.

"This place is hella creepy," Kennedy said.

Felix laughed. "I think it's cool. You know," he said, lowering his voice. "Rumor has it that the place is haunted. That the Caldwell brothers' great great grandmother hung herself from that very chandelier."

I looked up at the crystal chandelier. I wanted to call his bluff. A chandelier would snap if someone tried to hang themselves from it. *Right?* The crystals looked delicate, but the chandelier itself did look pretty sturdy.

I pulled my jacket tighter around myself. "Where is everyone?" There had been people everywhere when we'd gone into Felix's apartment. But there was no one in the foyer. Just that hint of music coming from the...left? I turned around in a circle. Or was it the right? I looked into a dark hallway.

"They're probably in the ballroom." Felix pulled out his phone and glanced at it. "But I gotta meet Mason and a few other people upstairs real quick. I'll catch up with you guys in a minute."

"No freaking way," Kennedy said. "We're coming with you."

He laughed. "They're upstairs."

They're? That could easily include Matt. I didn't like this. I didn't like this at all. But what was the alternative? Walking down that dark hallway alone? No thank you. I followed Felix and Kennedy up the winding staircase, trying my best not to look over at the chandelier.

The upstairs was just as creepy as the downstairs. I started envisioning the kind of coffins vampires slept in behind all the closed doors.

Felix stopped in front of one of the doors and knocked. I stepped back when a wave of smoke blew the door open. Kennedy gripped my arm for dear life and screamed at the top of her lungs.

The smoke laughed. Well, not the smoke. A hand swished the air, blowing the smoke away. Mason was standing there, a joint hanging from his upturned lips. "Sorry, I didn't mean to scare you." His eyes raked over Kennedy and I swore I heard her gulp.

"Congrats on the win," Felix said.

Smoke swirled in front of Mason's face. He removed the joint from his mouth and a puff of smoke masked his face again. "Thanks, man. It was a close one."

"That touchdown saved the day."

The smoke dispersed at Mason smiled. "I was just lucky my brother was there to catch it."

Matt. I wondered if he was in the room behind him. I tried to peer around Mason but his shoulders were too broad.

"Ladies, if you'll excuse us for just a moment," Mason said. He opened up the door and gestured for Felix to come in. The door swung closed a bit when Mason let go. I could only just see into the dark room. Mostly I could just see more smoke. If Matt was there, I couldn't make him out.

"I thought he was a smoke monster," Kennedy said.

I laughed but it sounded forced. "Me too."

"Do you think what Felix said was true? About their great great grandmother?"

"I don't know."

Kennedy kept ahold of my arm when the door squeaked open a little more. Maybe it was a gust of wind. Maybe it was something else. But now I could see inside. I watched Felix hand Mason a bag of something in exchange for an envelope. I was about to look away when I saw James wrap his arm around Felix's shoulders with a laugh.

The exchange was so fast that I would have missed it if I blinked. But Felix definitely slipped a much smaller bag into James' palm as they did some sort of weird hand-shake. James slid his hand into his back pocket and turned. I should have looked away. But I had never been able to look away from one of the Untouchables. James' eyes locked with mine. And it wasn't like that fancy party at the hotel when he'd smiled to be polite. Smiled to hide his sadness. Smiled because he was trained to. This time he didn't smile at all. Instead, he lowered his eyebrows and his beautiful features turned into a scowl.

A brunette I didn't recognize threw her arms around his torso and kissed his cheek. But his eyes didn't leave mine.

I stepped away from the door, pulling Kennedy with me. "This place really is creepy," I said. "Maybe we should just go."

"But we just got here," Felix said.

Kennedy and I both jumped. We hadn't heard him come out of the room.

"Come on, it'll be fun. I was kidding before. This place isn't haunted. Really, you have nothing to worry about." He slid his hand into mine and led us back down the stairs. Kennedy was still holding on to my arm and I was pretty sure it looked like we were huddled together like we were in a horror movie. And I swore to myself that I would not be the one that went off alone and got murdered in the haunted mansion.

We walked through the dark hallway for a few minutes, the music getting louder the farther we walked. Finally we made it to the ballroom and I breathed a sigh of relief. Even though the gothic design extended into the room, there was at least more light. And barely any smoke monsters. Just a few in the corners, and I could tell they were men because I could at least see their jeans under the puffs of smoke.

Felix led us over toward the bar and dropped my hand as he picked up one of the shots on the counter. "Here's to a fun night."

I didn't move to grab one of the shot glasses. "We promised my uncle we wouldn't drink," I said.

"I didn't," said Kennedy. "And I'm so scared if I don't drink I'm going to keep screaming all night." She grabbed the shot out of Felix's hand and downed it in one gulp. "Ow, it burns. But I'm going to feel so much better in a few minutes."

"That's the spirit," Felix said. He looked back at me. "It's just one drink."

"I don't know. Last time I drank I was kind of embarrassing." And I threw up the next morning. And my uncle got so mad. And I molested Matt's face.

"That was vodka mixed with all sorts of sugary shit. This is straight tequila. There's a big difference. You'll be fine." He handed me one of the glasses.

I wasn't sure if what he said was true. Wasn't all alcohol just alcohol? I looked down at the clear liquid. But the glass was so small. How much harm could one little sip do?

"I won't let anything bad happen to you, newb."

I'd already let him down by kissing Matt. Even if he didn't know it. I didn't want to let him down anymore. And I believed him. He wouldn't let anything bad happen to me. I tapped my glass against his and drank the whole thing like Kennedy had. "Ugh. That's so disgusting. I'd rather have punch."

Kennedy laughed. "The second one goes down easier." She pulled three more shots to the edge of the bar.

I knew it was a bad idea. I knew it but I still found myself reaching out to grab one of the glasses. It burned just as badly the second time.

"You still owe me that dance," Felix said to me.

"Let's do it!" Kennedy pulled us both out into the middle of the room where everyone was dancing. She shimmied her hips in what could only be described as a perfect backup dancer routine. How had I not known she was a great dancer? I kinda just stood there awkwardly. I didn't know how to dance. I looked at the people around us. Most of the girls were practically humping the guys on the dancefloor. And I definitely didn't know how to dance like *that*. I moved my feet a bit but I just felt awkward. Although the music was good. I closed my eyes. Oh crap, my arms were doing that thing where they felt heavy again. Two tiny glasses of tequila couldn't have been as bad as two glasses of punch. It wasn't physically possible.

"Can I speak to you for a second?"

I jumped when someone's hand landed on my shoulder. My eyes flew open. Felix was staring at someone over my shoulder. I turned and saw James Hunter standing there. The scowl was no longer plastered to his face. Instead it was the smile. The fake one that didn't reach his eyes.

"Um." I looked around but James was definitely talking to me. "Me?" I poked myself in the middle of my chest.

He leaned forward, his lips brushing against my ear. "Can you keep a secret?"

I wasn't a scholarship student. I'd probably kissed my brother instead of the boy I'd promised my first kiss to. My life was becoming one big secret. "Yes."

"You can't tell anyone what you saw tonight."

Or…what? I swallowed hard.

"Please," he added, taking the tone of a threat off the table. "I swear it wasn't what it looked like."

I pulled away and looked up at his face. Similar words to what Matt had said when I'd seen James come into school late. *I have it under control.* It wasn't what it looked like? So why wasn't he offering an alternative? My eyes dropped to the dark circles under his bloodshot eyes. I didn't want to keep his secret. I wanted to help him. "I think it was what it looked like." I didn't realize the words had even left my mouth until his fake smile melted off his perfect face.

"James! There you are," the brunette I'd seen him with earlier said. "I've been looking all over for you. I thought you left." She looped her arm through his. "Who's your friend?"

"Brooklyn Sanders. She's a new student at Empire High. A scholarship student. A sophomore. She just moved here from Delaware."

How the hell did he know all that?

"Nice to meet you, Brooklyn. I'm Rachel," she said and then turned back to James. "Come on, let's get another drink."

He nodded and then leaned toward me one more time. "Keep my secret and I'll keep yours," he whispered before Rachel pulled him away. He disappeared into the crowd of other students dancing.

Now *that* was a threat. The chill I'd felt when I'd walked up to the mansion returned. The problem with James' threat was that I didn't know what secret of mine he was talking about. I had so many it was getting hard to keep track.

I didn't want to be here anymore. I didn't want to be tied up with people like Matt and James. And most of all I didn't want my arms to feel so heavy. Or for the room to be spinning so fast.

I was in over my head. I needed to come clean to Felix. I'd tell him everything. I wasn't going to be blackmailed by some rich kid I didn't even know. Even if he seemed to know me. I turned around and ran right into someone, their drink splashing all over the front of my dress. *Shit.* I wasn't sure how, but this party was even worse than the one last weekend.

CHAPTER 18

Saturday

"Sanders!"

I looked up from the stains seeping into my dress to see Rob holding a now-completely empty cup in his hand. He was smiling brightly like always.

"I thought that was you! What the hell are you doing here?" He clapped me on the shoulder like his brother had just a minute ago.

Getting scared shitless, getting my favorite dress ruined, and getting threatened by your brother. I shouldn't have been here. That much was clear. "I was actually just leaving."

His fingers tightened on my shoulder. "Shit, I spilled my drink all over your dress. Let's get you to the bathroom to clean that up."

I stepped back from him. "I'm fine."

"Come on. I'll show you where it is." He slipped his hand around my upper arm and started pulling me off the dance floor.

Felix stepped in front of him, putting his hand on his chest. "I'll take her."

Rob glanced back down at me. "You here with him?"

I nodded, feeling incredibly awkward that Rob was holding my arm.

"Huh." Rob smiled. "This night keeps getting more and more interesting." He looked back at Felix. "I promise I'm not stealing your girl. But the bathrooms downstairs are getting redone. I know where the ones upstairs are. I'm just escorting her. I swear."

Felix didn't move.

I looked down at my dress. As much as I'd rather Felix help me find a bathroom, if I didn't get cold water on the stain right now, it would set. "It's fine, Felix. I'll be right back."

"I'll keep him entertained," Kennedy said and started dancing even though Felix was just staring at me.

Rob pulled me toward the doors of the ballroom. "I thought you stopped seeing Felix when you canceled on him Thursday night."

"I didn't cancel on him." I found myself getting closer and closer to Rob as he led me down the dark hallway.

"Very very interesting."

Why on earth did he think I canceled my dinner plans with Felix? I was pretty clear in class that I had no intention to.

"Well, I feel obligated to tell you that your friend likes him then."

"Who...you?"

Rob laughed. "As happy as I am to hear that you think of me as a friend...no. I'm not into dudes. I was talking about Kennedy."

"You're into Kennedy?"

He looked down at me. "Are you drunk?"

"No." I shook my head. "I don't know. Maybe?"

He laughed. "Kennedy likes Felix." We walked into the foyer and I was distracted by the chandelier. The death chandelier.

"She doesn't like Felix," I said. "She used to freshman year. Now I'm pretty sure she hates him."

"No way. She definitely wants him." He led me up the stairs.

"Wanna bet? Rob, are you sure there aren't any bathrooms I can use downstairs?" In such an enormous house it seemed ridiculous that there wasn't one, just one, I could use that wasn't up here. The higher we climbed, the colder it felt. And as we started walking down the hallway I knew something wasn't right. Why had I agreed to come up here with him? Why wasn't I running in the opposite direction? If there was one thing I'd learned in the past few weeks, it was that it was better to stay away from the Untouchables. The reasoning behind their nickname was becoming more clear every day.

"You know what? I have a different bet to make with you," Rob said, ignoring my question. He stopped walking and I almost tripped as he tugged on my arm.

We were alone in the hallway. It was possible that Mason was still in one of these rooms, but I didn't remember which one. I had the fleeting feeling that no one would be able to hear me if I screamed. "Is it true? The rumor about the Caldwell's great great grandmother?"

"You're definitely drunk. We were in the middle of a bet, Sanders." His fingertips lightly tapped the bottom of my chin, drawing my gaze up to his. "Focus."

I stared at him. That permanent smile was still on his face. And I found myself wishing that I liked him instead of his brooding friend. I quickly dismissed the thought. I didn't like Matt. I liked Felix. Felix, Felix, Felix.

"I bet you that I'll have you screaming my name in 60 seconds."

The first thing that popped into my mind was an image of Rob throwing me over the balcony. James wasn't the first person to threaten me from my new school. Charlotte told me I'd disappear. Was this it? Were she and Rob in cahoots? I'd forget about Felix because I'd be as dead as Matt's great great grandmother. I pulled my arm out of Rob's grip. I wasn't going to take another threat from a stupid Hunter. "Fat chance, asshole."

He just kept smiling. "Asshole? I thought we were friends, Sanders?"

I glared at him.

"Sixty seconds. If I'm right, you'll owe me a favor," he said.

That meant I'd still be alive? I tried to think back to what he'd said. *I bet you that I'll have you screaming my name in 60 seconds.* I had no plans on screaming in the bathroom. Honestly, the odds of me crying were significantly higher since he'd ruined my dress. This was an easy bet to make. "And if I win?"

"Not happening. But in the slim chance that it does…I'll owe you a favor."

A favor from Rob didn't sound like a bad thing to me. Maybe I could ask him to help get Isabella off my back. Or get him to let me know what James thought my secret was. Or get his bestie to stop leaving me notes. "Deal." I put my hand out for him to shake.

Instead of taking my hand, he leaned forward. For a second I thought he was going to kiss me. *Screaming his name.* Maybe I would scream, but it wouldn't have anything to do with him being a good kisser and wanting more. Because I had zero freaking plans to find out if he was or not. I was already a possible brother kisser. I wasn't planning on doubling my odds of that being true. I was about to reach my hand out to stop him, but he reached out first and lightly pushed me.

I fell backward into a dark room, landing hard on my ass. I glared at him standing in the hallway. He had the audacity to laugh. And then he slammed the door shut, bathing me in darkness.

"Rob!" I yelled and stood up, banging my palms against the door. My hands stumbled in the darkness, searching for the doorknob. I tried to turn it, but it didn't budge. He must have been holding the doorknob from the outside. "Let me out!"

I remembered earlier when I thought there were coffins in the bedrooms. Now it was all I could think about. The darkness felt like it was swallowing me whole. Now the tears that I thought were more likely than my screams started to burn my eyes. "Rob, open the door!"

I heard him laughing on the other side.

"Open the fucking door!" I slammed the door with my fists now, my tears cascaded down my cheeks.

Something brushed against my shoulder.

I screamed at the top of my lungs and threw a punch into the darkness. My fist collided with solid rock.

A grunt.

No, not a rock. I'd read Twilight. I knew vampires' muscles felt more like stone than flesh. God, I was going to die. Just not the same way the Caldwell's great great grandmother had. I was going to get eaten by a vampire. I screamed again and a strong hand clamped over my mouth.

I bit down on the vampire's palm.

"Jesus." He removed his hand. "Brooklyn, calm down. It's just me."

Matt. I'd recognize that voice anywhere. Even in the pitch black when all I could think about was vampires and death. Every ounce of me wanted to throw my arms around Matt's strong shoulders and have him protect me. But he wasn't protecting me. He was trying to scare me. He was part of whatever sick game Rob was playing. So instead of finding solace in his arms, I punched him again.

"Ow. Would you stop doing that?" He grabbed both my hands in one of his and pulled me into his chest. He was breathing fast, his cinnamon-scented exhales intoxicating me.

I tried to move my hands, but he kept them locked in his. "What is wrong with you?"

"You're still ignoring my notes. I needed to…talk to you. To see you."

I had nothing to talk to him about. And if he wanted to see me, wouldn't the lights be on? He literally had his friend push me into this room. This was…this was kidnapping. God, he was such a jerk face. "We have nothing to talk about."

"So you felt nothing after our kiss?"

"You mean the kiss you stole?" I couldn't see him in the dark room, but he laughed and I could easily envision his smirk. His stupid, sexy smirk.

"You gave it to me." He leaned forward, his warm breath on my neck. "Just like you'll give me the next one." He lightly kissed the side of my neck.

I wanted to tell him to go screw himself. To demand him to let go of my hands. Instead I stayed completely still. I closed my eyes, savoring the feeling of his lips on my skin. I was mad. And scared. And for some reason desperate for his touch. I couldn't tell him to stop. Because I didn't want him to.

"And the next." His lips lightly traced up my neck. "And the one after that. Because I know you feel this too." His lips hovered over mine. Waiting.

I swallowed hard.

"Tell me I'm wrong." He let go of my hands. "Tell me you felt nothing and I'll leave you alone."

I felt like I was on a sinking ship. A burning sinking ship. I was going under. But there was something about drowning with him that was a lot more appealing than drowning alone. Because that's what I'd been doing. Slowly drowning alone for weeks.

I couldn't stand here and lie to him. Because I didn't feel nothing when he kissed me, no matter how much I wished I had. I felt everything. Every. Single. Thing.

I closed the distance between us. My lips pressed against his, earning a groan from him that was quickly becoming my favorite sound. He pushed me backward, sandwiching me between him and the door, and deepened the kiss.

There was no way to say he stole the kiss this time. I'd initiated it. Maybe I did it because I was still scared. Maybe it was because I was drunk. There were a million ways I could describe my actions away. But I was pretty sure the truth was that I wanted this. Him. I wasn't dangling from a banister or being eaten by a vampire. I was alive. And I wanted to be alive with him.

His hands felt like fire as they trailed down the sides of my body, pulling me against him.

"You're mine," he said against my lips.

I breathed in his cinnamon exhales. I didn't push him away this time. I didn't tell him to stop. I didn't call him a thief. But he was most certainly a thief. Because he was trying really hard to steal my heart. And in that silent room, just the two of us breathing hard, it felt real. It felt like falling in love.

"Is Matt in there?" A female's voice drifted beneath the wooden door.

"Shit," Matt said and released me from his embrace.

"Nope," Rob said much louder than the girl was speaking. "Pretty sure he's downstairs! Matt is definitely not in his bedroom!"

"Why are you shouting? And why are you holding the doorknob?" She knocked. "Matt, are you in there?"

Matt grabbed my hand, pulling me farther into the dark room. "You need to hide," he hissed.

"What?" I pulled my hand out of his.

"Please. I'll explain everything in a minute." He opened a closet door.

"You're not serious?"

"Matt, I know you're in there!" There was pounding on the door. "Let me in!"

"I promise." He grabbed my face in his hands. "Just…please, Brooklyn. I swear I'll tell you everything as soon as she leaves. I need you to trust me."

I could just make out his features in the darkness. I had never seen him look worried before. Something was wrong. Really wrong. I heard the click of the door opening.

"Matt?" the girl was definitely in the room now. Now that I could hear her better, her voice sounded so familiar.

"Told you he's not in there," Rob said, his voice clear now too.

"Where the hell is the light switch?" she asked.

I wanted to trust Matt. But the kiss we just shared was the only reason I stepped back into his closet. I was holding on to that moment instead of all the other ones. Like when he'd let Charlotte make fun of me in class. Or when he ignored me in the halls. Or when he scared me half to death in that auditorium and then again tonight. I didn't trust him. But I wanted to.

Matt closed the door behind me. The light turned on a second later and I could see his bedroom clearly through a crack. A huge four-poster bed was in the center of the room. I thought there'd be decorations or posters or something that screamed him. But it just looked like the rest of the house. Dark red wallpaper. Cold. Creepy. My thoughts trailed off when Isabella came into view.

It felt like the blood in my veins turned to ice.

"Oh, my bad," Rob said. "Guess he is. I'll just leave you two alone then…I guess?"

"You can stay," Matt said.

But at the same time Isabella said, "We actually need a moment alone." Then she glared toward the door where I assumed Rob was still standing.

"Right. I will catch you two later then," Rob said and left, the door closing behind him.

I closed my eyes. This wasn't happening. I wanted to wake up. I pinched myself but it just hurt and I was still standing in a closet.

"What are you doing up here?" Isabella asked, stepping closer to Matt. "The party's downstairs."

He cleared his throat. "Changing. I spilled something on myself." Some of the stains from my dress had transferred onto his shirt. "I'll be right back down."

"I'll wait." She sat on the edge of his bed and crossed her legs. Her skirt was so short that if it rode up any more she'd be flashing him her underwear.

Matt glanced toward his closet. *Me.* And then back at her. He pulled off his t-shirt. I'd never seen him without a shirt before. And for a moment, I forgot that Isabella was sitting on his bed and I was hiding. Because his abs? If I wasn't so mad at him I probably would have been drooling. He grabbed another t-shirt from a drawer.

"You know," Isabella said and stood up, grabbing Matt's hand that was holding his shirt. "The party's kinda lame. Did you know that Rachel is here? It's so humiliating for me. Her throwing herself all over James in front of all my friends. Doesn't he know how that looks?"

"He probably thinks it looks like he's dating her. Because she's his girlfriend."

"That's not how everyone else sees it and you know it. Rachel doesn't belong here. She's not even smart enough to get a scholarship to Empire High. She attends public school. Public. School. It's sad, really. I'd pity her if she wasn't so horribly annoying."

"We're not at a party with our parents, Wizzy. James doesn't have to pretend to like you here. Cut the bullshit."

She huffed. "How many times do I have to ask you to stop calling me that? And you know I don't like it when you curse around me." She put her lower lip out like she was a child.

Gross.

"If you don't like the way I talk you can leave."

She sighed. "No. I don't think I can face seeing anyone else tonight. You know what would make me feel better? Hiding out up here."

Matt glanced over at the closet again. I was pretty sure he couldn't see me. Did he know I could see him?

He cleared his throat. "I'd rather go back downstairs."

"Are you sure? I could think of a lot of things we could do right here." She sat down on his bed again and I tried not to vomit all over the thousand dollar tuxes hanging in his closet.

"Maybe later. Right now, I was hoping we could…dance."

Dance?

Isabella smiled. "Now that sounds fun. Do you have any music up here?"

"I meant downstairs." He pulled on his fresh shirt.

"Oh. Well, I guess I could use another drink too." She stood back up and walked over to him. "But you have to promise to dance with me the rest of the night so I don't look like a fool. Or else I might make a scene with Rachel and that would really ruin James' night."

"One dance," Matt said.

"Oh, Matt." She pressed her index finger against his lips. "I wasn't asking." She trailed her finger down, pulling at his bottom lip. "Dance with me the rest of the night. I'll make it worth your while like always."

He didn't say a word. I held my breath. Waiting for his response. What did she mean when she said, *"I'll make it worth your while like always."* Why was she touching him? Why wasn't he pushing her away? I stared at Matt, willing him to tell her to leave. To kick her out of his freaking bedroom.

Instead, he nodded his head.

"There. That wasn't so hard, was it?" She grabbed his hand. "Tonight is going to be so much fun now." She pulled him toward the door and then the lights went out.

For a second tonight, I hadn't felt like a dirty secret. But now? I was literally sitting in a closet with a stain down the front of my dress. I was the definition of a dirty secret.

And for some reason I waited. A minute. Maybe two. Maybe freaking fifteen. And as the seconds ticked by in my head, I knew Matt wasn't coming back. He left me. He left me alone in his dark room. Locked away in his closet like the dirty secret that I was.

I wiped away the tears beneath my eyes. Matt Caldwell was an asshole. And I was done believing a word from his mouth.

I pushed open the closet door. I'd waited so long that my eyes had already adjusted to the darkness. I went to open his bedroom door, but paused. I needed to tell him what I hadn't before. I'd let him kiss me instead like an idiot.

I switched on his lights and walked over to his nightstand. The top of it was empty except for the bedside lamp. I opened up the first drawer. I swallowed hard. Like me, he had a huge box of condoms. But unlike me? It was open. *I'll make it worth your while like always.*

I rummaged through the drawer, looking for a notepad and pen. I found a pen but nothing to write on. I opened up the next drawer and froze. There was just one folder inside with Isabella's name on it. I lifted it out of the drawer and opened it, assuming it was old school notes or something. But it was filled with pictures. Candids. Of her. I lifted up one. Then the next. And the next. They were all of Isabella. Her laughing. Her with her friends. Her freaking eating at some posh restaurant. I thought about the way she touched him. The way he didn't flinch. He told me they weren't dating. But Matthew Caldwell was a liar. It was the only thing I knew about him for sure.

I grabbed one of the pictures and turned it over. I closed my eyes and it was almost like I could still feel his body pressed against mine. *Tell me I'm wrong. Tell me you felt nothing and I'll leave you alone.*

I opened my eyes and stared down at the back of the picture. "I feel nothing," I wrote out. I didn't sign it. He'd know it was from me. Besides, if he brought Isabella back to his room tonight, I didn't want her to see a note from me. She tortured me enough. I didn't need to give her any more ammunition.

UNTOUCHABLES

I walked out of his room, feeling the weight of the lie in the note. Because honestly? I didn't feel nothing. I felt…broken. And I was pretty sure it was exactly how Matt wanted me to feel.

CHAPTER 19

Saturday

"You're shivering," Felix said, breaking the awkward silence in the car. He shrugged out of his jacket.

I couldn't take his freaking jacket from him. I could barely even look at him. "No, it's okay." We were on a date and I'd made out with another guy. I wasn't that kind of girl. So why the hell did I keep kissing Matt in dark places? This wasn't me. I blinked fast, trying to hold back my impending tears. God, I was such an idiot. Felix was a good guy. A sweet guy who was literally holding out his jacket to me. And I'd kissed Matthew Caldwell instead. *Again.* I'd hidden in his freaking closet waiting for him even when it was obvious he was seeing Isabella. I was…the worst.

"I'm overheated anyway," Felix said, keeping his jacket outstretched toward me.

I was sitting in the back of his fancy car in a wet dress that was more suited for the summer than the fall. I couldn't even try to hide my shivering. But I deserved to suffer. I deserved it. And a part of me felt like I was shaking because I was angry. Angry with Matt, yes. But even angrier at myself.

Felix wrapped his jacket around my shoulders anyway.

The guilt was so heavy that his jacket felt like it weighed 50 pounds. I just needed to come clean. I needed to tell him the truth. That I'd made a mistake. Twice. But I'd never make it again. Matt was a thief. And a liar. He was such a freaking liar. I was done making mistakes.

"Are you okay?" Felix asked.

I pulled his jacket tighter, hoping the weight would suffocate me so I never had to have that conversation with Felix. *No.* I was so far from okay. "I'm fine," I lied.

"Tonight was fun, huh?" Kennedy asked, leaning forward so I could see her around Felix. "I love dancing. And Felix is such a great dancer, don't you think?" She put her hand on Felix's thigh.

I grimaced. "Mhm." I could see it now. Everything was so clear tonight. I'd learned the truth about Matt. And I'd learned the truth about Kennedy too. Rob was right. She clearly had a thing for Felix. Whatever had happened between them freshman year wasn't over. At least, not for her. Being alone with the two of them in the car was unbearable. I wanted to scream at the top of my lungs that I'd kissed Matt. That I was sorry. That I was so fucking sorry. Kennedy deserved a great guy like Felix. Not me.

Because I was a brother kisser. Potentially. A brother kisser that kept going back for more like the sick person I'd become. It would be easy to blame the tequila that I hadn't wanted. But that didn't explain the first kiss away. Honestly, nothing could explain either kiss away. And I was so upset with myself, because there was one more thing that had become clear tonight. I'd messed everything up with Felix. I'd messed it up and I couldn't undo it. And I wanted to. I really really wanted to undo it all. I wanted to be with Felix. But even if I became a genie and undid everything, I couldn't be. I couldn't be with him because Kennedy liked him. And I couldn't do that to Kennedy.

Felix smiled down at me as we pulled up outside my apartment building. "I'll walk you to the door."

"That's okay. Thanks for the ride." I started to open the door, but the driver got there first. I stepped out onto the busy city street without looking at the traffic. A car beeped at me as it sped by. I hurried to the sidewalk.

Before I could walk up to the apartment, Felix grabbed my hand, pulling me back to him.

"Are you trying to get yourself run over?" There was humor in his eyes.

Maybe I was. Maybe all the secrets were too much. Being here in this stupid city was too much. I just wanted to go back to being invisible. "I'm sorry that tonight was a disaster," I said. I was. Even if there was no way to fix it. I stared into his eyes. Why had I kissed Matt? Why? Why had I messed everything up? Felix had always been the right choice. The better choice.

"I can think of one way to make it better." He tucked a loose strand of hair behind my ear and then his hand stayed put on the side of my face.

He wanted that first kiss I'd promised him. I had to tell him the truth. He deserved to know the truth.

"I believe I promised you something." His face slowly lowered to mine.

This wouldn't be my first kiss. Not even my second.

He drew a fraction of an inch closer.

I couldn't kiss him. I couldn't. Not like this.

Even closer.

So why did I want him to kiss me anyway? I wanted him to kiss away tonight. To kiss away the pain in my chest. I wanted to pretend that none of the Untouchables had ever talked to me. That it had all been a nightmare.

He was barely a breath away.

I closed my eyes. And for a second I imagined that I was back in my hometown. That my mom was still alive. That I'd never been kissed. That everything was right in the world.

Felix's lips pressed against mine. I closed my eyes even tighter, wanting to believe my lies. I wanted to remember this moment. Ingrain it in my mind more than Matt's kiss. Because this kiss was the one I was meant to remember until I was old and gray.

His lips were softer than Matt's. He tasted like tequila instead of cinnamon. His fingers didn't dig into my skin with urgency, he held me like we had all the time in the world. He didn't make me feel like a dirty secret. He kissed me right there in the middle of the busy city sidewalk because he wasn't embarrassed of me. And his fingers felt like ice on my already cold skin as the apartment door beeped open behind me.

Kennedy. Shit. I opened my eyes and saw her disappear into the building. All my lies came crumbling down around me. I was in NYC. My mom was dead. I'd been kissed three times. Nothing was right. I pulled away. "I'm sorry."

"Brooklyn?" Felix called after me.

I ran to the door, catching it before it closed behind Kennedy.

"Brooklyn!"

I ignored him and ran after my best friend. She was the only constant I had now. The only person that was always on my side. What if she really did like Felix? What if I'd just messed everything up? "Kennedy!"

She turned around on the step she was on. "Good way to end the night," she said with a smile. Her arms were wrapped around herself like she was holding herself together.

"No. No, not really."

She pulled her lips to one side as she studied me. "Why? I strongly doubt it was a bad kiss."

I shook my head. I couldn't even focus on the kiss. Her words spun around in my head. She knew what it was like to kiss Felix. Wasn't that what she was saying? "Do you like him?"

"Who?"

"Felix."

She started to shake her head.

"Rob said that you had feelings for him. Is that true?"

"What? I don't even know Rob."

I joined her on the step she was standing on. "You didn't deny it. You can tell me. I would never date him if you liked him. Just tell me."

"Well, I'm denying it now. I do not, in any way whatsoever, like Felix Green. If anything, I hate him. He's so annoying."

I didn't believe her. I didn't believe her because of the way she said it. And the way she looked when saying it. And the way she'd been acting the last few days. And the way she'd run away when he'd kissed me. "Kennedy…"

"I like…Cupcake. Okay? Happy now? The truth is finally out." She threw up her arms like she had never been more exasperated with someone in her life.

Oh. Wait, what? "Cupcake?"

"Yes. Joe. Joe Dickson. Cupcake. And I didn't want to tell you because I don't know if he's into me. But there it is. I have the biggest freaking crush on Cupcake. Even though he has a stupid nickname and he's kind of short. I can't help it. And I have no clue if he likes me back. I feel so…pathetic."

"You're talking about Cupcake? The guy that hit me in the face with a dodgeball?"

"You can barely see the bruise anymore. And I'm sure it was an accident. Besides, Brooklyn, he's actually really nice. And have you ever tasted one of his father's cupcakes? He brings me test samples of new flavors all the time. They melt in your mouth."

"Yeah, they're good. My uncle loves them." I didn't mention the fact that they were pretty much banned from our apartment now.

"My whole plan tonight was to make him jealous. Which I'm pretty sure worked great. Especially since you disappeared for like half an hour trying to find a bathroom. I got to dance with Felix the whole time and you should have seen Cupcake's face. It was practically green."

"Well that's…great. That's awesome." I breathed a sigh of relief. It all made sense. The way she kept putting herself between me and Felix. She wanted it to look like Felix had asked her to the party. To make Cupcake jealous. *Cupcake.* Who would have guessed?

"God it feels good to get that off my chest. I love Cupcake!" she screamed in the stairwell.

"Shhh!" I tried to scold but I started laughing. I was so relieved. She wasn't mad at me. We were okay. And it left me hope that I could fix things with Felix too.

"So what is this about Felix being a bad kisser?" she asked.

Kennedy had just confessed her feelings to me. She deserved the same in return. And if I didn't tell anyone I'd kissed Matt soon, I was worried the weight of the lies would kill me. "You're spending the night, right?" I locked arms with her as we started to walk up the steps again.

"Of course."

"I have a lot to tell you."

"Okay…" We climbed the steps in silence for a moment.

I needed to be in my bedroom, the door locked securely behind me. I didn't want anyone eavesdropping. No one else could know what I did. Kennedy was the only person I could trust.

"This wouldn't happen to have anything to do with how long you were searching for a bathroom tonight?" she asked as we stopped outside my apartment.

I pulled out my key. "I'll tell you in a second. Keep your voice down. I'm hoping my uncle is already asleep." But before I could put my key in the lock, the door opened.

My uncle was standing there with a frown on his face. "You're fifteen minutes late," he said. "I was worried sick."

With everything that had happened tonight, I had completely forgotten about my curfew. It hadn't even crossed my mind.

"It's my fault," Kennedy said. "It took me forever to find the bathroom before we left. All the ones downstairs were under construction and…"

My uncle held up his hand. "And you're in love with cupcakes? Yeah, I could hear you yelling from the stairs."

"Actually Cupcake. Singular. He's a boy at our school."

"Have you two been drinking?" my uncle asked.

I swallowed hard. "No." How much could one more lie hurt?

He folded his arms across his chest. "You smell like a brewery. I told you two that I expected you to take better care of each other. But here you are again in the same state as last weekend. So I'm going to ask you one more time and I expect the truth this time. Have you two been drinking?"

"Someone spilled something on her dress," Kennedy said. "And we…"

"Kennedy, I think it's best if you head home," he said.
"But…"
"Home. Now. Brooklyn, get inside."
I cringed.
"But, Uncle Jim…" Kennedy started.
"One more word and I'll be talking to your mother. Go home, Kennedy."

Kennedy pressed her lips together, gave me an apologetic smile, and fled down the hall.

My uncle opened the door so I could come in.

I walked inside and started toward my room.

"Not so fast," my uncle said.

I froze in my tracks.

"I gave you a 1 o'clock curfew and you broke it. You told me you wouldn't be drinking tonight. But apparently you like to lie."

The tears I had been holding back all night started to spill down my cheeks. I was a liar. All I seemed to be able to do was lie.

"And you lied again tonight when you so clearly have been drinking. I told you that I'm not an idiot. I know that kids drink. But you said you wouldn't show up on my doorstep drunk ever again. And you're wasted, Brooklyn. You reek of alcohol. You can barely stand up straight. What the hell were you thinking?"

I wasn't. I hadn't been thinking clearly all week. Not since Matt kissed me.

"Not only that, but that boyfriend of yours was the one that told me 1 o'clock. He was the one that confirmed you wouldn't be drinking. He looked me in the eye and made those promises. I didn't even ask him to." He shook his head.

I thought about how Felix had pressured me to drink. How he hadn't mentioned the time at all. I didn't have a defense. I gave in to him. And I lost track of time when I was hiding in Matt's closet. But I couldn't tell my uncle any of that.

"He's clearly a bad influence like Kennedy said. I don't want you to see him anymore. End of discussion."

I wiped away the tears beneath my eyes. "What? You can't forbid me from seeing him."

"Actually I can. And I just did. I gave him a chance despite my reservations. I gave him a chance for you. Because I believed that you had good judgment. But he failed. And so did you. You will not be seeing him anymore."

"This wasn't his fault." I stepped forward and realized my uncle was right. My body swayed and I had to place my hand on the wall to steady myself. I was drunk. I was such a freaking idiot.

"You're right."

What? "I am?"

He coughed into his hand and cleared his throat. "It wasn't his fault. It was mine. I've been too lenient with you. You're grounded, Brooklyn. For one week."

"You can't ground me. You're not my mom." And my mother had never grounded me. I'd never given her a reason to. I didn't even know what being grounded entailed, but I assumed I wouldn't like it.

"I know, Brooklyn. I'm not your mom. I'm your uncle who took you in when you had no one else! I'm giving up everything for you. And if all I can do is teach you to make good on a promise, then so be it. I'll do whatever it takes. Now you're grounded for one month. Go to your room."

"I hate it here."

"I already know that. You've made that abundantly clear. I put a roof over your head. I sent you to the most prestigious school in the city. I've done everything to make this as easy for you as possible. And you hate it anyway! So I might as well give you a reason to actually hate it. You're grounded for the rest of the semester. Now go to your room before I ground you for the rest of your life." He sighed and turned away from me, like he couldn't even look at me anymore.

I needed air. I was used to being able to step outside to breathe. To clear my head. When my mom was sick I used to go on walks around the hospital. I'd get all my tears out and go back to her hospital room with all the optimism I needed for her. To show her I wasn't scared. To show her I believed in miracles. One that could save her. God, I had so blindly believed in miracles. I'd clung to hope like an idiot.

I slammed my bedroom door closed, gasping for air as the memories collided with my reality. I flung open the window and climbed out onto the fire escape. I gasped for air as I climbed out. But all the air did was make me cry harder. I sat down on the cold metal and let myself cry. Cry for my loss. Cry for my mistakes. Cry about everything my uncle said. He was right. I was ungrateful. But how could I be grateful in such a cruel world? A world that took my mom away. A world where I was allowed to talk to assholes like Matt but not sweet guys like Felix.

I gasped for breath, my lungs finally expanding and collapsing properly. I'd only been out on the fire escape once before, when I'd first moved here. I climbed out hoping to see the stars in the sky. I had this stupid thought that if I could see the stars that I could pretend that I was looking at them from my home back in Delaware instead of here. That seeing them would make me feel like I wasn't so far away from my mom.

But there were no stars in the city sky. I let my tears fall. And there were no miracles.

CHAPTER 20

Monday

I started running on the track before Felix had a chance to catch up to me. I'd had the rest of the weekend to think about what had happened Saturday night. Being home 15 minutes late shouldn't have mattered that much. And literally everyone at that party was drinking, if not worse. I thought about the smoke swirling in Mason's face. And the drugs James had bought. My uncle was being completely unreasonable. Being grounded for a week was one thing. But the whole semester? Screw him. I picked up my pace.

And I didn't know what to say to Felix. I wasn't allowed to see him anymore - not even at school. My uncle worked here. He'd know. And honestly? I didn't want to talk to Felix right now anyway. Because this mess was his fault too. He'd pressured me to drink. He'd ignored the time just like I had. Yesterday I'd spent the entire day staring at the ceiling of my room as the focus of my anger oscillated between Felix and my uncle.

"Wait up!" Felix called behind me.

I knew I couldn't outrun him on the track forever. His legs were longer than mine. And despite his laissez-faire attitude, he'd been lowering his mile time too. I didn't want to have to tell him I couldn't see him anymore. But I also didn't want to have to tell him that I'd kissed Matt. Telling him I had to stop seeing him at least saved me from that awkward conversation. And waiting wouldn't solve anything. My uncle wouldn't change his mind. I wasn't even sure he'd ever speak to me again. So I stopped right in the middle of the track and turned to face Felix.

He caught up to me. "What's wrong?" He was out of breath from his sprint behind me.

I watched the rise and fall of his chest. His kind smile. The way he pushed his hair off his forehead before it could stick from sweat.

I didn't want to stop seeing him. This wasn't fair. But I knew life wasn't fair. It just felt like I'd already been punished enough. I'd already lost enough. "I was home 15 minutes late on Saturday. And my uncle could tell I'd been drinking. I'm grounded for the rest of the semester."

"That's a little…extreme isn't it?"

"It's not even the worst part. He also forbid me from seeing you."

Felix laughed, but when I didn't join in, his smile fell. "He forbade you from seeing me? Are you serious?"

I could feel the tears welling in my eyes again. I thought I'd shed all of them this weekend, but apparently not. "He thinks you're a bad influence on me." It was such a joke. Isabella and Charlotte tortured me for sport. And Matt went around pulling me into dark spaces and making me kiss him despite the fact that we were probably related. And I wasn't forbidden from seeing any of them. Just Felix.

"Is that what you want? To stop hanging out with me?"

I thought about the kiss lie. The lie that I was a scholarship student. I was so tired of lying. My tears started to fall down my cheeks. I didn't want to have to give him up. "Of course not."

He stepped forward and pulled me into his arms. "Don't cry. We'll figure it out. I'll talk to him…"

"He hates you."

"I doubt he hates me. He's just worried about you."

I wasn't sure that was true. From our conversation Saturday night, I was pretty sure my uncle was just annoyed by me. Annoyed I was here. Annoyed by my presence. I was an inconvenience and he was finally fed up. He didn't want me here anymore. That much was clear.

"The answer is pretty simple," Felix said. "We just keep hanging out anyway. At least at school."

I looked up at him. "It's not that simple. He'll see us. He…"

"And what? He'll ground you again? He's already played all his cards."

That was true. What could be worse than being grounded for the rest of the semester? *Grounded for life.* But that wasn't possible. I'd turn 18 in a few years and he couldn't ground me then. "I guess you're right." I glanced at the school in the distance. Could he see me now? Was he already pissed?

"So he thinks I'm a bad influence, huh?" Felix whispered in my ear.

The way he said it made my heart beat faster.

"We've barely even done anything, newb." His hands slid down my back, stopping right above my ass. "Just one kiss." His breath was hot in my ear.

His words seemed to echo in my head. *Just one kiss.* If I was going to keep seeing him, I needed to pull off the Band-Aid. He deserved to know the truth. "It wasn't my first kiss," I said. The words came out by themselves. I probably could have thought of a more ceremonious way to confess, but there it was. The truth was out there. It was like I could feel it settle between us.

There was a smile on his face that I didn't quite understand. "Yeah, it was a little hard to believe that someone like you hadn't been kissed before. I don't know why you thought you needed to lie about that."

"I didn't lie." I pressed my lips together. "It was true. When I told you."

"Oh. Fair enough. Who'd you kiss?" He looked more curious than upset. Actually, he didn't really seem upset at all.

"It doesn't matter. It's over."

He shrugged. "Okay."

"Are you mad?"

"No. It's fine. We're not exclusive or anything."

Felix hadn't asked me to be his girlfriend yet. I knew that. But the way he said "we're not exclusive" made my stomach churn. Did that mean he was seeing someone else? This whole time I'd felt awful about kissing Matt. And he…what? What had he been doing?

He smiled like nothing I'd said mattered. "Maybe you can save me one of your other firsts then?"

I thought about what Matt had said in the auditorium. *"I'm going to be all your firsts, Brooklyn."* I tried to shove away the thought, but it still sent a chill down my spine. "Yeah," was the only response I could muster.

"Like…your first kiss on the track."

I laughed.

He leaned down and kissed me. "And your first kiss during gym class." He kissed me again.

I'd kissed Felix a total of three times now. That was one more time than I had kissed Matt. And I felt relieved. I stood on my tiptoes and kissed Felix again. I wanted to keep kissing him until the two kisses with Matt were a distant memory.

***

"So…Joe," I said and stared at Kennedy and Cupcake on the other side of the lunch table. "Where did the name Dickson and Son's Sugarcakes come from?" I had to stifle a laugh as the ridiculous name left my mouth.

I had no idea what to talk to Cupcake about. I kept waiting for him to apologize to me. He'd hit me at full force with a dodgeball and had never uttered an "I'm sorry." I thought it would come. But as lunch slowly ticked closer to coming to an end…nothing.

He swallowed down some water with a huge gulp. "My last name is Dickson. I'm my father's son. And we make sugarcakes."

What the hell is a sugarcake? How were we not talking about that? Or the fact that the name of their shop was practically pornographic. If you said it fast it was basically Dicks On Son. "I thought you made cupcakes?"

"Amongst other things."

Kennedy smiled at him. I glanced at Felix who just shrugged and kept eating.

Finally the bell rang, ending the awkward lunch.

"Catch you later," Kennedy said and pecked Cupcake on the cheek.

I turned toward Felix. Should I do the same? A kiss on the cheek? I shook away the thought. It felt too forced.

"I can give you a ride home today if you want," Felix said.

I smiled. "That would be great." My uncle would never know. He always got home a few hours after me.

"See you then." He leaned forward and kissed me. Not on the cheek. A full kiss on the lips right there in the middle of the cafeteria. My mind had been racing ever since he'd told me we weren't exclusive. But that kiss pretty much sealed the deal. Right? Who else could he possibly be seeing? *Unless they don't go to this school...*

As he walked away, I felt the hairs on the back of my neck rise. I knew Matt was watching. And for the first time since I'd stepped foot in Empire High, I wasn't watching him back. I hadn't glanced at him all day. I was going full-on cold turkey. It was easier than I thought. All I had to do was picture Isabella touching his chest. Or the opened box of condoms. Or the dozens of pictures of Isabella in his nightstand.

"I thought you were banned from seeing Felix?" Kennedy said as we walked out of the cafeteria together.

I'd caught her up this morning. Just not on the whole kissing Matt twice thing because we'd run out of time before the first bell. But I was glad I hadn't told her now. I'd decided to bury that secret. It was done. I'd told Felix and he hadn't pushed the question of who. And I didn't feel compelled to ever talk about it again. Ever. "I decided to ignore that suggestion."

She laughed. "Brooklyn the bad ass. I like it."

I smiled as I pulled some books out of my locker.

Something hit my back, making me spill my books onto the floor. If I had been a fraction of an inch to the left, I probably would have split my head open on the side of my locker.

Isabella laughed. "Clumsy me." She put her hand on her chest, feigning sympathy. Her minions giggled beside her.

I tried my best to ignore them as I crouched down and started picking up my books. But they didn't leave.

"I'm used to ignoring the help," she said. "I just didn't see you. Out of habit, of course." She kicked one of my books with the toe of her shoe, knocking it farther away from me. I leaned forward on my knees to grab it.

"We're not the help," Kennedy said. "Go bother someone else."

"Oh, sweetie. Just because you go to this school doesn't mean you're one of us. Were you or were you not catering Mr. Caldwell's birthday party a few weeks ago? An event that I was *attending*?"

That was Matt's father's birthday party? No wonder he only helped me in the bathroom, away from prying eyes.

God forbid his parents found out he associated with *the help*.

Kennedy just stared at Isabella.

"Good, we agree."

I stood up, clutching my books to my chest.

"I saw Rachel all over James at the party this weekend," Kennedy said. "They make a cute couple."

Isabella lowered her eyebrows. She always looked mean. But the action made it look like she was about to rip Kennedy's head off. "Oh, were you there? I didn't see you." She laughed. "Right, we were just talking about that. I never notice the help."

"Well I bet you noticed Rachel."

"That's really none of your business, but just to clear the air since everyone seems to think they know what's going on…my parents want James and me together. However, James and I have mutually decided that our own wishes are more important than our parents. We both like different people. My relationship with James is nothing more than theater put on for the sake of our parents."

I thought about the way she'd sat on Matt's bed like she'd been there a million times before. I held my books a little tighter. I didn't know if what she said was true. Maybe she did like James. Maybe she didn't. Regardless, she was definitely screwing Matt.

"Oh, really?" Kennedy said. "Because it didn't look like you had a date on Friday."

"It didn't look like you did either, sweetie."

Kennedy smiled. "I thought you didn't notice me there?"

Isabella opened her mouth and then closed it again. "Charlotte told me you were there," she said and gestured to her favorite minion. "Right, Charlotte?"

Charlotte nodded. "Sad, really. Who goes to a party without a date?"

Kennedy glared at her. "You would know. No one would date someone as hateful as you."

"Or as poor as either of you," Isabella said.

All of them laughed. But the joke wasn't funny. Poor people dated all the time. And Kennedy and I were both dating people. This conversation was ridiculous. But for some reason I still didn't open my mouth.

Isabella turned her attention to me like she could hear my silence. "The party is at my house this weekend."

There was a long awkward pause. Kennedy and I both looked at each other.

"Oh." Isabella touched her chest again. "You didn't think...oh no. I should clarify before you get the wrong idea. Because I want to be very clear about this." She leaned forward slightly. "Neither of you are invited." She was talking to both of us, but only staring at me with her demon eyes. "Not just to my party. But anyone's party. *Ever* again. Unless you're handing out appetizers." She turned on her heel and walked away, her minions hot on her trail.

"Bitch," Kennedy said under her breath.

"The joke's on her," I said. "I'm not allowed to go to a party even if I wanted to."

Kennedy laughed. "I bet I can convince Uncle Jim that we can still hang out."

"I hope so. Or my weekends are going to suck. And my weeknights. And all my days."

Kennedy laughed and looped her arm through mine. "He won't keep us apart. He loves me."

I nodded. I was pretty sure my uncle did love Kennedy. I just wasn't sure he loved me.

CHAPTER 21

Monday

The chair squeaked in front of me. I didn't look up. My eyes were scanning the same page of my entrepreneurial studies book over and over again, even though I wasn't retaining an iota of it.

"Brooklyn."

It was Matt's voice. I ignored him, squinting at the page in front of me.

His forearms rested on my desk as he leaned forward. "We need to talk," he whispered.

The time for talking had passed. He'd been promising me a talk for a week but he never talked. He just assaulted my lips. I pressed said lips together, trying to ignore the memory of what it felt like to kiss him. It was easy because the memory of me sitting in his closet was easier to focus on. He'd promised he'd come back *to talk*. He hadn't.

"What day this week works for you to meet up after school?" he asked.

So now he was being reasonable? He didn't have a ballet to attend every other night but Thursday this week or some other dumb excuse? "No days work. Sorry." I lifted up my book, trying to block him from view.

"I'll make whatever day you want work. Just pick a day and time."

"I can't. You and Rob will have to start the website without me. I'll write some workout descriptions or something while you two do the coding."

"We agreed to do it together."

"I never agreed to that."

Matt placed his hand on my book, lowering it to my desk so I could no longer hide behind it. "Brooklyn, please."

I finally looked at him. And he looked...not good. It was the first time I'd ever describe him that way. There were dark circles under his eyes. His hair was askew like he'd just woken up from a nap. Maybe he had. The Untouchables could pretty much do anything they wanted at this school and not get in trouble. I pulled my book away from his hand, but I didn't hide behind it again. Instead I slammed it closed. "Why are you even talking to me right now? Class is about to start." The last thing I wanted to do was get in trouble in Mr. Hill's class again.

"But it hasn't started yet." Matt smiled in that annoying charming way of his.

And something in me snapped. "You're both assholes," I said, first glaring at Matt and then at Rob. "I think I have a right not to speak to either of you after what happened Saturday."

Rob laughed. "Sorry, Sanders. It was just a classic Hunter-Sanders mess around. I didn't mean any harm."

So it was fun for Rob to torture me now too? "A what? You pushed me into a dark room and held the door closed. You made up lies about Kennedy. And you ruined my dress."

"A shame. That dress looked great on you."

I glared at him.

"And I didn't lie about Kennedy."

"Yes you did. Felix and her are just friends." Like Felix was just friends with me? Because we weren't technically dating. He'd said it himself. Was it possible that Kennedy was the other girl Felix was seeing? The thought swirled around in my head. No. Definitely not. That couldn't be true. I swallowed down the lump in my throat.

"If you say so," Rob said. "Better get to the bottom of that, though. It seemed like you were getting pretty close to Felix in the cafeteria. Wouldn't want to see you get hurt."

The lump was already back in my throat. "Like you care."

"I care," Matt said.

You've got to be kidding me. "Yeah, right. Like you cared about me on Saturday when you stuffed me into your closet like a dirty shirt?" Thinking about his shirt made me think about him removing his shirt. His abs. His strong arms. *Stop.*

Rob laughed. "Who puts dirty shirts in their closet? You're a weird one, Sanders."

"We'll talk about this later," Matt said when Mr. Hill walked into the room. "Just pick a day."

"I literally can't. I'm grounded. For the whole semester."

"Why?"

I ignored him.

"Why?" Matt asked again.

"Miss Sanders are you planning on talking during my whole class?" Mr. Hill asked.

Are you kidding me? Matt was the one turned around talking to me. And words had left his mouth more recently than mine. Why wasn't he in trouble?

"No, Mr. Hill," I said. "I'm sorry," I added, hoping he'd let me off the hook this time.

"Good. Since you're in such a chatty mood, why don't you start us off today by reading from the top of page 47?"

Not again. I started reading. And kept reading. And reading. My throat started to grow hoarse again and still Mr. Hill made me read. I hated this class. I hated this school. I cleared my throat for what felt like the hundredth time. And I hated Matthew Caldwell.

***

My uncle and I were sitting in silence eating dinner. The silence was killing me. He was probably waiting for me to apologize. But I wasn't in the mood. I pushed around some of my rice with my fork.

He cleared his throat.

I waited for him to say something, but he didn't. Maybe he heard that I'd eaten lunch with Felix. He just as easily could have been waiting for a confession instead of an apology. He wasn't going to receive either from me.

The minutes ticked by.

He pushed his plate aside. "Do you want to watch a movie tonight?"

It was a peace offering. I knew that. But maybe I wasn't ready for peace. I didn't respond.

He sighed. "Kiddo…"

"I'm not a kid." I dropped my fork onto my plate. "May I be excused?"

"I know you're not a kid. But…"

"I only have two friends at school. If you make me stop talking to Felix you're cutting my friend count in half."

"You know that's not what I want. But that boy…"

"You don't know him."

My uncle sighed. "I know enough."

I was about to protest when the phone rang. I looked back down at my half-full plate. No one ever called me. The only person that had my number was Kennedy, and she never called. She always just walked over.

My uncle stood up and grabbed the phone. "Sanders residence."

There was a long pause.

"Yes, but that won't be possible."

Another pause.

"Because she's grounded."

I looked up from my plate.

My uncle was staring at me. "For school you say?"

Pause.

"Yes. I see."

Another pause.

"She stayed out past her curfew."

"Who are you talking to?" I mouthed silently at him.

He ignored me. "I couldn't agree more," he said into the phone.

Pause.

"Sure, sure. Tomorrow night is fine."

Another pause.

He smiled. "You too. Goodnight." He hung up the phone and turned to me. "Now he seems like a good boy."

"Who?" But my stomach had already turned over halfway through the conversation. I knew exactly who. I just had no idea how he got my phone number. Or why the hell he was calling. I'd made myself more than clear today.

"Matthew something or other. He says you have a group project together?"

I nodded because that was all I could do. Matthew Caldwell was absolutely not a good boy. I was pretty sure he was sent straight from hell just to annoy me.

"He wanted to make sure it was okay to work on it tomorrow afternoon. I'll drop you off to do your project with him after work. Make sure to get the address from him at school."

He even assured that I'd talk to him tomorrow? *Confident prick.* "I'm grounded though," I said. "I can just split up the work with my group. We don't have to meet after school."

"School work always comes first." He grabbed his plate and placed it in the sink. "I'll do the dishes if you want to pick the movie."

I wanted to tell him that Matt was a liar. A cheat. A bully. But I didn't know how to tell him that without admitting that I'd kissed him. That confession might just tip the scales to me being grounded for eternity. Especially if I was related to him. *God, what is wrong with me?*

I could ask. I could ask right now and put the issue to rest. But I kept my lips closed. Not knowing the truth was better than knowing in this case. Right? I took a deep breath. None of it mattered because I wasn't going to kiss him again. I needed to focus on what mattered. "Please don't make me stop seeing Felix," I said. "Can't I just do chores around the house? Or like…write I'm sorry 100 times on a sheet of paper? Or something else to satisfy this whole grounded thing?"

My uncle placed one of the plates in the dry rack. "Your mom never grounded you, huh?"

I sighed. "No. But I also never did anything bad. I was a little preoccupied taking care of her."

He rinsed off his soapy hands and turned to me. "I can't stop you from talking to a classmate in school. But right now, I don't feel comfortable with you hanging out with Felix outside of school."

"What if he just comes here? While you're here?"

"Are you actually sorry? Because I haven't heard you say it yet."

"Of course I'm sorry."

He didn't say anything.

"I didn't mean to worry you." I knew how terrible worrying felt. Like a vine encircling your heart and slowly crushing it. "I'm sorry."

He nodded. "We'll discuss Felix another week. What kind of guardian would I be if my semester-long grounding only lasted 2 days?"

"A really good one?"

He laughed and started doing dishes again. "Ask me again next week."

"What about Kennedy?"

"Ask me again next week," he repeated.

I wasn't allowed to hang out with Felix or Kennedy but my uncle was forcing me to hang out with Matt? What kind of sick twisted nightmare was I living?

CHAPTER 22

Tuesday

"I'll pick you up at 8," my uncle said.

I stared out the taxi window without moving. When I'd seen the Caldwell's house on Saturday night, I thought it looked like a haunted mansion. I was picturing the same thing for this house. But the Hunter's mansion didn't have the same feel. The gray stone exterior reminded me of a restored estate that had been turned into a museum back home. It wasn't scary. But it looked equally as cold.

"Kiddo?"

"Yeah?" I turned away from the window.

My uncle was smiling at me. "8 o'clock, okay?"

"You don't have to pick me up. How much trouble can I get in on the subway?" We'd taken the subway halfway here and a taxi the rest. It was completely insane of him to go so out of his way. Back and forth and back and forth again. But he insisted that grounded kids didn't ride the subway alone.

"I'll be waiting right here," he said.

I knew he didn't want to have to come up to the door. He didn't want the people who lived in such an ostentatious expanse of a house to judge us. But I was pretty sure they all had more secrets than me. And they were judging me regardless. "Sounds good," I said. "See you then." I opened the car door and stepped out.

The cool autumn air made me pull my jacket tighter around myself as I made my way up the gray stone steps. Well, not my jacket. I'd tried to give Felix his coat back today, but he'd insisted that I keep it. And I was grateful. Because it was a hell of a lot warmer than mine.

Before I lifted the knocker, I watched my taxi disappear out the main gate. Part of me wanted to run after my uncle. Beg him to not make me go into this house. He was abandoning me for four hours. *Four.* I wasn't sure I could handle Matt playing with my emotions for that long. Or Rob who was probably going to cash in on his bet soon. Or James who was blackmailing me with one of my many secrets.

But if I learned one thing from my mom, it was that we didn't back down just because something was hard. We fought. We fought until the very end. Even if the end was sooner than either of us hoped. I could make it through four hours. I was about to lift the knocker when the door creaked open.

Oh God, this place is haunted too.

But instead of a scary gust of wind or smoke monster, there was a man standing there in what could only be described as a butler uniform.

"Hello, ma'am," he said, keeping the door ajar with a white-gloved hand. "Can I help you with something?"

"Um…" I was expecting Rob or Matt to open the door. James if I was unlucky. Not a strange man who didn't know why I was there. "I'm Brooklyn."

"I'm sorry, Brooklyn. I think you might have the wrong house."

"This is Rob's house, right?"

He frowned.

"Robert Hunter?"

"Yes."

I wasn't sure why this man wasn't letting me inside. "He invited me to work on a school project. I might be a few minutes late." I swallowed hard when the butler just stared at me. The longer he stared, the more certain I was about what was happening. A prank. This was all some stupid joke. Invite the new girl to your house and pretend you didn't? Were they planning on throwing me out? Filming the whole thing? Wasn't making me sit in the closet in the dark bad enough?

"No, I don't think so," the butler said. "I'm expecting a young man for a school project. Sanders is his name."

I breathed a sigh of relief. "That's my last name."

"Oh." He laughed. "Well it would have been nice of young Robert to tell me he was expecting a girl. He made it very clear when we spoke that Sanders was a boy."

I heard familiar laughter behind the butler.

"Just a bit of fun, Eric," Rob said. "Because she's one of the guys." He threw his arm around my shoulders, pulling me into the foyer. "Right, Sanders?"

"No. Not really."

He laughed. "See? Always jesting. Right this way," he said, keeping his arm around my shoulders. "Bring up the snacks in a bit, will you Eric?"

"Of course, sir."

My sneakers looked out of place on the marble floor. And on the ornate twisted staircase Rob was leading me up.

"Aren't we going to work downstairs?" I asked. "In the kitchen or something?" The last thing I wanted was to hang out in Rob's room. I'd had this fear all day that I'd wind up in a closet again. It would be best if the only hiding option was a pantry. At least then there would be food.

"Nah, James' computer is in his room."

I swallowed hard. I didn't want to be in James' room either. Or his house. Or anywhere near any of these people.

"What? Are you afraid I'll lock you in again?" he asked. "Don't be. I already won the bet. Now it's just a matter of what I'll make you do."

"You could do the gentlemanly thing and forget about the bet altogether."

"James is the gentleman. Me?" He let his arm fall away from my shoulders. "I'm the youngest son. And as you can probably tell…the youngest sons of prestigious families aren't held to the same standards as their older siblings. I'm anything but a gentleman, Sanders. Nice jacket by the way. Are you trying to make this evening unbearable on purpose?"

"What?" I was too focused on the fact that Rob thought his brother was a gentleman. We were talking about the same James, right? The blackmailing druggie with the sad smile?

Rob slid his index finger and thumb down the zipper of Felix's coat. "He's not going to like this."

"Who? James?"

Rob laughed. "Naïve as ever, Sanders. You're driving him mad you know. Playing hard to get. It's his weakness."

I wasn't as naïve as he thought. Because I knew now that he was referring to Matt. "I'm not playing hard to get. I have a boyfriend." I didn't. Felix had made that pretty clear. He'd been kissing someone else. *I think.* Regardless, it was easier to pretend that Felix and I were exclusive. I didn't want Matt to try to kiss me again. Or get anywhere near me at all. I was going to set some ground rules fast on this stupid after-school project hangout.

"Huh. If you say so."

The way he said it made it seem like he knew I was lying about Felix being my boyfriend. What did Rob know? I realized it was possible that he knew who else Felix was kissing. Before I could ask him, he opened the bedroom door.

"Sanders has arrived," Rob said and strolled into the room.

I waited a moment, trying to clear my head. I wished I was about to walk into some random sunroom or second kitchen, but there was a nameplate on the door. This was definitely James' bedroom. I took a deep breath. All I had to do was not engage with Matt. Or James. Rob would be the only person I talked to. And I'd keep it to a minimum.

James' room wasn't anything like Matt's. There was no fear of coffins or vampires as I walked in. But still…that same coldness had me crossing my arms in front of my chest. Everything in the room was baby blue. Like his parents had found out they were having a boy and vomited the color everywhere. There were also a few posters on the wall of Giants' players. It could have been any boy's room in New York. The only thing unique about it was that one wall had floor to ceiling shelves filled with books. It was practically a library. Which didn't exactly make the room feel any homier.

"Sanders, this is James," Rob said.

I looked over at James.

He was sitting at his desk staring at me staring at his room. It looked like he wanted me to disappear as badly as Charlotte always did.

"We've actually met," I said.

"Right, right," Rob lightly slapped my shoulder. "I forgot that you two were talking at the party last weekend. You can just sit on his bed. I already filled him in on everything yesterday and he's almost done."

I just stood there. I didn't want to sit on James' bed. And not just because it was James' bed. I had purposely not looked at Matt since walking into the room, but he was on the bed. I felt locked in place. James' eyes on me. Matt's eyes on me. "Then why the heck am I even here if it's almost done? You said you needed my help."

Rob laughed. "We just thought it would be fun to hang out for the night. Right, Matt?"

I finally mustered the courage to look over at him.

Matt was sitting on the bed, leaning forward, his elbows on his knees. His hair was wet. He'd probably just showered after football practice. Or maybe he just showered because he was dirty from all the sex he was having with Isabella. Too bad you couldn't scrub away an STD.

And even though I knew he was sleeping with Isabella, my heart still started racing when I saw him. I didn't know what the term was for being a brother lover off the top of my head. All I could think of was pedophile. Was I worse than a pedophile?

"What are you wearing?" Matt asked.

Suddenly the jacket felt warm. The room was no longer cold. I was pretty sure they'd turned the heat up to 80 to make me sweat. "Can I borrow your phone?" I asked Rob. "I need to call my uncle to come get me."

"Don't be that way, Sanders," Rob said. "Come on, we just want to get to know you better. Here, a drink will help." He gestured over my shoulder.

Eric had just walked in holding a tray of glasses filled with amber liquid.

I thought he was supposed to be getting snacks. Not alcohol. Where were Rob's parents?

Rob lifted up two of the glasses and held one out for me.

"No thank you."

"Have you ever even tried bourbon? You might like it."

Alcohol was not my friend. None of it. "I'm already grounded."

"We're not going to tell on you, Sanders." He kept his hand outstretched. "We're pretty great at keeping secrets."

I was sure they weren't. "Where are your parents?"

Rob laughed. "Geez, what is it, Tuesday? My mother's downstairs, probably a few drinks in herself, berating the housekeeper. My father is most likely picking up a call girl in a bar on Wall Street."

I was pretty sure my mouth was hanging open. He was kidding…right?

"And if my dad isn't doing that, he'll be home soon and my mom will start berating him instead of the housekeeper. A classic Hunter Tuesday." He took a sip of his drink.

"That's enough," James said.

"What? We're supposed to be getting to know each other."

"She doesn't need to be privy to our parents' personal lives. I've got this covered. She's right…she can go." James grabbed the glass from Rob's hand and downed it. Then he took another from the tray and went back over to his desk. In a few seconds that glass was empty too.

He was mad that I was here. Clearly. But I wasn't the one blackmailing him. *Asshole.*

"Who rammed a stick up your ass?" Rob asked.

I laughed.

James turned from his chair and locked eyes with me.

The smile fell from my lips.

"How about we just go downstairs," Matt said and walked over to us. "Let James work in peace and we'll come back up in a bit."

I was happy to get away from James' room. But significantly less happy when Matt wrapped his arm around my back.

"Don't touch me," I said and tried to maneuver away from him, only to bump into Rob in the hall.

Rob caught me in his arms. "She has a boyfriend, man. You should probably lay off."

I pushed myself out of Rob's arms. Why did they all keep touching me? I didn't want to be touched. I folded my arms across my chest, trying to look as uninviting as possible.

"She doesn't have a boyfriend," Matt said.

"She swears she does. She's even wearing Felix's jacket."

"Felix? Do we really need to talk about this again?" Matt asked me.

I tried to hold my head up a little higher. "There's nothing to talk about. Felix and I are dating. Exclusively," I added.

"Take off his jacket."

Was he serious? "No. Felix gave it to me. So I'm going to wear it."

"Rob, if you'll excuse us for a second." Matt veered me away from Rob and into…a dark room.

Son of a bitch. Not again. "Matt, stop." I pushed on his chest, but he didn't budge.

"We need to talk. Alone. Now." He switched the lights on, stepped into the bathroom behind me, and then locked the door.

"What can't you say to me in front of Rob?"

He lowered his eyebrows. "You know what we need to talk about. But first I need you to take off that pothead's jacket."

"Screw you. There's nothing to talk about. You promised you'd leave me alone if I told you I felt nothing. Do you need me to say it again? I. Felt. Nothing."

He looked so angry. "That's not true."

"You're such a prick. And how'd you get my phone number anyway? You're not just a prick. You're a creepy prick. Are you stalking me?"

He stepped forward and I stepped back. But I had nowhere to go. My butt collided with the vanity.

"Take the jacket off. Now."

"Take it off yourself." I had no idea why I said that. I meant it to be a retaliation, but I was very aware of the fact that I'd just asked him to strip me.

The anger in his eyes was suddenly replaced by something else. I swallowed hard. He was looking at me like he wanted to devour me.

I cleared my throat. "I meant…"

I couldn't finish my sentence because he grabbed the back of my head and slammed a kiss onto my lips. His kiss was hard and frantic. Like he really did want to devour me.

And I kissed him back. I didn't know how not to. It was so easy to get wrapped up in everything Matthew Caldwell. And I wasn't sure I was capable of keeping my hands to myself anymore. My fingers wandered into his wet hair, pulling him closer.

He groaned into my mouth as he shoved the jacket off my shoulders. I didn't need the jacket when his hands were on me. His fingertips felt like fire on my skin. He groaned again and I was very aware of the fact that the kiss was even more smoldering than his touch. He lifted me up onto the vanity and my thighs slid around his waist. It was like my body had a mind of its own.

"Nothing?" he asked, as he pulled away. "You don't look at me like our kisses mean nothing." His chest rose and fell as he caught his breath. "You're looking at me like you want to kiss me again right now."

My fingers were still buried in his hair. I quickly pulled them away. "I most definitely do not want to kiss you."

Idiotic. Stupid. I had just kissed him. I had no rebuttal. Especially because he was right. I could stay right here in the bathroom until 8 o'clock with him and be perfectly content. But that wasn't an option. Because I hated him. "Now, if you'll excuse me…" I tried to slide off the counter, but his hand caught my hip.

"This is about the pictures, right? I know you saw them."

I rolled my eyes and tried to get past him.

His fingers tightened on my hip, keeping me firmly locked in place. "It's not what you think."

"And how the hell could you possibly know what I'm thinking? You know nothing about me."

"I know that you're the only one that calls me out on my shit."

"Well, someone has to."

"And I know your mom passed away a couple months ago. I can't even imagine how much that hurts."

It hurt like hell.

"And I know that you never met your father. And you put on a brave face, but I see your pain, Brooklyn. I see it."

I felt tears prickling the corners of my eyes. There was no way I was going to cry in front of him. "You don't know me." All he knew was how to kiss me when I didn't want him to.

"I know your face lights up when you see me. It's the only time when you don't look sad."

"That's not true." Was it true?

"I'm addicted to that look. Like I'm the only one that can make you happy." He lightly touched my bottom lip with the pad of his thumb. "The only one."

I swallowed hard.

"I know I've been an ass. All I'm asking is that you hear me out." He leaned forward so our lips were only an inch apart.

I could smell his body wash. The sweet smell was making me dizzy. But I wasn't dizzy enough to forgive him. Or believe him. "I've been waiting to hear you out for weeks. I don't care what excuse comes out of your mouth. I'm seeing someone else. And if you don't let me out of this bathroom in five seconds I'm going to scream bloody murder." I was trying to be strong, but I was pretty sure I was whispering.

"Isabella's blackmailing me. And I've been trying to turn the tables on her. I'm trying my best here."

That was not at all what I thought he was going to say. But as surprising as it was, I knew it was bullshit. "You expect me to believe that? I know you're sleeping with her."

"What? No. No," he said more firmly. "Remember what I told you when we first met? She's toxic. Her whole family is. I would never. Ever. Sleep with Isabella Pruitt."

"Even if she was blackmailing you?"

"I swear, Brooklyn."

"I saw the way she touched you. How comfortable she was on your bed…"

"She's been spending time with me because she can." He ran his fingers through his wet hair. "But I haven't slept with her. I haven't even kissed her. She's just stolen all my freaking time. Time that I'm very aware that I'm not getting back. Time I'd rather be spending with you."

"Why should I believe anything you say?"

"I wouldn't lie to you."

I laughed. "You said you'd come back for me on Saturday night. I sat in your closet for fifteen minutes. All you do is lie to me, Matt."

"And I'm sorry…"

"If you're really sorry, tell me what she has on you."

He pressed his lips together. "I can't."

I shook my head. "All that time you feel like you've wasted with Isabella? That's how I feel about you. I'm done, Matt. I'm done wasting time on you." This time he let me slide off the vanity. But I didn't get far because he grabbed my wrist.

"I'm having someone follow her. That's what all those pictures were. It's just surveillance, but my guy hasn't found anything."

"So you're trying to blackmail her back? That's your solution?"

"It's the only solution."

I pulled my wrist out of his grip. "Fighting fire with fire is never the solution."

"It is in this case."

I stared at him. If Isabella really was blackmailing him, it would explain why he didn't talk to me at lunch or in the halls. Just in class where we were assigned a project together. And even then he never came to my defense against Charlotte. *Charlotte.* "What about Charlotte?"

"What about her?"

"Are you sleeping with her too?"

"God no. I'm not sleeping with either of them. I swear."

I wanted to believe him. But I was pretty sure lies fell from his lips more often than the truth.

"I have to be careful around all of Isabella's minions because they'll report back to her," he said. "Even just a friendly hello in the hall and Isabella will lose it. And I can't let this thing come out. I can't."

"So you're trying to tell me that Isabella asked you not to talk to me as part of the blackmail? Why?"

"Apparently she doesn't like the way you looked over at our lunch table on the first day of school."

God, I had been trying to break that habit. I knew it would get me in trouble.

"And she figured out that I like you. She's trying to make my life hell. The only way I can see you at all is thanks to this group being randomly assigned." He put "randomly" in air quotes.

"It *was* randomly assigned. Why are you using air quotes?"

"Everything in Mr. Hill's class can be bought for the right price."

"How much did you pay him to put me in your group?"

"Does it matter?"

"Of course it matters."

Matt shook his head. "It doesn't. What matters is that I like you. I really like you, Brooklyn. And I know you like me too."

I did. *I don't. Screw me.* I shook my head. "Then just tell me the truth. Tell me what Isabella knows."

"I would if it was just about me. But it's not. And if it comes out…it's not me that will get hurt."

I took a deep breath. "I heard you out. And I'm sorry that you're being blackmailed." But I was being blackmailed too and I wasn't going around being a dick. I was just getting all of Isabella's wrath because of Matt apparently. He'd made my life hell. I picked up Felix's jacket off the floor. "I hope it all works out for you."

"It can't work out for me if you're dating Felix."

I just stared at him.

"Stop seeing him."

"Are you kidding me? You just told me we can't be together anyway. What's the point of us both being miserable?"

"Don't play games with me, Brooklyn. We both know you don't even like him…"

"I do like him. I like him a lot actually."

Matt shook his head. "You don't. And my private investigator will find something on Isabella any day now. Until then we have to keep our relationship private. But it's only temporary."

I'd discovered something new about Matthew Caldwell. He'd lost his mind. "You and I don't have a relationship. You're an insane person."

He reached out and tucked a loose strand of hair behind my ear. For some reason I didn't move away or punch him, both of which crossed my mind. And I didn't do either when he leaned down and kissed me.

And kissed me.

And kissed me.

I should have tried to push him away. But his kiss made me weak in the knees. And turned my mind to mush. My fingers dug into the skin of his neck, pulling him closer. I had the same feeling that I did the first time he'd kissed me. Like it was easier to breathe when his exhales were what I was inhaling. Like I wasn't drowning anymore.

"You're mine and we both know it," he said against my lips. "And you do drive me crazy. Especially when you hang out with other men. Now I need you to hand me Felix's coat so I can burn it."

I pulled away. What was I doing? I was kissing the enemy. *Again.* "No." I took a deep breath and tried to step away, but now he had me sandwiched between him and the door. "I'm no one's dirty little secret, Matt."

"That's not how I see you." He dropped his forehead against mine. "You're a very clean large secret."

I laughed even though I really didn't want to. His time was up. I should have been screaming at the top of my lungs for help. Instead, I breathed in his exhales and tried to stop myself from kissing him again.

"All I'm asking for is time, Brooklyn. I just need you to wait a few more days until my PI finds something. But in the meantime…we can sneak around."

"So you'll still ignore me in the halls?"

"And pull you into dark rooms to kiss you senseless."

My throat made a weird squeaking noise. "And I wouldn't be able to tell anyone that we're together?"

"Not a soul."

For some reason I wanted to say yes. The word was at the tip of my tongue, but I swallowed it down. There were a whole lot of buts. Despite what Matt called it, I would be a dirty little secret. I'd have to sneak around. I'd have to lie to my only two friends. And I was a bad liar. I'd be grounded until I was 18 at this rate. And then there was another really big reason to not be with him. I didn't know who my father was. I stared into Matt's eyes. But I didn't look anything like him. Not even a little bit. I couldn't be related to him. Right?

"What do you say?" Matt asked. He gave me that perfect smile of his.

And I nodded. I have no idea why I did it. It was like a horrible reflex to that smile. My mind knew not to nod. It was like my heart had taken over my whole body. Which was probably why I really wanted him to lift me up on the vanity again. *Stop it, stupid heart.*

"Great," he said and grabbed the doorknob. "Make sure you return Felix's jacket tomorrow, because if I see you wearing it again, I'm pretty sure I'm going to lose it." He walked out of the bathroom.

Matt needed to learn what the word no meant. But I was very aware of the fact that I hadn't actually told him no. I'd nodded like the fool that I was. I looked down at Felix's jacket in my hand. What had I just done?

CHAPTER 23

Wednesday

I opened my locker to grab my gym clothes before class. But instead of a neat pile of clothes staring back at me, there was an insulated lunch box. I looked over my shoulder. Part of me expected to see Matt, but as promised, he'd been ignoring me all day. Isabella had been attached to his hip as he walked past my locker this morning. He'd kept his eyes trained ahead, laughing at something Isabella whispered in his ear. The more I saw them together, the less I believed him. He liked to whisper me promises in dark places. But in the light of day? I was invisible.

The lunch box was placed exactly where one of Matt's notes had been last week. The note showing up in my locker could be explained away. But a lunch box could not fit through the slats. There was no doubt about it now. Matt somehow had access to my locker. And my phone number. What else did he have access to? I unzipped the lid on the lunchbox and looked down at a note on top of a salad.

Thought you might like this better. See you tonight.

Tonight? The note wasn't addressed to me. And it wasn't signed by Matt. It was definitely from him though.

But what on earth was he talking about? We didn't have plans tonight. I'd be spending the rest of my nights this week in my room. Grounded. And honestly, I was a little relieved. All this drama with Matt and Felix and the rest of the Untouchables was too much.

Last night I'd sat outside on the fire escape thinking about all the ways Matt and Felix were different. But there were a lot of similarities too. And honestly, a lot of those were bad. I knew if I made a pro/con list for either of them, they'd both have more cons. I wasn't sure there was a right choice between the two. All I should be focused on right now was putting one foot in front of the other. Establishing a new life here in New York. Matt and Felix only complicated things. And my life was complicated enough without them.

I pushed Matt's note to the side and looked down at a prepared Caesar salad with extra parmesan shavings on top. We'd ordered pizza last night at the Hunters' mansion. Or estate. Or whatever rich people called their too big homes. I'd barely touched the pizza though because I was too nervous with Matt watching me.

So he'd bought me a salad for lunch today. Which could have just been a weird thing he did with everyone he dated. Or it could have been the fact that he was worried I didn't eat enough last night. Paired with the fact that I ordered a Caesar salad with extra parmesan shavings almost every day at lunch. He'd noticed. He'd definitely noticed even though he sat across the cafeteria. He noticed me. I zipped the lunchbox shut. It was sweet that he'd been paying attention. Sweeter that he bought me a salad for lunch. I wasn't sure why, but thinking about how sweet it was made my eyes watery. It had been a long time since someone had taken care of me. A really long time.

I grabbed my clothes, tucked them under my arm, and hurried to gym. I wasn't going to break down crying in the halls of Empire High. That would be asking for trouble. Isabella would probably slip on a puddle of my tears and sue me. She'd do the whole thing right in front of Matt, and he wouldn't say a word.

I delayed going to the gym for as long as possible. Just like Matt had been avoiding me today, I'd been avoiding Felix. I didn't know what to say to him. Matt had made it clear that he wanted me to end things with Felix. But I hadn't exactly agreed. I did like Matt. I really did. But I liked Felix too. So what if Felix didn't know what kind of salad I liked to eat? Although, Felix literally sat next to me at lunch. If anyone should know what I ate, it would be him.

None of it mattered. I knew what I had to do.

After roll call, Felix caught up with me on my way to the track.

He threw his arm around my shoulders. "How was your third night of being grounded?"

I pressed my lips together. I knew what I needed to say to him. But I had all class to break the news. I looked up at him. "Actually, I was allowed out of the house for a group project."

"Oh, that's brilliant. What kind of group project can we make up together?"

I laughed. "I doubt my uncle would believe I had a gym project. Especially with you."

"I can be very persuasive."

Like when you persuaded him you and I wouldn't drink at that party and then pressured me to? Or when you persuaded him that you'd have me home by 1 am? Maybe Felix was good at persuading people to do things, but he wasn't good at keeping his word. He was a liar. Just like Matt.

I tried to shake away the thought, but it was locked in place. I wasn't sure how I had gotten so tangled up with both of them. Going back to being invisible was going to be a blessing. All I needed was Kennedy and my uncle. I ignored the voice in the back of my mind saying I needed my mom too. She would have been able to help me sort through all of this. We hadn't had enough time. I needed more motherly advice. I needed her.

"I was thinking I could steal another first today," Felix said as he pulled me in the opposite direction of the track.

The tears that had been threatening to escape all day finally slid down my cheeks. He was being sweet, just like Matt. And all I felt was…lost.

We stopped under the bleachers. "How about the first time anyone's kissed you under the…" his voice trailed off. "Hey, what's wrong?"

There was a lot wrong. But instead of one of the million excuses I had rolling around in my head, I settled on the truth. Because honestly, it all came back to this. My uncle was right. I needed someone to talk to. "I miss my mom. I miss her so much."

"Oh." His arm fell from my shoulders.

I swallowed down the lump in my throat. *Oh?* I was trying to have a conversation with him. "Oh" didn't cut it. I needed him. Didn't he see that? I needed someone to help me. "Sometimes it feels like it's hard to breathe knowing that she isn't."

"I'm sorry, Brooklyn." He shoved his hands into his sweatpants pockets.

And I never saw anything so clearly in my life. I took a step back from him. He didn't want to hear me. He just wanted to make out under the bleachers with the new girl. It was just some game to him. But the joke was on him, because if I was a game, I was missing tons of pieces and had been left out in the rain for months. Abandoned. Forgotten. Broken. "I can't do this." I turned around.

"Do what?"

I started walking away, but he grabbed my wrist.

"I've never lost anyone that was close to me, Brooklyn. I don't know what to say that could possibly make it better. All I know what to do is say I'm sorry because I am. I'm so fucking sorry."

I turned back to look at him. "I hate that phrase. 'I'm sorry.' It doesn't mean anything. You have nothing to be sorry for. It wasn't your fault."

"But I'm sorry that you're going through something on your own. I'm sorry that I don't know how to react. I'm sorry for a lot of things."

I took a deep breath.

He pulled me into his arms, resting his chin on the top of my head. "Or if you'd prefer it…I'm not sorry."

I laughed into his soft t-shirt. "Better." I kept the side of my face pressed against his chest.

"If you ever want to forget for just a few hours…you know I can help you with that."

I closed my eyes. God, Kennedy was right. He just wanted to sell me drugs. I should have slapped him. Or pushed him off of me. But I was in desperate need of a hug. So I just stayed where I was. For one minute. Maybe five. But his sentence hung awkwardly in the air the whole time. "I will never buy drugs from you, Felix." There. It was out there.

"I wasn't asking you to buy them, newb. I'd just give them to you."

I closed my eyes tighter. So maybe he wasn't trying to sell me drugs. But he was still pushing them. "Being numb is no way to live," I said, quoting my uncle from my night over the toilet bowl.

Felix ran his hand up and down my back. "Okay."

Another awkward silence stretched between us.

Felix cleared his throat. "You know, my parents are never around," he said. "It's probably one of the reasons we get along so well."

I knew he was trying to understand. But he didn't. His parents were coming back. I was never going to see my mom again. Or hear her laughter. Or dance with her around the kitchen. She wasn't coming back. And I didn't know how to let her go. But this helped. "Probably," I said into his chest.

"So this can be written down in the books," Felix said. "The first time you skipped gym class to hug someone under the bleachers."

I laughed and looked up at him. I was supposed to be telling him I just wanted to be friends. Not because Matt had told me to. But because I'd planned on telling both of them that today. Friendship was all I needed. But would

Felix still hold me like this if we were just friends? Would he still try to listen to me when I was sad? I had a feeling that he wouldn't. And I didn't want to have to say goodbye yet. I hated goodbyes. The only one I'd ever had to say before was permanent.

***

My uncle turned off the TV and looked over at me. "You've been awfully quiet tonight. Something on your mind?"

I shook my head. "The movie was great. I was just really into it." I hadn't been paying attention at all. I didn't even know what movie we had been watching.

"It was crazy when that guy stole the horse," he said.

"Mhm. So crazy."

"We were watching Office Space, kiddo. There were no horses."

I laughed. "I must have zoned out."

"Right, right."

"I should probably get to bed." I stood up.

"Brooklyn?"

I looked down at him. He'd lost weight. His shirt looked a little baggy and his cheeks weren't as plump. I was good for him. It was good that I was here. Maybe it's where I was supposed to be. I couldn't save my mom. But I could still save my uncle.

He smiled. "I may have been a little hard on you the other night. How about you invite Kennedy over after school tomorrow to do homework like usual?"

"Really?"

He nodded.

"Thank you." I leaned down and hugged him. "Goodnight, Uncle Jim."

"Night, Kiddo."

Once I'd washed up, I changed into a comfy old t-shirt and slid under the covers. I was about to switch my lights off when I remembered Matt's note. I pulled open the drawer to my nightstand. Ignoring the mega box of condoms, I grabbed the stack of notes Matt had given me. I reread the top one again. *Thought you might like this better. See you tonight.* The salad had been delicious. Better than the ones they made in the cafeteria. But I hadn't gotten a chance to thank him. Both him and Rob hadn't been in class today. I'd sat there by myself wondering how much Matt had paid Mr. Hill to put us in the same group. And I wondered if Mr. Hill was so mean to me because Isabella had slipped him some money too.

I wasn't going to see Matt tonight. I had no idea why he'd written that. But tomorrow I'd have to make a choice. My resolve to end things with Felix had faded fast. Would the same thing happen when I saw Matt? It was easy to tell myself I needed to walk away. It was another thing entirely to actually do it. Because I was pretty sure Matt was right. My face did light up when I was around him. It was easy to forget about how sad I was when I stared into his eyes. Especially when he stared back.

I looked through the other notes. It had become kind of a nighttime ritual. But it felt different tonight. Like reading his handwriting somehow made me breathe easier. Almost like I was with him.

There was a knock on my door.

I waited for my uncle to say, "Kiddo, can I come in?" like he usually did. But when his words didn't come, I climbed out of bed.

Another knock made me spin around. I almost screamed but immediately swallowed down the cry. The knock was coming from my window. Matt was standing on my fire escape. With a bouquet of red roses and a black eye. For a second we just stood there staring at each other through the glass. My gaze lifted from the flowers to his eye again. What the hell was he doing? What the hell was I doing? He was hurt. I ran over to my window and lifted it open.

"Why are you so surprised to see me?" he asked and smiled. But the action made him wince. "I told you I was coming over tonight."

He hadn't. Not in those words. But I couldn't focus on that right now. "Jesus, what happened to your face?"

"It's nothing. These are for you," he lifted up the flowers, blocking his black eye from my view.

I didn't care about the flowers. Even though no one had ever bought me flowers before. I grabbed them and pulled them away from him so I could see his face again. "What happened?"

"Nothing. Keep your voice down. Are you trying to get double grounded?" He climbed through the window and into my room.

I swallowed hard. I was definitely not trying to get grounded again. But having a boy my uncle hadn't met climb through my window wasn't exactly precedent for not being grounded again. "Matt."

He turned away from me.

I knew I should have told him he couldn't be here. But he was hurt. And he'd come to me for help. I walked over to him and put my hands on either side of his face. "Tell me what happened."

He winced, pulling away from me. "I'm fine." He looked around my room for a moment as he pulled off his varsity jacket. Then he sat down on the edge of my bed. "Come here."

Why wasn't he answering my question? I placed the flowers down on my nightstand. "Let me go get some frozen peas or something…"

He grabbed my waist and pulled me on top of him. My thighs straddled him, pushing the hem of my baggy t-shirt up. I froze. I wasn't wearing any pants. I was straddling Matthew Caldwell on my bed in my underwear. And not cute lacy underwear. Underwear that came in a pack of five from Target that I'd had for years. I was pretty sure there was a hole in one of the seams.

"This is all I need," he whispered. "You." His hands stayed firmly on my hips as he stared into my eyes.

His left eye was almost swollen shut. The other one was red, almost like he had been crying. But I couldn't picture that. I couldn't picture Matt breaking. Everything about him exuded strength. My hands settled on his shoulders. "I can't help with the swelling."

He dropped his forehead against mine. Maybe he was worried I could see him. Really see him. Like he claimed he could see me.

"Tell me what happened," I whispered. "Please."

"I messed up. I was trying to find another way."

"Another way for what?"

His hands slid slightly lower, his fingertips resting right above my ass.

It felt like all the air left my lungs. "Matt."

He spread his fingers, his thumbs running along the top of my thighs, as the rest of his fingers squeezed my hips. "You're perfect."

For the first time I realized that the smell of cinnamon wasn't wafting off of him. I lifted my forehead from his. My heart was beating so loudly that I swore he could hear it. The bloodshot eyes. The way he was acting. "Have you been drinking?"

"No. Just…" He sighed as he blinked faster. "I was trying to fix it."

"Fix what?" I had no idea what he was talking about.

He didn't respond.

"What did you mess up?"

His eyes finally met mine again. "I need your help, Brooklyn."

That wasn't an answer. Or maybe it was. He'd done something bad. And he was coming here to get me to fix it. "Okay. How can I help?" Matt had all the resources in the world at his fingertips. How on earth could I help him?

"I need you to ask Felix to stop selling to James."

I stopped breathing. I couldn't do that. It was the one thing that I actually couldn't help him with. I wasn't sup-posed to know what James was doing. He'd already threatened me. If I asked Felix to stop selling to him…that would be spreading James' secret. I could already picture James going to Felix and Felix telling him what I'd said.

But really…what was the worst that could happen? James probably just knew that I wasn't a scholarship student. I didn't really care if that came out. Or maybe James knew that Matt and I kept hanging out together. If that came out, Isabella would tell everyone what she had on Matt. My mind was spinning. What did Isabella have on him?

Matt's fingers slid down my thighs.

The action made my thoughts come to a halt.

"I hate that he touches you," Matt said.

Felix. I put my hands on top of Matt's to stop them from moving. But not because of my feelings for Felix. Or because I wanted Matt to stop. It was because I was finally piecing together Matt's night. At first I thought he might be high. I was pretty sure it was smoke that I smelled on him. But by the way he was acting…I knew he wasn't high. He was hurting. And it killed me to see him in pain. "Matt."

He looked back up at me.

If he hadn't been smoking, it meant he'd been around someone who was. "Did Felix do this to you?"

This time Matt didn't wince when he smiled. "Do you really think Felix could take me?"

Honestly no. Matt was every bit the football player. He was taller and stronger than Felix. My mind raced back to the only other person Matt had mentioned. *James.* "You were with James then?"

Matt shook his head. "James certainly feels better when he punches things. But no, he would never hit me. He's one of my best friends. He would never hurt me." Matt dropped his forehead back against mine.

I didn't know what to say to that. James and I weren't friends. He had no problem threatening me. But maybe he was as loyal to his friends as Matt was. I hoped so. And I wanted to be let in. "You can tell me what happened."

"I like this," he said as his fingers played with the hem of my baggy t-shirt. "You'd look even better in one of my shirts though."

I tried to hide my smile. "Matt, we need to talk about this. If we're going to work you need to trust me."

That seemed to get his attention. He sighed. It sounded so labored. "I went to Felix's dealer. I wanted to go above his head and cut off his supply. I tried to buy it all. Pretty sure they thought I was a rat."

Oh, Matt. He was trying to take care of his friend. He had a heart of gold to match his golden hair. But this wasn't the way. James needed more help than a 16-year-old could provide. Just because Matt had a good heart didn't mean it was enough to get his friend sober. I put my hand on Matt's chest.

A low groan escaped his lips. Not one like when he kissed me. He sounded like he was in pain.

I looked down at where my hand was on his chest. "Matt?"

"I'm fine."

"They hurt more than just your eye, didn't they?"

"I'm fine," he repeated.

"Take your shirt off."

He chuckled. "You first."

I ignored him and pushed up the fabric of his t-shirt. Bruises laced around his abs. I let his shirt drop back into place. "You need ice." I tried to climb off his lap, but he tightened his grip on my thighs.

"Please. Don't go."

"Matt…"

"I didn't come over here for you to take care of me. I just wanted to see you. I needed to see you. You're so beautiful, Brooklyn. Have I ever told you how beautiful you are?"

I tried to hide my smile. "You're not so bad yourself."

"I can't get you out of my head."

"How hard have you been trying?"

"Harder than I'd like to admit. But I don't want to give Isabella the satisfaction of ruining my life too. I don't want to give you up."

There was a lot to that sentence. It was sweet. And…troubling. "Who else's life has she ruined?" She'd only been attempting to ruin mine so far. But I wasn't surprised to hear that I wasn't the first person to get in her way.

"I'd rather talk about your big box of condoms."

Oh, shit. I turned to my nightstand. The drawer was still open, fully displaying the condoms my uncle had bought me. I was about to explain when Matt cut me off again.

"Tell me I'm not too late."

It was the same thing he'd asked before our kiss. My first kiss. He'd promised to steal all my firsts. But the more time we spent together, the less likely he was to have to steal them. I was pretty sure I'd be giving him everything I had. "You're not too late, Matt."

"Hmm." He leaned back on my bed, pulling me with him.

I thought he was going to kiss me, but instead he rolled to the side and placed me gently on the mattress. My weight against his torso had probably hurt him. I was about to apologize when he started talking.

"I wish I'd waited for you." He placed his hand on the side of my face. "But I can wait now. Until you're ready. I'll wait for you."

I thought about his equally big opened box of condoms. He must have known I'd seen it, like he'd known I'd seen the pictures of Isabella. But honestly, I didn't care if he'd used a handful of condoms. Especially if he hadn't used them with Isabella. And he swore he hadn't. "I'd like that," I said. I knew my life was still tangled up with Felix's. But it was easy to forget when my limbs were tangled up with Matt's.

"You said your mom was young when she had you." His voice was barely a whisper. "How old was she?"

I hadn't expected that question. "She was 19."

"Tell me about her."

"My mom?"

He kissed my forehead, pulling me closer. "Yeah. I want to know all about her."

This was the conversation I'd wanted to have earlier today. But Felix never asked me about my mom. Neither did Kennedy. My uncle barely even brought her up. I closed my eyes and let Matt hold me. I finally had someone who wanted to listen. "She was so full of life. And she had so much hope. I don't know how she stayed so optimistic during her treatments. And before she was sick we used to have so much fun just the two of us. Fall was her favorite season. Up until last fall we even still raked leaves and jumped in the piles. Her laughter was one of my favorite sounds. And sometimes I'm worried that I'm going to forget what it sounded like."

"It probably sounds a lot like yours."

I pressed my lips together. I liked to think so. "Maybe." But I wasn't sure I had enough laughter in me to fill a whole room. I barely laughed anymore at all.

"I wish I could have met her," Matt said.

"Me too."

"You look just like her."

I thought about all the pictures on my walls. I guess Matt had opened his eyes again. But I kept mine closed. "How did you know I like Caesar salads?"

"You order one almost every day at lunch."

I was right. He'd noticed. It wasn't just some lucky guess. "It was even better than the cafeteria ones. Thank you."

"I'll bring another one tomorrow."

I laughed. "I wasn't implying that you needed to. I just wanted to let you know I appreciated it."

He pulled me even closer. "I want to bring you another one tomorrow. Tell me more about your mom. And your life back in Delaware. Tell me everything."

I smiled against his chest. I told him all my favorite things about each season. He especially liked my story about the snowplow that came to my cul-de-sac and left huge natural snow forts. I'd had so much fun having snowball fights with the other neighborhood kids around those forts. And then there was the delicious hot chocolate my mom used to make for all of us afterward to warm us up.

I told Matt all my favorite stories as he held me tight. I wasn't sure when we fell asleep. But I found drifting asleep in his arms effortless. There was no staring at the ceiling. No sleepless night. I slept better in his arms than I had in months.

But when I woke up the next morning he was gone. I would have thought I'd imagined the whole thing, but my sheets smelled like him. And there were roses wilting on my nightstand. He'd also left his varsity letter jacket with a note.

You'll be able to wear this soon. I promise.

I pulled on his jacket. The fabric swam around me, the jacket stopping mid-thigh. And I wished I didn't have to take it off before going to school. I took a deep breath, the smell of cinnamon wafting around me. I finally had my answer. There was no way I could just be friends with Matt. Not when I was hoping he'd show up again tonight. And the next night. And the next.

I ran my finger down the large 'E' for Empire High on the front of the jacket. All the football players wore their jackets to school every day. Except for a few players that had given them to their girlfriends. Matt would be missing his. People would notice. Him leaving this here meant something. I just hoped it meant he was falling for me too.

CHAPTER 24

Thursday

I tried to focus on moving my legs faster instead of the pit growing in my stomach. I'd been dreading gym all day. And now that it was here, I felt even worse. Although, maybe it was just the fact that I was running and had a terrible cramp. I was pretty sure secrets gave me cramps.

"Are you okay?" Felix asked as he jogged beside me. "You're acting…off."

"I'm fine." My voice came out weird. God, I needed to just come out with it. I had to put the brake on things between Felix and me, I knew that. All I could think about all day had been falling asleep in Matt's arms. It wasn't fair to Felix. But I also didn't know how to break the news without saying I had feelings for someone else. I'd promised Matt we could keep things between us a secret for now. I was tossing around the idea of blaming it on my uncle. After all, he had forbidden me from seeing Felix. It was the easy way out. The un-honest way. The coward's way.

I shook the thought away. I had to lie about having feelings for Matt. But that didn't mean I needed to throw my uncle under the bus for no reason. And it wasn't just the lies holding me back. I had to figure out how to ask Felix to stop selling drugs to James in a way that couldn't come back to me. The last thing I needed was for James to tell everyone about me seeing Matt…if that was the secret he meant. But there were lots of things he could be referring to. Matt knew my phone number, my address, my locker combination…all without asking me. He had resources. Surely James had the same ones. He could know anything.

"Hey," Felix grabbed my arm, pulling me to a stop. "Seriously, what's going on?"

I leaned down and put my hands on my knees, pretending to catch my breath. Really I just needed to figure out what to say.

"Is this about yesterday?"

I looked up at him. "Yesterday?"

"When you mentioned your mom, I didn't know what to say. And I kept saying I'm sorry, which you hate." He smiled. "And I regretted the drug thing as soon as I said it. I know drugs won't help make you feel better."

I looked back down at the track. "It's not about yesterday."

"Then what is it? You can barely look at me."

I squeezed my eyes shut, took a huge breath, and then opened my eyes again. "No matter what happens, we'll always be friends, right?" I asked as I stood back up.

His eyebrows lowered. "Brooklyn, what's going on?"

I was hoping he'd agree to stay friends. He hadn't. But that didn't change anything I needed to say. It just made it hurt more to end things. *Say it. Spit it out!* "I really think I'm not in the right headspace to be dating right now, Felix. I think right now all I need is a friend."

"Is this about that other guy you kissed?"

"No." I hoped my voice sounded even. God, I hated lying. "I'm just...struggling. With a new city and a new school and a new home. I mean, I fell apart yesterday crying about my mom in the middle of gym." I tried to smile. "But I really, really want to stay friends."

Felix pushed his sweaty hair off his forehead, but didn't say anything.

I didn't expect him to look so upset. I knew he was kissing other girls. It wasn't like he was serious about dating me. "Nothing really has to change. We can still hang out at school. Maybe my uncle will even let me see you after school now that we're just friends. And you can keep seeing whoever else it is that you're seeing."

His eyebrows lowered even further. "I'm not seeing anyone else."

"But when I told you that our first kiss wasn't my first kiss ever you said it was fine because we weren't exclusive..."

"Brooklyn, I said that because you told me you kissed someone else. You wouldn't even tell me who it was. What the hell was I supposed to say?"

I pressed my lips together. "So you weren't dating anyone else?"

"Of course not. I really like you, Brooklyn. I have no time to think about kissing other girls because you're all that I think about."

"I didn't know that." I felt like such an ass. This whole time he had only been seeing me? I tried not to think about all the times I had hooked up with Matt.

He shook his head. "I guess I should have told you I was mad that you kissed someone else. But I didn't want

to come off like this super possessive guy. That's not me."
He shoved his hands into his sweatpants pockets. "It *wasn't*
me. But just thinking about you doing that really messed
with my head. I wanted to ask you to be my girlfriend. I
wanted to make it exclusive. But you keep pulling back. I
didn't want to freak you out by asking when it didn't seem
like you were ready. And now you're pulling back more
anyway."

I wanted to cry but I blinked fast so none of my tears
would spill. If I had known that he hadn't been kissing
other girls, would it have changed anything? I didn't know.
Probably. But it was too late. I'd already kissed another
boy…a lot. A lot a lot. I couldn't undo it. And I couldn't
undo how I felt about Matt. "I'm sorry."

"I thought you hated that phrase." He smiled.

And I laughed because the tension needed to escape
somehow. "I do."

He just stared at me, like he was waiting for me to say
something else.

But I didn't know what else to say.

"Does me telling you that change anything?" Felix
asked. "If I asked you right now to be my girlfriend, would
you say yes? Because I'm asking. Brooklyn Sanders, will
you be my girlfriend?"

As soon as he asked, my initial thought was to say yes.
It's what I'd been waiting for. It's what I wanted. I just
wasn't sure I wanted it with him anymore. The knot was
back in my stomach. Maybe I really wasn't ready to date
anyone. Maybe all I actually needed was friendship from
both Matt and Felix. "Everything I said before was true.
I'm really struggling. None of this has been easy for me."

"I know." He took a step forward. "But why can't I be the one you lean on through all of it?"

Because I already leaned on Matt all night. And I couldn't tell Felix that. I didn't want him to ever find that out. I didn't want to hurt him. "You can. As a friend."

"I'll always be your friend, Brooklyn. But don't think for a second that I don't want it to be more. I'll be waiting, whenever you're ready." He smiled and reached out to tuck a loose strand of hair behind my ear.

"I don't know when I'll be ready. I'm not asking you to wait. Really I'm telling you to date other people."

"No thank you," he said.

I laughed.

"I'd rather just hang out with my friend…if that's okay?"

"I'd like that."

He closed the distance between us and hugged me. My stomach still felt uneasy. He'd agreed to be just my friend. That's what I wanted. But I hadn't expected it like this. Knowing that I'd been the only one he was seeing. Knowing he was waiting for me to change my mind. Him being my friend felt heavy. Or maybe I just felt weighed down because I still had a favor to ask him. And I didn't deserve anything from him. He was too good. I was a liar. And a cheat. I didn't want to be those things. I hugged him back. I didn't want to let go. "There's one more thing we need to talk about."

He pulled back so he could look down at me. "You're not breaking up with me as a friend now too, are you?"

I laughed. "No. Definitely not. I have a small favor to ask you though."

"Okay…" He didn't sound excited about this development.

"You can't ask why. And you also can't tell anyone I asked you."

"So you just want me to agree to this favor blindly without any questions?"

"Yes."

He smiled down at me. "You do realize that maybe it would have been better timing to ask me this before you broke up with me?"

"I didn't break up with you. We weren't technically ever dating."

He put his hand on his chest. "That hurts, newb. Just spill it already instead of turning the knife in my heart."

I smiled, glad he was still using my nickname now that we were just friends. "I need you to stop selling drugs to James." *There. Done.*

"And why would I do that?" Felix asked. "James is one of my best customers."

"I said no questions."

"And I never actually agreed to that."

"Please." I didn't know what else to say. I kind of just hoped he'd agree with my random request.

"Is he the guy you kissed?"

"What? No."

Felix shook his head. "He has a girlfriend. You're better than that. You deserve better than that."

"It wasn't him."

"So why do you care if I sell to him?"

It was more than just Matt's request. I'd been awkwardly watching all the Untouchables since school started.

Staring from a distance. It didn't take much observation to realize that James was in trouble. He was sinking. *Just like me.* "Because he's using way too much of whatever you're giving him. And combining it with alcohol and God knows what else."

"Brooklyn, I'm a drug dealer. I have to sell to addicts. If I just stopped selling to my best customers, I'd be out of business."

James is an addict? "You're better than that." I threw his words back at him. "You have tons of money. You live in a fancy apartment on the Upper East Side. You don't need to be dealing."

"And how do you think my parents made all that money?"

"Your mom sells art."

Felix shook his head. "It's a front. It's dirty money. And dirty money doesn't get you the same prestige as old money, newb. Look around." He lifted up his hands. "The only reason people tolerate me here is because I have access to something they want."

"I'm only asking you to stop selling to one person."

"And that one person will tumble into the four most popular kids at our school. And then the whole football team. Soccer team. The cheerleaders. You're asking me to give up my business."

"Maybe I am." I hated what he did. He was hurting people. Didn't he see that? Maybe it had been bothering me more than I realized.

His eyes softened. "Is that the real reason why you don't want to date me? Because of what I do? I'd never get you tangled up in this."

IVY SMOAK

"Standing next to you tangles me up in it, Felix. It's dangerous." I thought about Matt's black eye and the bruises on his torso. Felix's suppliers had beaten him up. Did Felix know that? Did he ask them to do it?

"Pot doesn't hurt anyone."

"But you're not selling pot to James. Are you?" I saw him slip James something else. And it had to be bad, or James wouldn't have threatened me.

He opened his mouth. But before he said anything, he closed it again. His Adam's apple rose and fell as he stared at me. "Okay, newb. I'll think about it."

It wasn't a yes. But it wasn't a no either. "Thank you."

"Being your friend comes with a lot of strings, huh?" He smiled at me.

"I'd say it comes with a normal amount of strings," I said with a laugh.

He started walking backward on the track. "Race you to the finish line? As your friend, I'm not going to let you win this time."

"You've been letting me win?"

He winked and started running.

My heart skipped a beat. Felix was going to risk his whole business just because I'd asked. He hadn't been seeing anyone else. And he'd been letting me win at our mile races this whole time? I started running after him. What if I just made a terrible mistake?

CHAPTER 25

Thursday

I took another bite of the delicious salad. Matt had left me another one in my locker, just like he'd promised. A girl could get used to this. Although, it was hard to get used to being ignored by him all day.

"Earth to Brooklyn," Kennedy said and tossed a French fry into my salad. If that wasn't enough to get my attention, her camera also flashed, momentarily blinding me. "Did you hear what I said?"

I blinked, trying to remove the dots from my vision. "Sorry. What?"

She threw her arm behind Cupcake's back, snuggling into his side. "Joe asked me to homecoming! It's going to be so much fun. Tell me you two are going together." She motioned to Felix and me.

I forced myself not to look over at the Untouchables' table. Matt wouldn't be asking me. Unless he somehow got out from Isabella's thumb before then. Which meant I wouldn't be going to homecoming. It was for the best. I hadn't exactly put my best foot forward at any of the parties I'd been to. I'd probably just accidentally drink spiked punch and make a fool of myself anyway. It would be better if I stayed in my room all night and studied.

"We actually hadn't talked about it yet," Felix said. "But now that you mentioned it…how about it, newb? Be my homecoming date?"

Had Felix totally forgotten our conversation from twenty minutes ago? The one where we'd agreed to be friends? I slowly chewed my bite of lettuce. I was stalling. Trying to find anything to say that wasn't completely awkward. I hadn't had a chance to tell Kennedy that Felix and I had put the brakes on things. It would be weird to just blurt it out now.

He leaned over and whispered in my ear. "As friends. Come on, it'll be fun."

I could not under any circumstances go to homecoming with Felix. First of all, my uncle wouldn't let me. Second of all, I was pretty sure Matt would freak out. And third, it would send the completely wrong message to Felix. *Think. Say anything.* I took a deep breath. "Sure." *Sure?* What the heck did I say that for? Sure was not the appropriate response to that question!

"Awesome. Maybe we can all meet at my place for pictures?" Felix said. "We can get a limo and the whole deal. It'll be fun."

"Sure." *Stop saying sure!*

"Speaking of homecoming, we should catch the football game beforehand too," Felix said.

"Sure." *Damnit!* I was pretty sure I just had a seizure and the only thing I could say now was "sure." *Screw me.*

"Great." He smiled down at me.

"That sounds wonderful," Kennedy said. "And speaking of the opposite of wonderful…what the heck happened to Matt's face?"

I wanted to thank her for stopping my sure seizure, but why on earth did she have to bring up Matt of all people? I swallowed a crouton wrong and started choking.

"You okay?" Kennedy asked and handed me my bottle of water.

"Fine," I mumbled between huge sips.

"So what do you think happened to Matt's face?" she asked again.

"How should I know?" I did my best not to turn around and stare at Matt's black eye. And I waited for Felix to say something. Did he know what Matt had done? He must have.

"I heard he got beat up by a pimp for refusing to pay an ugly prostitute," Cupcake said.

"Yeah, right," Kennedy said with a laugh. "Where did you hear that?"

"Everyone's saying it." He shrugged. "The guy's a total whore. I heard he slept with the whole cheerleading squad. Together. In one night."

"Really?" I asked.

Cupcake nodded.

My throat still felt dry from the crouton choking. It was like reading aloud in Mr. Hill's class sore. And I felt that same sense of defeat that I did in Mr. Hill's class too. Probably because all the excitement I felt about Matt seemed like it was being flushed down the toilet. A whole cheerleading squad? At once? I'd never even had sex before. He'd told me he'd wait for me now. I knew that meant he'd already had sex. I knew that from the condoms in his drawer, or lack of condoms left in his drawer. How many were missing? I could get over a few. Hell, I already knew he wasn't a virgin. But screwing the whole cheerleading squad? I felt like I was going to be sick.

Kennedy's smile dropped, probably when she saw my reaction. "I don't think that's true," she said. "His older brother is a total man whore. But I think Matt's kind of sweet."

"The Caldwells are all the same," Cupcake said. "One and done. Wham, bam, thank you, ma'am. Ask anyone."

"No they're not, Joe," Kennedy said. "And it's unbecoming to spread rumors."

"Babe." He pulled her back into his side. "What do either of you care about Matthew Caldwell anyway?"

"We don't," I said and pushed my salad aside. But I did. I really did. But I couldn't say that out loud. And I couldn't defend Matt, because for all I knew, what Cupcake was saying was true.

Kennedy cleared her throat. "Exactly, we don't."

"Cupcake?" Cupcake asked and pulled out a box of cupcakes from…I have no idea where. Seriously, where had those been a minute ago?

"Absolutely," Kennedy said and grabbed one with chocolate frosting.

He held it out to me.

"No thank you," I said.

"Felix?" Cupcake waved the box in front of Felix's face.

"Actually, can we talk for a minute?" Felix asked. "I have an idea I want to run by you."

Cupcake closed the lid. "Sure, what's up?"

"Let's talk just the two of us," Felix said.

"Okay. Later, babe," Cupcake said and kissed the side of Kennedy's forehead.

After an awkward hug with Felix, I watched them walk away. "What was that about?" I asked.

"I don't know." Kennedy shook her head. "But I don't like it."

I watched the two of them leaning against the cafeteria doors talking. *Me either.*

"Is something going on with you and Felix?" she asked. "It looked like you panicked when he asked you to homecoming."

"I didn't panic. I said sure." I said sure a lot, actually. I pushed some lettuce around with my fork. At least I could be honest with her about one thing. "But we did decide to just be friends."

"Really?" She sounded a little excited, but I didn't blame her. She'd made it clear that she hated him. "Does that have something do with Matt? Because Joe's information about him seemed to really bother you, despite the fact that you always insist that he's a jerk. I kinda thought you'd agree with him."

"It has nothing to do with Matt." I desperately wanted to tell her that Matt came over last night. That he'd given me his varsity jacket. But I'd promised not to. I wished I could just go back to last night when Matt was holding me in his arms. Everything made sense then. Before the cheerleader sexcapades.

"You sure about that? Because he still looks at you like something's going on."

I glanced back at the Untouchables table. Matt was staring directly at me. A scowl slicing across his perfect face. His swollen and bruised perfect face. I quickly turned away.

"Nothing's going on," I said.

"Good."

"Good?" I looked up at her. "Why is that good? I thought you wanted me to date Matt?"

"I *did*. And you'd make a much cuter couple than you and Felix. But…I think it's probably a bad idea. At least right now."

Did she think he was a slut too? I was worried I'd learned more about Matt in the last five minutes than I'd learned during all my time here. All I could think about was that box of opened condoms in his nightstand. I wish I'd counted how many were left. Had he used five? Twelve? Seventy-two? I felt like I was going to throw up my salad.

Kennedy pushed her tray aside. "I've been dying to tell you this all day. I just didn't know exactly what to say. And I thought it might be best if I got to the bottom of it before even telling you anything. But I don't want to keep it from you. I overheard a conversation between my mom and Uncle Jim. He stopped by this morning early before work."

"Okay…" I waited, but Kennedy didn't offer any more information. "What were they talking about?"

"You. And someone at this school."

I held my breath. Did my uncle know that Matt had spent the night? He was going to ground me until I was old and gray unless he decided to kill me instead. "Who?" I asked.

"I didn't catch the name. But I heard one thing clear as day." She leaned forward.

I leaned forward too. Waiting. My heart pounding.

"Brooklyn, you *are* related to someone at this school. I don't know any more than that. But I promise I'll keep digging."

My throat felt even drier than before. "Are you sure?"

"Positive."

"Am I related to another student?"

"I don't know. It might be a faculty member. Or it might be…Matt."

I didn't know how to react to that news, so I just stared back at her.

"It was great that you were dating Felix because Uncle Jim flat out said you weren't related to him. But now that you guys aren't dating…you need to be careful. You don't want to accidentally make out with your brother," she said with a laugh.

My stomach churned. Yeah, I was definitely going to throw up my salad.

"I know I said I'd help figure out this whole missing father mystery and I've been a little MIA. But we can figure this out together. We already have our first real clue other than the fact that your father at one point lived in the city."

"But you think Matt's father is my dad?" *God, I am a brother kisser!* I was pretty sure there was a special place in hell for people like me. I'd probably be forced to kiss my brother for eternity as punishment. Although…if Matt really was my brother, the punishment sounded pretty good to me. *No! Stop thinking about kissing your brother, you monster!*

"I think that your uncle would have no other reason to be concerned enough to talk to my mom about it if it wasn't someone you were hanging out with. And you just had that after school project the other day. So I was thinking it was probably Matt. Or…Rob."

Rob joked around with me like an annoying brother. I tried to remember what he'd said about his father the other night. Something about picking up call girls on Wall Street. I swallowed hard. I didn't want Rob's father to be my dad. I wanted someone caring and kind. But I knew that wasn't the case. A kind caring man wouldn't have abandoned me and my mom.

As soon as I thought it, I realized I already had the best father figure I could. My uncle was kind and caring and patient with me. I wished I could forget about the whole father thing completely. I didn't even really want to meet my father. But I also didn't want to accidentally date my brother. I had to talk to my uncle. "He said you could come over and do homework with me after school today," I said. "Will you help me ask him?"

Her face lit up. "Are you ungrounded?"

"Only for you and schoolwork."

"I knew he'd cave," she said with a smile. "It hasn't even been a week, the big softie. Okay, so now we just have to figure out how to ask him about it."

"Yeah. Please tell me you have a plan?" Because I had nothing but flat out asking. Which maybe would have been suitable, but I'd already done that. And he'd denied my very reasonable request.

"Well, first I think it would be easy to just start talking about how hot both of them are."

I laughed.

"And then we can gauge his reaction to see if he's disturbed or not."

"That's not a bad idea."

"We got this. We'll just study his reaction and I think we'll be able to figure it out before you go to sleep tonight."

She was so confident that I found myself nodding my head. We'd figure out who my dad was before I went to bed. Also before Matt came over tonight. *If* he came over again tonight. I hoped he would. I wanted to kiss him again. *Oh, God, what is wrong with me? Please don't let me be related to Matt.*

CHAPTER 26

Thursday

Kennedy flopped down on my bed. "What's with the flowers?" she asked.

The roses Matt had given me were in a vase on my nightstand. It had taken me forever to find a vase this morning. I'd eventually found it tucked all the way in the back of a cabinet I couldn't reach unless I was standing on a chair. I had completely forgotten that the flowers were there, or I would have suggested we watch TV instead of hanging out in my room once we were finished with our homework. My thoughts came to a halt. The flowers weren't the only evidence of Matt's visit. His jacket was slung over a chair in the corner. Luckily Kennedy was busy staring at the roses.

"Did Felix send you these?" she asked when I didn't respond to her first question.

"Yup," I said without even really listening to her, as I tried to slowly slide over to the chair.

Kennedy started to turn and I threw myself into the chair to block the jacket from her view.

"I never took him as the sending flowers type," she said and shook her head. "I can't believe you broke up with him right after he sent those."

I pulled my blazer off and tossed it behind me on the chair to cover up the jacket. I breathed a sigh of relief that it was successfully hidden. The roses could be explained away. But Felix didn't have a varsity jacket. Especially not in whatever large size Matt's broad shoulders needed.

"Did he do something?" Kennedy asked. "To make you just want to be friends with him instead?"

I shook my head. "No. I'm just trying to focus on myself right now. And with everything with Uncle Jim…"

"He told you?" Kennedy asked.

I frowned. "Told me what?"

She stared at me for a minute, her eyes scanning mine, before looking back at the flowers. "Told you about who you're related to. Duh."

I laughed. "No, I didn't corner him at school and demand answers. Don't you think I would have told you instead of going over English notes? I'm pretty set on our plan for tonight. I just meant the whole me being forbidden to see Felix outside of school thing."

Kennedy waved her hand through the air. "He's already letting you see me outside of school again. I'm pretty sure he'll ease up on Felix too. Just give him a little more time."

I made sure my blazer was perfectly covering Matt's jacket before standing up. "Regardless, I think it's best if I'm just friends with Felix." I plopped down on the bed next to her. "How are things going with Cupcake?"

"Delicious."

I laughed. "I'm serious. Are you happy?"

She crossed her arms behind her head and looked up at the ceiling. "How can I not be happy when he brings me cupcakes every day? He literally showers me with sweets. And he's cute. Don't you think it's cute that he calls me babe?"

"Mhm. So very cute."

She kicked my ankle with her foot. "Don't patronize me."

"I'm not," I said.

"You hate him."

I pressed my lips together. "I don't hate him. I was just surprised to find out that you liked him. I thought maybe you would have mentioned your crush on him after he nailed me in the face with a dodgeball."

"Well, that hardly seemed like the time," she said with a laugh.

"Fair enough," I said, laughing too.

There was a knock on the front door.

I sat up. "Weird. Uncle Jim must have forgotten his key or something." When I answered the door, Kennedy's mom was standing there with a smile on her face.

"Hi Mrs. Alcaraz." I turned away from the door. "Kennedy! Your mom is here!"

Kennedy ran into the kitchen. "Can I stay a little later? Por favor?" She drew out the "o" in "favor" in a way that made her mom smile.

"I came to fetch both of you for la cena. Jim called and said he'd be home late, Brooklyn. You're stuck with us for the rest of the evening."

As much as I loved Mrs. Alcaraz's cooking, I really needed to talk to my uncle. "But…"

"Mi amor, you look hungry. Come, come." She started walking down the hall toward her apartment before I even got a chance to protest.

"Come on," Kennedy said and slipped her arm through mine. "She's making empanadas…your favorite."

Darn Mrs. Alcaraz and her mouthwatering empanadas.

"Plus…she knows who you're related to too. And I'm pretty sure she'll cave before your uncle does."

Kennedy was right. I quickly locked the door behind us and followed Mrs. Alcaraz. The secret of my father's identity was spreading. All I needed was for it to spread to me.

The smell in their kitchen was heavenly. Mrs. Alcaraz placed a dish of steaming hot empanadas down in the middle of the table and I was the first to dig in.

"God, they're both so hot. You couldn't go wrong with either," Kennedy said through a mouthful of steaming beef and pastry dough.

We hadn't talked about how we were going to broach the subject with her mom, but I should have expected that we'd be sticking to the original plan. But now it felt awkward as her sentence hung in the air.

"Wait for them to cool then," Mrs. Alcaraz said. She reached over and pulled the empanada out of Kennedy's hand.

"I'm talking about the two boys Brooklyn has a crush on at school." Kennedy grabbed the empanada back and took another bite.

I cleared my throat. "Right. Robert Hunter and Matthew Caldwell are both so dreamy."

"But Kennedy told me you were dating Felix," said Mrs. Alcaraz. "El narcotraficante."

I just stared at her. "I'm sorry, I have no idea what that means." I tried to swallow down my bite so I wouldn't be talking with my mouth full.

"It means she likes him," Kennedy said.

Her mother glared at her. "No. The drugs," she said. "He has the drugs."

"No." I shook my head. "That's not…" was there even a point in arguing with Mrs. Alcaraz about this? I sighed. "You're right. Which is why I like those other two boys now."

"Mis niñas." She leaned forward and put one hand on my cheek and then her other hand on Kennedy's cheek. "You're both too young to date." She removed her hands and started eating like that was the end of the discussion.

"But Brooklyn really likes both Robert Hunter and Matthew Caldwell," Kennedy said. "A lot."

Mrs. Alcaraz ignored her and kept eating.

"A lot a lot."

Her mother continued to ignore her. Or was she just hiding her gaze? Was she actually avoiding eye contact?

Something in my stomach churned. And it wasn't the delicious food.

"She's thinking about sleeping with them," Kennedy added.

Mrs. Alcaraz spit her food out onto her plate and started coughing. "Perdóneme?" she asked after a huge gulp of water.

"At the same time," Kennedy added.

Mrs. Alcaraz turned to me with so much shock on her face. "Grupo de tres?"

I didn't need to understand Spanish to know that the words group and three were a part of that sentence. As in…threesome. "No," I quickly said. "Nunca."

Mrs. Alcaraz sighed. "Kennedy, what has gotten into you?" She grabbed the empanada from Kennedy's hand again.

"Hey! I was trying to eat that."

"Explain. Now."

"I heard you talking to Uncle Jim this morning. You said Brooklyn was related to someone at school. I didn't catch the name. And we thought maybe it was Robert Hunter or Matthew Caldwell?" She emphasized each of their last names.

Kennedy was a worse liar than me. But I wasn't mad about it. The question was out there now. We should have just flat out asked to begin with. Then her mother wouldn't think I was a hussy.

"I…" Mrs. Alcaraz's voice trailed off. "It's not my place to say."

"But, Mama."

"This is not our place, Kennedy."

"But I know that you know. And Brooklyn deserves to know who her father is. You can't keep this from her."

"It's not my place to say," her mother repeated.

"But what if she ends up sleeping with her brothers…"

Brothers? Plural? "Kennedy stop," I said. "Please stop saying I'm going to sleep with both of them." I was pretty sure my face was bright red. "But Mrs. Alcaraz, I really do need to know. I want to know." *I think*.

"You have to talk to your uncle about this, mi amor. Not me."

"I've already tried."

Mrs. Alcaraz started eating again like the conversation had come to another end.

"Where is he tonight?" I asked. "Did he say?" That annoying feeling of a clock ticking down in my head had returned. And I had no idea why. If Matt showed up again tonight, I wasn't going to sleep with him. But still the clock was ticking.

"He had to take care of some business," she said.

"What business?" Janitorial work didn't have a night shift. Well, maybe it did. Wait, did it?

"Por favor!" She threw up her hands. "Would you two both just eat? I made your favorite, Brooklyn. Por favor."

"Sorry," I said.

Kennedy locked eyes with me and gave me a sympathetic smile. "Lo siento, Mama."

"Sí sí." Mrs. Alcaraz lifted up her fork and started eating again. And this time it was the end of the discussion.

***

I was filling out the daily crossword puzzle my uncle always did when the door to our apartment finally opened.

"I thought you'd still be at the Alcaraz's," my uncle said as he placed a satchel down on one of the kitchen chairs. A satchel I had never seen before. He was also in a suit. I didn't even know he owned a suit. It was a little baggy on him because of the weight he'd lost. I wanted to comment on it. To give him a compliment. But the air felt heavy between us.

"I had dinner there. Hours ago. Where were you? I was worried."

"I'm the adult." He kissed the top of my head. "Let me do the worrying, kiddo."

"You didn't answer my question."

"Six across is colonel," he said.

I glanced down at the crossword puzzle. It was one of the only answers I didn't know. And he was right. That definitely fit. I looked back up at him. "I meant the 'where were you' question."

"It's late, kiddo." He yawned. "You should be getting to bed. We can talk about this tomorrow, okay?"

He did look tired. And honestly, I was tired too. Asking him about my dad wouldn't get me anywhere tonight. Besides, I wasn't going to go on and on about how hot the Hunter and Caldwell brothers were without Kennedy to back me up. But for some reason my mouth opened anyway. "I broke up with Felix," I said. I wasn't sure why I said it. No, that wasn't true. I said it because I wanted him to know that he could trust me. And because it had been weighing on me all day. And maybe I wanted him to be proud of me too.

"Are you okay?" he asked.

It wasn't the answer I was expecting. But for some reason it was better. He wasn't worried about the fact that I did what he wanted me to. He was just worried about me. "Yeah. I think so."

He smiled. "I'm sorry I wasn't here earlier for you to talk to."

"Honestly, I think all I really needed was a hug."

He leaned down and hugged me. "Better late than never," he said.

I hugged him back. "Will you be home tomorrow at the usual time?" I asked, without letting go.

"Yeah, kiddo. I'll even let you pick out the movie."

I smiled and hugged him a little tighter.

He pulled back and started coughing.

"Are you okay?" I was pretty sure I had just squeezed him too hard.

He took a huge breath. "Fine." He cleared his throat. "I finally picked up some Nyquil like you suggested. I'll take it tonight."

"Good." I'd been pestering him about taking some cough medicine for weeks. I guess whatever fancy thing he'd had to do tonight in a suit had made him want to not be coughing everywhere.

"Now go get some rest, kiddo."

I stood up and hugged him one more time, this time not quite as hard. "Goodnight, Uncle Jim."

CHAPTER 27

Friday

Matt had shown up again last night. This time bearing two cups of hot chocolate. He said even though it wasn't snowing, he hoped it reminded me of my mom. I was pretty sure I would have cried if he hadn't been staring at me so seductively the whole night. And holding me. And kissing me senseless when I told him Felix and I were just friends *and* that I'd asked Felix to stop selling drugs to James. I was a pretty great girlfriend. *Girlfriend?*

The smile faded from my face as I knocked on the Alcaraz's door. Despite our wonderful night together, Matt hadn't asked me to be his girlfriend. But what did I expect? Sneaking around was hard enough. Being a secret girlfriend would be even harder. Or would it? Wouldn't it just be the same? I bit the inside of my cheek. Why did everyone I date never ask me to make it official? *Felix did, you idiot.*

Kennedy burst out of her apartment with a pancake hanging out of her mouth, hopping on one foot as she finished pulling on a shoe. And I was immediately distracted from my pesky thoughts.

"Um…I can come in if you're not ready," I said.

"No." She slammed her foot on the ground, shoving the shoe on. "I have a huge update." She pulled me away from her apartment.

"What kind of update?"

"On Project Undercover Daddy."

Ew. "Do we have to call it that?"

"Project Who's Your Daddy?" she said as we hurried down the stairwell and out into the blustery fall weather.

"Let's put a pin in the name for now. What did you find out?"

"Actually...I don't think it's related. But did you see your uncle last night? He was in a suit!"

"Yeah, I saw him right before I went to bed." *Right before I hung out with Matt all night.*

"Do you think he was on a date?" she asked.

I honestly hadn't thought about that option. "I don't know."

"Well I think I know what's going on," Kennedy said. "It's going to sound crazy, but just hear me out."

"Okay..."

"Uncle Jim has always been in my life. And he's always helped my mom out, especially after we lost my dad. And I don't know why, but I kind of always assumed that they might end up together."

"Your mom and my uncle?"

Kennedy nodded.

She was right, that was definitely crazy. Mrs. Alcaraz and my uncle were friends. Not lovers. "Kennedy..."

"So I think he was on a date. He even called my mom to make sure you'd have dinner with us, just so he could make sure that she knew that he was on a date."

"Wait…what?"

"I think he was trying to make my mom jealous! Because he loves her! And when he came over last night he just wanted to show off his fancy suit and give her some papers to sign."

"Papers?"

"Not important. Brooklyn, if they get married, we'll be sisters!"

That wasn't how that worked. Jim was my uncle, not my father. "Wait, how does all this relate to Project Undercover Daddy?" *Oh God, why did I just call it that?*

"I guess it's more about my soon-to-be new dad." She shrugged. "Sorry."

"But you said there were papers he had your mom sign?"

She clapped her hands as we made it up the steps outside Empire High. "You're right. It was probably a marriage certificate!"

I laughed. "So you think he went out with another woman to make your mom jealous. And then immediately married your mom?"

"Well when you put it like that…" Kennedy laughed too. "So scratch the marriage thing. But they really might be in love."

Maybe. "It always just seemed like they were friends to me."

"I don't know…my mom was certainly agitated last night while Jim was out on his date. She kept yanking food out of my mouth and trying to change the subject."

"That's because you kept implying that I was down for threesomes."

She laughed. "Maybe. Or maybe she's been pining for Uncle Jim this whole time. And even if they're not already married, they still might get hitched one day. It's going to be weird when I have to stop calling him uncle, huh?" She shook her head. "I'm going to go tell Cupcake all about it. See you in English class!" She practically skipped away.

I shook my head as I stopped by my locker. Uncle Jim and Mrs. Alcaraz? I hung up my jacket and grabbed a few books. I wasn't sure I could picture it as easily as Kennedy could. Although if they did get married, I'd get to eat Mrs. Alcaraz's delicious pancakes every morning. And those empanadas. And even though I wasn't my uncle's daughter, Kennedy was right. It would practically make us sisters. Was it possible that the conversation Kennedy had overheard the other night was about that? That I would be related to someone at the school *if* Uncle Jim and Mrs. Alcaraz got married? If that was the case, Mrs. Alcaraz didn't know who my father was. It also meant that the secret wouldn't be spreading to me anytime soon either.

I sighed and closed my locker. And then I'm pretty sure I jumped out of my skin. Because James was silently leaning against the locker next to mine, his arms folded across his chest, a frown on his face.

"I thought we had an agreement," he said.

I swallowed hard. "We do." I looked around. There were students walking around. Unlike Matt, James didn't seem to care if anyone saw us together.

"You don't think I noticed you getting closer to Felix these last few weeks? And now he just randomly decides to stop selling to me? You want me to believe that's a coincidence?"

"He stopped selling to you?" I would have smiled if James wasn't staring daggers at me. Felix had done what I'd asked. He'd risked his whole business for me.

"Don't play games with me, Sanders."

He used my last name like his little brother always did. But he wasn't joking around with me like Rob. James looked…really pissed. "I'm not." I tried to keep my voice even. "I didn't tell Felix to stop selling to you."

"You did." He dropped his voice. "And you have until lunch to fix this, or everyone in the whole school will know your secret."

"James. I've been friends with Felix since almost the beginning of the school year. Way before I saw what he gave you," I said, lowering my voice. "I didn't get close to him to get him to stop selling to you. That's ridiculous."

He leaned forward. "Ridiculous? Are you calling me ridiculous, Sanders?"

"No." My voice was small. "But maybe…maybe you have a problem, James. You can take this opportunity to get clean."

"So that's what this is? You care about me?" The corner of his mouth ticked up a notch. "And here I thought you were fucking Matt."

So that was the secret he had on me? He knew I liked Matt. But he didn't know I could be related to Matt. That was a relief. Besides, his intel was all wrong. Matt and I had only kissed. "I'm not sleeping with Matt. So if that's the big secret you're going to share…go ahead. I'll be the one laughing at you."

"That's not a secret, Sanders. Matt didn't even tell me that in confidence. He was joking around about it in front of Mason and Rob. Even Isabella. Everyone knows about it."

"That's a lie." Matt said no one could know about us. He wouldn't have told anyone that. Especially *that*. Especially not Isabella. Because it wasn't even true. He hated Isabella. He wouldn't be joking around about anything with her. I knew that, and yet, I felt my bottom lip tremble.

"No, a lie is when you stare me right in the eye and tell me I'm ridiculous. Because we both know you had Felix cut me off. Have a nice morning, Sanders. Because if you don't fix this, your afternoon's going to be hell."

*****

I had played it cool all morning. Even through gym. But as I made my way to lunch, I was starting to panic. I was glad that Felix had stopped selling to James. He'd even confirmed it to me while we were running earlier. And I had no intention of asking him to start selling to James again.

I didn't know what secret James would reveal at lunch, but I figured it would be about my uncle. And I could handle that. I wasn't embarrassed that my uncle was a janitor. If it had been up to me, I would have been honest about it from the start. It was my uncle's idea to keep it a secret.

It was definitely going to be about that. James had already said his piece about Matt. And yet…I had a bad feeling. What he'd said about Matt was a lie. A definite lie. Maybe he knew there was more to that story. What if I was related to Matt? What if James announced it to the whole school…which would make Isabella spill whatever she had on Matt. And I knew it was something bad.

It'll be fine, I tried to tell myself as I took a deep breath.

But then I saw my uncle through the cafeteria doors. He rarely had lunch duty, probably because he was trying to avoid me. But there he was…pushing around a trashcan, waiting for students to toss their trays. I could handle the teasing. But I wouldn't be the only one subjected to it. They'd be making fun of him too.

Screw me. I grabbed Felix's arm before we went into the cafeteria.

"What's up?" he asked.

"I need you to go up to James right away and tell him you'll sell to him again." I couldn't risk it. I was banking on the fact that the secret was about Matt and me. And I was banking even more on Matt being honest. Because if he really had told everyone we were sleeping together…I didn't care what Isabella had on him. As far as I was concerned, they could both go to hell. But right now, I was believing in Matt. And if it wasn't about him? I didn't want my uncle to witness the rest of the students making fun of me because of him. Or worse…making fun of him.

Felix started laughing, but he stopped when he saw my face. "What? Are you serious? I gave it up. For you. Because you asked me to."

"I know. And I'm so so thankful. But I need you to go sell whatever you were selling to James right now."

"Brooklyn, what's going on?"

"Please."

"Brooklyn…"

"Please. Please, please, please. You have to. Right freaking now."

"I don't…"

I grabbed the front of his blazer. "Felix, please. I'll do whatever you want. Anything. Just go sell James drugs!"

"Would you lower your voice," he hissed.

I grabbed his hand and pulled him through the cafeteria doors. "We'll do it together. I'll sell them."

"Brooklyn, can we please just talk about this for a second?"

I pulled him toward the Untouchables' table. "There's no time to talk! James needs drugs and you have drugs…"

"I don't have any on me."

"It'll be an I owe you kinda thing then. Please, Felix. I'm in trouble. I need you to do this. Please." I was hysterical. I was pretty sure I lost it somewhere between my locker and the cafeteria doors.

"Okay. I'll handle it. But first I need to find Cupcake…" He started looking around the cafeteria.

"What? No. I swear to God, Felix, if you don't go right now I'm going to…murder you in your sleep."

He stared at me like I'd lost my mind. Which I most definitely had. "Are you high?" he asked me.

God, I was going to kill him. "No! And you don't have time to talk to Cupcake about cupcakes right now. It's now a life or death situation. So go sell James whatever he wants. All of it. Anything. And give him a nice discount while you're at it." I tried to shove him in the direction of the Untouchables' table, but Felix didn't budge.

"I said I'll handle it, Brooklyn. I just need to talk to Cupcake first…"

"Oh, there you are, Brooklyn!" Isabella shouted and waved me over to the Untouchables' table.

I froze.

Felix froze.

"Brooklyn Sanders," she continued when I didn't move. "Geez…Sanders…wait…" her voice trailed off. "God, that sounds so familiar. Why does that sound so familiar?"

The squeaky wheels of the trashcan my uncle was pushing stopped. "Miss Pruitt," he said. "The cafeteria is for eating. Let's lower your voice now."

"Oh." She looked at my uncle. Then at me. "Oh," she said a little louder.

There was a lump in my throat that wouldn't go away. It was like she set up the whole scene. Baiting my uncle to talk to her since he was the closest faculty member to her.

"Sanders," she said. "Jim Sanders." She stared at my uncle like she was in shock. "Brooklyn, darling…are you related to Janitor Jimbo?"

I cringed at the nickname that the students had given him. *Say something.* But my lips felt like cement. *Say anything.*

A few students nearby snickered.

"Oh, it all makes sense now," Isabella said. "I knew you couldn't be a scholarship student. Poor? Yes. Direly so," she said and glanced at my uncle. "But you're incredibly dumb too." She smiled sweetly at me as more students started laughing. "Just like your fat janitor uncle."

How dare you. But the words didn't come out. I looked at my uncle. He looked ashamed. But not of what Isabella was saying. He looked ashamed of himself. I felt tears start to trail down my cheeks. *Say something!*

"Miss Pruitt, go to the principal's office right now," my uncle said. But there was no authority in his voice. He sounded so defeated.

"Excuse me, janitor. The help doesn't talk to me," she said.

"Shut your troll face, Isabella!" Kennedy grabbed my hand. I wasn't sure when she had appeared by my side. But her having my back finally made it feel like my lips were unfreezing.

"Kennedy, I wouldn't butt into this," Isabella said. "There's low." She looked at Kennedy. "And then there's loooow." She turned to me. "Brooklyn is as dumb and poor as a janitor. Literally. You better cut ties with her now before you're both the laughingstock of the school." She flicked a green bean onto the floor at my uncle's feet. "Pick it up," she said to him. "It's your job."

My uncle started to lean down. And something inside me snapped. "His name is Jim, not Jimbo." I let go of Kennedy's hand and went over to the Untouchables' table. "And he's smarter than you'll ever be. He does those impossibly hard daily crossword puzzles in the papers every day in record time. And he knows how to fix everything. From my shoes you tried to ruin to anything that breaks down at this school. All he can't fix is your vile attitude." I leaned down and snatched up the green bean before my uncle could.

"He took me in when I didn't have anyone else," I said. "He's the best uncle in the whole world. He's kind and caring and so full of love. You'd be lucky to have someone like him in your life. Maybe if you did you wouldn't find it so necessary to put other people down to feel good about your hateful self. Oh yeah…and one more thing. My uncle is also a faculty member here. Not the help. Which means you have to listen to him. I believe he told you to go to the principal's office, Wizzy."

I still didn't know what that nickname Matt called her meant, but the look on her face was priceless.

She cleared her throat. "You're not making a good point when you're already doing janitorial work," she said, eyeing the green bean in my hand. "And no wonder Janitor Jimbo had to take you in. Your parents were probably embarrassed that they spawned a trash child."

I'm pretty sure I snapped again. Because the green bean in my hand somehow ended up smacking against Isabella's perfectly contoured cheek. She gasped.

"Before you tell the whole school about my personal life, you should get your facts straight. My parents didn't give me up. My mom died."

The little laughter left in the cafeteria died away with my words.

For some reason I glanced at Matt. He was studying the food on his plate like it was the Mona Lisa. *I tried to save your secret from coming out, Matt. At least look at me. Look at me!*

He didn't. And in that second, I lost faith in him. I believed what James had told me. I was just a conquest to joke about with his friends. I glanced at James. I thought there would be a smile on his face, but he didn't look happy at all. His Adam's apple rose and fell as he stared at me. Something about the way he was looking at me sent a shiver down my spine. This was his fault. He'd clearly told Isabella about my uncle. So why did I feel bad for him right now?

IVY SMOAK

Another teacher finally came running over. *Screw me.* It was Mr. Hill.

"Miss Sanders, principal's office. Now," Mr. Hill said with all the authority in the world.

Isabella laughed.

God, why did it have to be Mr. Hill on cafeteria duty today?

"Jason," my uncle said. "Miss Pruitt started it."

For the first time ever, I saw Mr. Hill's demon eyes soften. "Okay, Jim. You too then, Miss Pruitt."

"But…" Isabella started.

"Don't make me repeat myself," Mr. Hill said.

I had never seen him be mean to anyone but me.

"You should probably come too, Jim," Mr. Hill said. "To let the principal know what actually happened here."

He nodded.

All four of us started walking out of the cafeteria, but I grabbed my uncle's arm, holding him back for a second.

"Don't listen to anything Isabella said. She just hates me."

"I'm so sorry, kiddo. I never meant for it to come out like that." He shook his head. "I embarrassed you in front of all your classmates."

"What? No."

"You're literally crying because of what she just told everyone." He lightly tapped the bottom of my chin to cheer me up like I was a two-year-old that had fallen and scraped my knee. Something about the action made me appreciate him even more.

"I'm crying because I'm angry. Furious. I'd never be embarrassed of you. I love you." I stopped in the middle of the hall so I could hug him. I thought Mr. Hill would yell at me any second, but his words never came. "I meant everything I said back there."

I'm pretty sure I heard him sniffle.

"As your guardian I should probably reprimand you for throwing a green bean at another student's face. But as your uncle…nice aim, kiddo."

I laughed.

"Let's go sort this mess out."

I stayed tucked into his side as we walked the rest of the way to the principal's office. I really hoped that Isabella's Prada ass was about to get expelled.

CHAPTER 28

Friday

Every time I catered, my arms still ached. But I was definitely getting better at it. And fortunately for me, I was pretty sure that tonight's catered event had been exclusively for old people. There hadn't been a single person from our school in attendance.

"I'm so tired," Kennedy groaned as we made our way up the stairs of our apartment building.

"Me too. But at least it's a good arm work out."

"What?" she asked when we came to our floor. "No, I'm not talking about work. I'm talking about stupid Isabella. I can't believe she only got a week's detention too. She should have been expelled."

I didn't disagree with her. The fact that Isabella started it but got the same punishment as me wasn't really fair. But it wasn't like I was learning the whole "life isn't fair" thing for the first time. Honestly, I was surprised she even got in trouble. "I really don't care."

"You don't care? She made fun of you in front of the entire school. And Uncle Jim. She's such a bitch."

I shrugged. "But I put her in her place."

"Yeah, you kinda did. When you threw that green bean at her face I thought she was going to scream." She started laughing. "The expression on her face was priceless."

"I should have grabbed Matt's tray and dumped it on her perfectly coiffed hair."

"That would have been epic," Kennedy said with a laugh. "Maybe next time."

"I'm really hoping there won't be a next time." I stopped at my uncle's apartment door.

"Yeah, me too."

"Do you want to hang out? Uncle Jim and I are going to rent a movie and I'm going to make popcorn."

"Homemade? As in that garbage without any butter?"

"That healthy treat without any butter."

"Um…no thanks. I'm going to scour the internet for the perfect second-hand dress for homecoming. Want me to keep a look out for you too?"

"Yeah. Sure."

"Where's your enthusiasm? It's our first big dance together. We're going to have so much fun."

"I haven't even asked my uncle if I can go yet."

"Then ask him tonight. I'm sure he'll say yes. And while you're at it, freaking ask him if he's secretly in love with my mom, because the suspense is killing me."

"I'll see if I can squeeze that into the conversation," I said, even though I had no intention of doing that. I just wanted to watch a movie, relax, and forget about today.

"Great. I'll come by tomorrow and show you some dress options. Have a good night with my soon-to-be father."

I laughed. "Night, Kennedy."

My uncle was sitting at the kitchen table doing his crossword puzzle when I came in. He looked up. "Hey, kiddo. How was work?"

"Good. No spills," I said and gestured to my clean apron.

He smiled. "Ready for that movie?"

"Yeah. Just let me go change real quick." I hit the lights on in my bedroom and went straight for the closet. I pulled my shirt off as I rummaged around for a clean pair of pajamas.

"Brooklyn?"

I was pretty sure my heart had jumped into my throat or else I would have screamed bloody murder. I turned around. Matt was there. Right in the middle of the bed-room. With his eyes glued to my chest.

Jesus. I threw my arms in front of my bra. "Are you crazy? How long have you been here?"

"I don't know." He looked down at his watch. "An hour. Maybe two."

"My uncle is out there."

"I've been quiet."

I held up my hand. "You know what? It doesn't mat-ter. Because you're leaving. Now." I marched over to the window and pushed it open.

"Brooklyn…"

"Now," I said again and gestured to the fire escape. *I should have locked my freaking window.* But I never thought he'd show up again after today. After he had sat there silently, watching Isabella mock me in front of the whole school. He'd told her about us. He'd lied and said we slept together. He'd been making fun of me behind my back with his friends this whole time.

"I thought you might be upset with me," he said.

"You thought I might be upset with you?" I said it slowly, like I was trying to comprehend his ridiculous words. "I'm more than upset with you, Matt. You just sat there and let Isabella tear me and my uncle apart. You did nothing. Do you have any idea how that made me feel?" I didn't wait for a response. "I'm done with you. Get the hell out of my room."

"I'm sorry about what happened today. I told you I can't talk to you in front of Isabella. Today was awful, but…"

"There are no buts. I don't want you to be here. I don't want to talk. I don't even want to look at you. Just go."

He didn't move. Not an inch.

"Did you or did you not tell all your friends that we had sex?"

"What?" His eyebrows lowered. "No."

I shook my head. I didn't believe him. How could I? "Whatever game you're playing with me is over. I don't ever want to see you again. Now get the hell out of my room."

"Brooklyn, I have no idea what you're talking about." He finally moved, stepping toward me.

"James told me. Are you really going to stand there and deny that you told all your friends we were sleeping together? Including Isabella?"

"What? Yes, I'm going to deny it. Because it's not fucking true. And James never would have said that."

I folded my arms across my chest, trying to cover myself more. "So now you're calling me a liar? You trust your addict friend over me? I broke up with Felix…for *you*. I got Felix to stop selling to James…for *you*. I've been sneaking around behind everyone's backs…for *you*.

"James isn't an addict. He's just going through a hard time." He ran his fingers through his golden hair, momentarily distracting me.

I turned away from him and picked up the pajama top I'd been looking for earlier. "Now you're just lying to yourself. My uncle thinks I'm changing. We're about to watch a movie. If I take any longer he'll wonder what I'm doing. You have to go."

"I'm not going anywhere until we talk about this. I'm sorry about lunch. I'm sorry if you heard some rumor that claimed I was telling people we had sex. I'm sorry I didn't step in to help. I'm so fucking sorry. I don't know what else I can say."

He was sorry? I hated when people said that to me after my mom died. Because it didn't make any sense. And in this case? It didn't make any sense either. Because there should have been a stronger word than sorry. I'd never accept his lame apology. He could shove his I'm sorry up his ass. "You're not sorry. You're defending James when the only reason Isabella knew anything about my personal life was because of him. He was blackmailing me, Matt. Your perfect friend isn't so perfect."

"I never said he was perfect. But blackmailing? Really? He's not Isabella."

God, I wanted to strangle him. "I saw Felix sell him something other than pot at that party last weekend. James said if I told anyone, he'd let everyone know my secret. And to think I actually tried to stop what happened at lunch today. Because I thought maybe, just maybe, the secret he knew was that you and I were together. And that if he said it in front of Isabella...whatever she had on you would come out too. I tried to fix it. I begged Felix to sell to him again. I'm glad Felix didn't get to him in time though. Because now I know exactly what kind of person you are."

"And what kind of person am I, Brooklyn?" His chest rose and fell as he said it, like he was barely holding on to all his pent up anger. But I didn't care how he felt.

"The kind of person I want nothing to do with."

He closed the distance between us. "We both know that isn't true."

"Go to hell." I shoved his chest. But as soon as my hand hit the fabric of his shirt, I found myself grabbing hold of it with my fist.

"Make me."

His lips crashed against mine. Or maybe mine crashed against his. I had no idea. All I knew was that I was furious at him. And somehow this made it better. Or worse. I was pretty sure I had lost my mind.

He groaned into my mouth. That sound that I found so addicting. That sound that made me want to forget all reason.

But I didn't forget this time. I pulled back. "Stop." I took a step back from him, trying to get his stupid cinnamon scent to stop swirling around my head. I quickly pulled on the same shirt I'd worn to work. I was pretty sure my face was bright red.

"I really am sorry, Brooklyn. If you say James black-mailed you, I believe you. I'll talk to him. I'll get him to leave you alone. You should have just told me."

And you should have stepped in today during lunch. I closed my eyes and took a deep breath. "Imagine on a scale of one to ten how today made me feel. Now multiply that by ten because every day that I wake up it's hard to breathe. I'm barely holding on. I didn't just lose my mom, I lost my best friend. I lost my home. I lost everything." I wiped the tears from my eyes, angry at myself that they were even there. I wanted to open my eyes to look at him, but I couldn't. I was worried that if I looked into his eyes I wouldn't have the courage to keep going. "I'm finally put-ting myself back together. Mostly because of my uncle's generosity." I tried to even my voice. "Maybe if Isabella had just been making fun of me, I could forgive you for doing nothing. But she made fun of my uncle. You could have defended him. He has nothing to do with whatever Isabella has on you. You let her make fun of a bystander. I didn't sign up for that. And I will never forgive you."

"I didn't know Mr. Sanders was your uncle."

I finally opened my eyes. It was refreshing that he hadn't called him Janitor Jimbo. But the fact that he had nothing more to say sealed the deal. "Yeah, well you do now. So go ahead. Call him Janitor Jimbo behind my back. Go tell all your friends that you and I are fucking. But if you ever show up at my window again…I'll…I'll…push you off the fire escape."

He smiled. "I know you don't mean that."

"I was falling for you, Matt. And I'm too tired to fall anymore. I've already hit rock bottom once this year. And

I don't want to hit it again. I can't hit it again. Because I won't be able to keep going this time." Matt's jacket was still lying on the chair by my bed. I walked over and lifted it up. "So take your varsity jacket and give it to someone you're not embarrassed to talk to at school." I shoved it into his chest.

"I'm not embarrassed of you."

"Really? I needed you to speak up today. Not on my behalf. On my uncle's. You're a fucking coward, Matt. I thought I could rely on you." I shook my head. "Today you found out that I'm the janitor's niece. And like the rest of the school, you said nothing. But I heard you loud and clear. You can let yourself out." I left Matt alone in my room.

"You forgot to change," my uncle said with a laugh.

"I changed my mind. I'm happy exactly the way I am." I plopped down on the couch beside him. "Now, what movie are we going to watch?"

He lifted up the remote as I settled under a fuzzy blanket. He turned on Wedding Crashers, probably because we'd watched it last week and we'd both laughed so hard. I knew he was trying to distract me from my crappy day. But I couldn't focus on Vince Vaughn and Owen Wilson's hilarity tonight.

There was a knock on the door.

"Now who could that be?" My uncle yawned and stood up. "Keep watching, kiddo. I'll be right back." He patted the top of my head.

The movie wasn't funny anymore. It was more about love than I even realized the first time I'd seen it. And I wasn't in the mood to watch their love stories unfold when

I'd just set mine on fire and threatened to push it down the fire escape.

"Mr. Sanders, my name is Matthew Caldwell. We talked on the phone earlier this week. I'm the one your niece is doing that school project with."

Fucking Matt. He was like the plague. Following me around. Hiding in dark corners. Making me feel like my heart was dying. I'd told him to leave. Not show up at my front door. I paused the movie. But I didn't know whether to run to the front door and make him leave or just hide out in here.

"Matthew, it's a little late," my uncle said. "I think it would be better if you came back tomorrow. Or maybe some other time when you're not sporting a black eye."

I breathed a sigh of relief. My uncle would get rid of him for good.

"I know it's late. And I know Brooklyn is grounded," Matt said. "But I really like her. And I was hoping to get your permission to take her to homecoming."

What the hell?

"Does she want to go with you?" my uncle asked.

Go, Uncle Jim! Kick him out!

"I really hope so. But I messed up today. The way Isabella acted at lunch…I should have said something. I should have stepped in. And I'm sorry. I'm not just here to ask you for permission to take Brooklyn to homecoming. I'm here to apologize to you too, Mr. Sanders."

There was an awkward stretch of silence. I was clutching the remote so hard in my hand that my knuckles were turning white.

"You have nothing to apologize for, Matthew. It was my fault for wanting to keep it a secret in the first place. I was just trying to protect her. You can see how much good that did me."

Apparently my uncle was a lot better at forgiveness than I was.

He cleared his throat. "But Brooklyn's been through a lot. And I think she'd appreciate an apology too. Why don't you come in?"

Traitor! But even as I thought the word, my heart softened. Or maybe it was because Matt appeared in the living room staring at me like he truly was sorry. Sorrier than he had been in my room. I just stared at him.

"Brooklyn, I'm sorry about today," Matt said. "When Isabella started talking about you and your uncle I should have said something. And I promise if she or anyone else at school is ever mean to you again, I'll be there. I'll have your back. You can rely on me."

He couldn't promise that. What about the blackmail? I kept my lips pressed together. I couldn't mention any of that in front of my uncle. It felt like Matt cornered me into forgiveness. He was as asshole-ish as ever.

My uncle cleared his throat, saving me. "I'm going to give you two a minute. I wanted to stop by and talk to Mrs. Alcaraz anyway. I'll be back."

I waited for the front door to close before I stood up. "You shouldn't make a promise you can't keep," I said. "And homecoming? Seriously? That doesn't exactly keep us a secret."

"But I believe you. If I'd had any idea that James was blackmailing you…screw him. And screw Isabella. I'm done. They deserve each other."

"Is that whose Isabella's secret would hurt? James?"

"I'll tell you everything as soon as I talk to both Isabella and James. What he did to you…I don't care what excuse he gives. But I owe him this. He's one of my oldest friends. Hell, he's one of my only friends. Or at least, he *was* one of my oldest friends."

I nodded. I didn't fault him for wanting to talk to James first. He was loyal to the people he loved. I understood that. I just hoped James didn't lie to him about what happened. It was my word against his. And I didn't have sixteen years of friendship with Matt on my side.

"Everyone will know that we're together by Monday. I promise. So what do you say? Come to homecoming with me?"

I'd already said yes to Felix. But just as friends. If Matt could figure out a way to get out from beneath Isabella's thumb, I could figure out a way to break the news to Felix. "Okay."

Matt smiled. "And no more threatening to push me down the fire escape?"

I laughed as he pulled me into his arms.

"I'm falling for you too," he whispered as he held me tight.

"I said I *was* falling for you. As in…past tense." I was smiling so hard that my cheeks actually hurt.

He laughed. "Maybe you can just pick up where you left off then?"

I already had. Right when he apologized to my uncle. "Yeah. I think I can manage that."

When my uncle came back, we all sat down on the couch to watch the movie together, me between the two of them. Matt laughed at the movie in all the same places that my uncle and I did. And the longer the night went on, the more normal it felt for Matt to be there with us. Matt didn't even make fun of the non-buttery popcorn I made. Although I'm pretty sure he did make a weird face after his first bite. I gave him credit for continuing to eat it though.

He smiled down at me as he stole some of my fuzzy blanket for himself.

I could really get used to this.

CHAPTER 29

Monday

Kennedy and I sat on the front steps of the school as I filled her in on everything about Matt. The good, the bad, the in-between. All of it. I would have told her over the weekend, but I didn't want to jinx it. Matt would be walking up these steps any minute now. The time for jinxing had passed.

Once I started talking, it was like I couldn't stop. I was done with secrets and lies. It kind of felt like a storm cloud had been following me around this school ever since I'd stepped foot inside and learned about the Untouchables. But it was sunny today. A perfect autumn day. The kind of day where my mom and I would rake leaves and jump in the piles.

"So you're definitely not related to him?" Kennedy asked.

"I think my uncle would have said something if we were. Matt asked his permission to take me to homecoming. I can't think of a much better segue to make Uncle Jim tell us."

Kennedy laughed. "Right. Something like…you have my permission," she said in a low voice. "But only as friends. Because she's your sister."

I started laughing halfway through her impersonation of Uncle Jim. "That was terrible."

"Almost as terrible as the segue." She pulled her camera out of her bag and snapped a picture of me.

"What was that for?"

"To commemorate the day you finally admitted that you're desperately, madly, head over heels in love with Matthew Caldwell."

"I never said I was in love with him." The words lacked conviction as they left my mouth.

She shrugged. "The picture says it all. And I'd like to take a moment to also remember that I called all this weeks ago." She turned the camera around, made the sassiest face ever, and snapped a picture.

"I could just take a picture for you." I held out my hand.

"You wouldn't properly capture the 'I knew it all along' look." Her smile faltered. "Speaking of which…how are you going to break the news to Felix?"

"I don't know yet." I told him I didn't want to date anyone. I thought I'd have more time before all this came out. "I'm hoping we can still be friends."

She shook her head. "Boys and girls are never really just friends, Brooklyn. That's high school 101. The only reason Felix agreed to be your friend last week was because he knew he still had a chance to make it more."

"I don't think that's true," I said.

"Trust me. It's true." She kicked a leaf off the step in front of her. "You could have told me all this, you know. I would have kept your secret."

"I know. Honestly, I think I was just trying to lie to myself. I didn't want to fall for him. What if Isabella's right? What if I'll never fit into this world?"

"Screw Isabella. You do fit. Matt chose you out of all the girls in this school, and they all come from the right zip code. Plus, you'll fit in better than ever now that you have that pretty thing on your arm."

I almost looked down at my arm, but then realized she was referring to Matt. "Oh, yes," I said with a laugh. "He'll be quite the accessory."

"I know, right? Do you think he'll surprise you for homecoming by buying you something other than a second-hand dress?"

"I think that only happens in movies. I'm fine buying my own dress."

"If you haven't noticed…you dating one of the Untouchables is just like a movie. Ah! Here he is!" She lightly slapped my arm and then lifted her camera. "I also want to capture his face when he finally gets to love you in the light of day."

I didn't even bother to hide my smile as Matt stepped out of the car. Followed by Mason, Rob, and James. I was pretty sure my heart stopped beating as they started to climb the steps. This was it. Kennedy was right. Suddenly my life really did feel like a movie. Playing in slow motion.

I stood up and waited for Matt to turn my way.

Kennedy snapped the picture to capture Matt's expression.

But Matt didn't turn my way. Had he not seen me? "Matt," I said. He still didn't turn my way. Maybe he hadn't heard me either. "Matt," I said a little louder.

He passed by me and disappeared into Empire High.

Kennedy stood up and grabbed my hand. "It's okay. He probably just didn't see you."

"Or hear me?"

"Let's just meet him at his locker," Kennedy said. "I'm sure everything's fine."

I released the breath I didn't know I'd been holding. Kennedy was right. This was just a misunderstanding. Matt promised me. He'd promised.

"I wouldn't do that if I were you," Isabella said. Her gaze trailed from my beat-up shoes to my hair and she rolled her eyes like the sight of me disgusted her. "It seems to me like he's ignoring you for a reason." Her minions standing behind her laughed.

"Shove off, Isabella," Kennedy said. "Don't you have detention to go to or something?"

"Lame comeback. Detention is after school. Not that I'd really know…seeing as it's not something I'd ever attend. My father called and got that silly punishment thrown out the window. He's one of the school's biggest donors. The principal even apologized," she said with a laugh. "I'm untouchable. Just like the Caldwells and Hunters. And just to make myself clear…I mean untouchable to the two of you." She smiled her asinine sweet smile.

"Oh really?" Kennedy said. "Because Matt and Brooklyn are dating."

"Dating?" Isabella laughed. "Did you not see…" she pointed to the school doors. "You didn't…" her voice trailed off and she put her hand over her mouth pretending to be shocked. "Oh no. Darling," she said as she stared at me. "That was Matt's way of telling you that you two will literally. Never. Happen. Not in your wildest, poor girl fantasies. For goodness sakes, you live with a janitor."

I opened my mouth to talk, but I didn't have a witty comeback. And I couldn't stand up for Matt. He'd walked right by me. Without a glance.

"Close your mouth," sneered Isabella. "You look like a fish."

Her friends snickered behind her.

"Well, I should be going. I don't want to be late for class. Not that I could get detention or anything." She walked away laughing. The sound of her heels clicking up the stairs sent a chill down my spine.

I wasn't sure how long I stood there before Kennedy pulled me toward the doors. "Take a deep breath," she said as we stopped by my locker. "We'll figure out what's going on. Let's hatch a plan in English, okay?"

I was barely paying attention. I'd opened my backpack to remove the books I didn't need, but Matt's jacket was staring back at me. All weekend I'd been picturing how this morning would go. After we walked through the halls hand in hand, I'd pull his jacket on as he kissed me good-bye at the door to my first class. Now my dream had been lit on fire and thrown into the dumpster. "Yeah, that's fine," I said.

"I'm sure Matt has a good explanation," Kennedy said before hurrying off to class.

He probably did. He always did. But I was done hearing them. I slammed my locker shut. Part of me wanted to walk back out the front doors. But unlike Isabella, I could get more detention. I walked into my first period class, my backpack feeling impossibly heavy with Matt's jacket in it.

UNTOUCHABLES

***

I'd hung out in the nurse's office for the past two hours, pretending to have cramps. Apparently girls hung out in her office all the time for this reason. Kennedy had given me the tip when we'd failed to come up with any possible excuse for Matt during English class. I couldn't focus today anyway, so lying in bed in the nurse's office seemed like the only viable option. Besides, something was definitely wrong with my body. I was pretty sure I was having a heart attack. Although the nurse had quickly ruled that out as she handed me a Midol and a glass of water.

My period wasn't until next week. But I took the Midol anyway, hoping it would somehow help the pain in my chest. Wasn't that what people did at this school anyway? Took things they didn't need? Like James taking whatever drugs he was on. And Matt taking my heart. The medicine didn't help with that.

I wanted to hide out in here for the rest of the day. But when it was time for my entrepreneurial studies class, I knew it would be better to get it over with. Besides, I was used to Matt ignoring me in school. He'd been doing it all year. The perfect actor playing his role flawlessly. I just wasn't sure how I'd been the one who ended up getting played.

The nurse smiled at me as I left her office. Like she was proud of me for braving the world with cramps. I wished that was my only problem.

I sat down in class and pulled out my notebook. The worst part about all this was that we still had our stupid project. I'd still have to work with him.

"Brooklyn," Matt said as he sat down in front of me in class.

I didn't look up.

"James didn't know about your mom. He feels awful about what happened."

"Good. He should." I kept my eyes on my notebook.

"He swore that he's going to apologize to you. I made sure of that."

"Great. And what about you?" I finally looked up. "Are you going to apologize to me about this morning?"

"That's what I'm trying to explain."

"Okay." I folded my arms across my chest. "Well, you're doing a great job." I said it sarcastically, but for some reason he smiled. It was true, I may have loved his smile yesterday. But today I hated it. He looked stupid. No one's teeth should be so straight and white. He looked like a photoshopped magazine cover. Fake.

Students around us started talking louder. They were probably making fun of me. But I drowned them out, waiting for the asshole in front of me to explain to me why on earth I should trust him yet again.

"James was a mess on Saturday when I went to talk to him," Matt said. "He confessed about the blackmailing. And he really does feel bad."

"So James told you the truth…which means we can't be together? Cool. Class is about to start, you should probably turn around."

"Brooklyn, I'm trying to explain…"

"Oh, no. I get it. You were willing to throw your friendship with James away when you thought he hurt me on purpose. But now he's sorry. So I'm just collateral damage."

"That's not…"

"It doesn't matter if James is sorry now. He still did it. He had information on me that he thought would humiliate me. But the joke was on him because it didn't." I leaned forward. "I don't care about what James did. I care about why you lied to me. Did you even talk to Isabella?"

"Yes. But I didn't want to leave James out to dry after I saw him. I couldn't do it. But I'll find a way. Before homecoming. I promise."

I shook my head. I was tired of believing in him.

"Brooklyn…" Matt reached out and grabbed my hand. In front of the whole class. "You're asking me to hurt one of my best friends. I can't do it. Please, I just need more time to figure out another way. I want to be with you. Just not like this."

"Hey, Sanders," Rob said. "Geez, what the hell is going on out there?"

I finally looked toward the other students. They were standing by the window, staring out at the city street. All I could see were red and blue lights flashing. I quickly turned away. Matt's hand was still on top of mine. I was vaguely aware of the fact that he'd only touched me because no one was paying attention to us.

"Brooklyn? Are you okay?" Matt asked.

I felt like I couldn't breathe. It could have been a police car or a fire truck. But all I could think about when I saw those lights was an ambulance. Like the one I had to call when I found my mom unconscious on the kitchen floor. The one I'd rode in with her to the hospital during her last stay there.

"Hey. Look at me." Matt reached out his other hand and touched the side of my face. "What's wrong?"

The last time an ambulance had pulled up, it was the beginning of the end. I knew that wasn't what was happening here. But I felt frozen. Like I was stuck in the past. I could see it all so clearly. I could feel that same terrible fear that had gripped my heart. I had thought she was already dead. I couldn't find her pulse.

Mr. Hill cleared his throat. "Class has started. Everyone take their seats. Now."

Matt didn't move. Even though our classmates started to come back from the window, his hand stayed on my cheek. Everyone could see us together. "It's okay," he said. "You're okay."

I would have nodded, but I was afraid his hand would fall. I didn't want him to move. Not because he was finally showing that he cared for me in front of everyone. But because his hand was warm. My mom's had been so cold.

Mr. Hill cleared his throat again. I was positive he was about to yell at me, even though Matt was the one turned around. But when he said my name, it sounded too loud. Too distant.

I looked up and Mr. Hill was staring at the speaker system.

"Brooklyn Sanders." My name came over the loudspeaker again. "Brooklyn Sanders, please come to the principal's office immediately." The voice sounded frantic.

I was scared to breathe. I was scared that my past was repeating. What if the voice on the loudspeaker sounded frantic for a reason? What if the ambulance was here for my uncle? But I was imagining it. I had to be imagining it. It was just a nightmare.

"Brooklyn Sanders, please come to the principal's office immediately," the voice repeated.

I heard it again. Not the speaker. But that clock ticking down in my head. The same one that had been ticking down as my mom slipped away. The same one I'd heard my whole life. Like I'd always been running out of time. But it should have stopped. My mom was already gone. Why hadn't it stopped?

"Brooklyn." Matt's voice broke through my thoughts. The only thing that sounded real in the past minute. A pen dropped. The lights continued to flash outside.

"I'm going to take you to the principal's office, okay?" Matt stood up and reached for my hand.

The warmth from his touch faded from my face. And I'd never been so cold. I didn't take his hand. Because I was already on my feet, running toward the door. Tick tock. Tick tock. Tick tock.

"Miss Sanders, you need a hall pass!" Mr. Hill yelled as I sprinted out of the room.

Tick tock. Tick tock. Tick tock.

I knew this fear. I knew this pain. But for the first time in my life, it wasn't my mom I was terrified of losing. It was my uncle.

CHAPTER 30

Monday

I ran through the hallway, racing toward the principal's office. Part of me expected to find my uncle being carted away on a stretcher toward the ambulance. Or unconscious on the floor. Cold. Not breathing. Just like my mom.

But the hallways were empty. All the students and faculty members were in class. I picked up my pace. *They're just calling me in to talk about detention again. Maybe Isabella tried to blame something awful on me. Maybe James planted drugs in my locker for revenge. Maybe. Maybe. Maybe.*

But the clock in my head just kept ticking down. And I knew it in my gut. All those maybes weren't real. Something had happened to my uncle. *Please don't let me lose him too.* I yanked open the door to the front office.

The school receptionist looked up. Her mascara was smeared, like she'd hastily wiped away tears after calling me to the office.

"Am I in trouble?" I asked. *Please let me be in trouble. Let me be expelled. Anything but this.*

She shook her head. "There's been an incident with your uncle."

For a second we both just stared at each other. Wishing this wasn't happening. An incident could mean anything. Maybe he was getting fired. But she wouldn't be hiding tears if that was the case. She wouldn't be barely holding on.

No. No, no, no. "Where is he?" My voice cracked. "I need to see him. Is he here? Is he here?" I could feel myself growing more hysterical by the second, but she just stared at me. With pity. With all the pity in the world. *Stop looking at me like that. Stop.* I grabbed the corner of her desk, preventing my knees from buckling as the tears ran down my cheeks.

"Dear." The school receptionist put her hand on her chest. "The ambulance just left. His number was the only emergency contact in your file, so we called a car to come pick you up to take you the hospital with him. It'll be here any minute. Why don't you sit down and wait."

I couldn't move. "What happened?"

"He started coughing up blood." She shook her head. "I don't know. He couldn't breathe."

"But he's okay, right? He's going to be okay? The ambulance got here in time?"

She wiped beneath her eyes, smudging more of her mascara. "Mercy Hospital has the best doctors in the city."

That wasn't an answer. My body wanted so badly to crumble to the floor. But I couldn't sit and wait like she'd asked. There wasn't enough time. There was never enough time. And I wasn't ready to run out of it.

Mercy Hospital was only a few blocks away. So I started running. Hoping I wasn't too late. But I was never the one with hope. That had been my mom.

***

I was somehow still standing after running to the hospital and bypassing the slow nurse in the emergency room who didn't realize that I was in an emergency. But whatever energy I had left dissipated as soon as I walked into my uncle's hospital room.

Some kind of mask was over his face and tubes were attached to his arms. His breathing sounded labored despite the equipment. He looked so pale. I swallowed hard.

"Uncle Jim?" I said softly. "I'm here."

The only response I got was a labored breath. His eyes were closed. The nurse said he was resting. But I wasn't sure why doctors weren't swarming around trying to figure out what was going on. The school receptionist said he couldn't breathe. That he'd coughed up blood. I saw a trickle, dried and black, on the corner of his mouth.

I pulled a chair closer to his bed and sat down. "Uncle Jim?" I slipped my hand into his and tried not to cringe at how cold his skin was. "Wake up, okay? I need you."

As the minutes ticked by, I felt calmer. I was used to sitting in hospital rooms waiting. And waiting didn't necessarily mean bad. Waiting for a clean bill of health for my mom. Waiting for the results of the experimental treatment. Always waiting. If something was seriously wrong, there would be no waiting. He'd be in surgery. Or something.

Besides, my uncle was healthier than ever. He'd lost weight since I'd moved in with him. He was eating more vegetables than sweets. The only thing that had seemed off was his cough. And even that had gotten better. It was just a cold. He wasn't supposed to be lying here. Not for a cold.

"Wake up," I whispered. "Please wake up." I squeezed his hand.

"Are you Jim's niece?"

I turned around. There was a doctor standing there, staring at me. I hadn't heard him come in over all the beeping of the machines.

"Yes." I dropped my uncle's hand and stood up. "Is he okay? Why isn't he waking up?"

He looked down at his clipboard. "We gave him something to help him rest."

I breathed a sigh of relief. "So he'll wake up soon?"

"In a few hours. We've given him some morphine for the pain."

"When can I take him home?"

"Home?" He shook his head. "I'm afraid that's not possible."

"But it's just a cold. He needs rest. And hot soup." I laughed, but it sounded forced.

"It's not a cold." The doctor put the clipboard under his arm. "I just got off the phone with his oncologist. He fought it for years, but he stopped his treatment months ago. It wasn't working anymore."

"Fought what?" I didn't know what an oncologist was. But it sounded fancy and I'd learned that any fancy medical name usually meant something horrible. "He just has a bad cough. I tried to get him to see a doctor, but he insisted it was nothing. So…it's nothing. It's nothing, right?" I didn't even believe my own words.

"He has stage IV lung cancer. I'm so sorry. I figured you knew."

I felt like I couldn't breathe. "So get him back on his treatment."

"That's not how it works. It's too late."

"It's not too late. He's here right now. Give him the treatment."

The doctor shook his head. "Like I said, he's resting. I've given him morphine for the pain. It's the best we can do. I'd recommend that you start making arrangements."

"Arrangements for what?" My brain couldn't process his words. I refused to. This doctor was clearly a lunatic that had escaped from the crazy part of the hospital. Was there an asylum at Mercy? I couldn't remember.

"Funeral arrangements," the doctor said perfectly calmly, like his words weren't killing me.

I shook my head.

"Is there someone else we can call?" he asked. "Your parents? Or other relatives?"

I shook my head again and turned back to my uncle. And I heard his labored breathing. I saw the blood in the corner of his mouth. I thought about all the weight he'd lost. He wasn't healthy. He was sick. He was dying. "How long does he have?"

"A few days at the most. More likely a few hours. I'm really sorry."

I didn't hear the doctor leave. I couldn't hear anything over my uncle's labored breaths and my own sobs.

CHAPTER 31

Monday

"Hey, kiddo," my uncle said.

I lifted my head off the rough sheets of his hospital bed and looked up at him. He'd taken off the oxygen mask. His breaths sounded more even. I could have sworn we'd just fallen asleep during a movie. That we were back home on the couch. Except for the beeping. And the fact that he was lying in a hospital bed.

I didn't know how I had any more tears left. But they started to spill down my cheeks all over again. "Why didn't you tell me?"

"I stopped treatment a few months before your mom passed away. When you showed up…I didn't want to burden you with more bad news. I thought I had more time."

"But even before that. The doctor said you fought it for years. You never told us."

"You and your mom were going through enough."

"You shouldn't have had to do it alone." I wasn't sure what made me hurt more. The fact that he'd gone through all those treatments all by himself, or that he'd sacrificed the last few months of his life to take care of me.

He squeezed my hand.

"Isn't there something else we can try?" I asked. "My mom tried all these experimental treatments."

"I'm tired of fighting, kiddo. I'm so tired."

"Okay." I tried to stop crying. I tried to be strong for him. But I couldn't. I could feel myself breaking into a million tiny pieces. "It's okay."

He shook his head. "I get why your mom was able to hold on as long as she did. You're a good kid, Brooklyn. You're worth fighting for."

So was he. I would have given up anything for him to keep breathing. Anything so he wouldn't leave me too.

I held his hand until he took his last breath. Until his fingers turned cold. Until the nurses pulled me away.

CHAPTER 32

Wednesday

Mrs. Alcaraz took me in. She'd signed papers agreeing to be my guardian before my uncle passed away. Kennedy had thought those papers meant they were getting married. But my uncle wasn't planning a new beginning. He was planning for the end. An end that I was the only one who hadn't seen coming. Kennedy and her mom had both known my uncle was sick. But unlike her mom, Kennedy didn't know my uncle had stopped treatment. She thought he was getting better. She was as heartbroken over my uncle's loss as me. I heard her sniffling as she tried to fall asleep every night. And I didn't have it in my heart to be mad at either of them.

I glanced over at Kennedy in the bed that we shared in her small room. Her breathing had slowed. I slipped out of the bed, trying not to disturb her. I tiptoed out of her bedroom and to the front door. Mrs. Alcaraz snored. I could hear her through her bedroom door. I was already growing used to their sounds. Like I had been here all along. But I didn't want to forget about my uncle. I hadn't known him long, and I wasn't ready to let go. I wasn't sure I ever would be.

I quietly slipped out and walked down the hall to my uncle's apartment. Most everything inside was already packed up in boxes. There'd be a new tenant by the end of the month. But until then…coming back was my only solace. The apartment still smelled like him. And if I closed my eyes tight enough, I could still picture him at the kitchen table doing crossword puzzles.

I opened my eyes. The table was gone. The memory just as fleeting. I pushed open the door to my old bedroom. The floor was covered in flowers in various states of decay. Apparently Matt thought the right bouquet might make me happy. So there were roses, lilies, daisies, tulips, chrysanthemums, and more I didn't know the names of. My room was like a nursery. Except I wasn't watering them. The thought of scouring Kennedy's apartment for dozens of vases wasn't at the top of my mind. So the roses were dry. The daisies wilted.

But then there was Matt. Sitting on a sleeping bag in the middle of my room where my bed used to be. He'd come every night. Like clockwork. And he was brighter than any flower. He made my heart smile, even if I couldn't make my lips mimic the feeling.

There were never any words. Just flowers. I was comforted by the silence. He didn't offer a lame "I'm sorry." He offered to hold me as I fell asleep. And that was what I needed. Him coming each night spoke louder than any words.

I sat down next to him on the sleeping bag and let my head drop onto his shoulder. His arms gave me comfort. I didn't care if our relationship was a secret. I didn't care about any of it. All I knew was that I didn't feel so broken in his arms. They were strong enough to hold me together. And I needed that. I needed him.

But I eventually had to say something. We'd fought right before I found out about my uncle. I'd been so mad at him. But now it all seemed…so insignificant. "I don't want you to ruin your friendship with James," I said.

"I don't care about any of that. I just want you to stop crying."

I wiped away the tears on my cheeks. I hadn't even realized I was crying. "Then tell me something happy." I looked up at him.

"This is my favorite part of the day," he said.

"Mine too."

"Do you want to talk about it?"

I rested my head back on his shoulder. "No." My voice sounded so soft that for a second I thought he hadn't heard me.

"But the funeral's tomorrow. Do you know what you're going to say?"

"That I thought I lost the most important person in my life three months ago. That I never thought anyone could come close. But that losing my uncle hurt just as much as losing my mom. That he gave up living the last months of his life to take care of me. He was selfless and kind and funny and smart. And he loved me more than I deserved. Because I pestered him a lot. Mostly about my birth father. And after my uncle died, I knew I'd lost the hope of ever uncovering my birth father's identity. But it doesn't matter anymore. Because I just lost the only father figure I ever wanted. And I wished he'd let me in sooner. Because he was worth fighting for." I swallowed down the lump in my throat. "Those were his last words to me. That he understood why mom was able to hold on for so long. Because I was worth fighting for."

"I wish I'd gotten to know him better," Matt said. He kissed the side of my forehead. "It sounds like he was an amazing man."

"He was." The past tense made my eyes grow watery again. "You know one of the main reasons I pestered him about my dad so much?" I looked up at Matt. The bruise on his eye was mostly faded now. His chocolaty brown eyes stared back at me with so much warmth. "I was worried that we might be related."

Matt smiled. "You could have just asked. My parents have been happily married for over twenty years. They even make out in public. It's weird."

I laughed. I was pretty sure it was the first time I'd laughed in days.

Matt's smile grew. "You know." He lifted up my hand. "Maybe one day you'll be a Caldwell." His index finger and thumb ran down my ring finger. "When I make you my wife."

I laughed again.

"What, you don't believe me? All your firsts are mine, remember?" His lips lightly brushed against mine.

"You want to be my first husband? Hmm…"

"Your *only* husband," he said.

"You're ridiculous."

But he wasn't looking at me like he was kidding. "I want you to know that I'm not going anywhere, Brooklyn. You'll never lose me."

My eyes started tearing up again.

"No, don't cry again," he said with a laugh and pulled me into his arms.

But for the first time this week I wasn't crying because I was sad. I was crying because I was happy. I hadn't really lost everything. I still had Kennedy and Mrs. Alcaraz. And I had Matt. I knew I had him. He wouldn't lie about this. Not now. I closed my eyes and listened to his heartbeat. I willed it to keep beating for me. I willed his heart to be as strong as his arms. *You'll never lose me either.*

***

My hands gripped the podium so tightly my knuckles were turning white. I sniffed, trying to force my last lines out. I looked out at the pews that were filled with people from our school. Felix. Cupcake. I recognized so many faces. And they all came out because they loved and respected my uncle too.

Even Mr. Hill, who apparently was friends with my uncle. He had given a nice speech before mine. The first thing I'd thought when he got up to the podium was that I was surprised he wasn't making me read his eulogy for him. I was pretty sure I even smiled.

And then there were the Untouchables in the back row. All four of them lined up in their crisp black suits. Their parents all in attendance beside them. I stared at Mr. Caldwell and Mr. Hunter for just a moment. Their sons were the spitting images of them. And none of them looked like me. Not that it mattered. None of it mattered.

I locked eyes with Matt. It also didn't matter that Matt wasn't sitting in the front row with me. It didn't matter that his friends didn't know I was his. Because I knew it. And I knew he'd come tonight and help me through this. And he'd keep coming until I was whole again.

Matt gave me a nod, encouraging me.

I took a deep breath. "I just lost the only father figure I ever wanted," I said, my voice shaky. "I just wish he'd let me in sooner. Because my uncle was worth fighting for." I made my way toward my seat between Kennedy and Mrs. Alcaraz. They both hugged me as I sat down.

"Mi amor, that was a beautiful speech," said Mrs. Alcaraz. "Jim would have been proud." She kept her arm around my shoulders as the priest began speaking again.

After the priest said his final words, Mrs. Alcaraz and Kennedy stood at the front of the church with me as people paid their respects. Each hug and shake of the hand made me feel empty.

"I know you hate people saying they're sorry," Felix said. He leaned forward. "So instead…this really fucking sucks, Brooklyn."

I smiled at him. "Thanks for putting that so eloquently."

He smiled back. He gave me a quick hug and I felt a little less empty.

"Hope to see you at school again soon, newb."

I nodded even though I wasn't sure that I was allowed to go to Empire High now that my uncle was dead. I wasn't a scholarship student. And I didn't have a penny to my name.

When Matt got to the front of the line, I was surprised when he leaned down to hug me.

I put my hand on his chest. "What about Isabella?"

"She's not here."

She was probably one of the only students that wasn't.

"Your speech was beautiful. Just like you." He kissed my cheek. "I'll see you tonight, okay?"

I grabbed his hand before he walked away. "I actually need some air."

"Do you mind if I steal her for a second?" he asked Mrs. Alcaraz. Even though he snuck into my old room every night to see me, he'd already introduced himself to Kennedy's mom. He'd even been over for dinner. I was pretty sure he liked the empanadas more than my butter-less popcorn.

Mrs. Alcaraz nodded. "Sí, sí."

Matt smiled and led the way down the altar. We walked outside onto the front steps of the church, hand-in-hand.

I took in a huge gulp of air. One thing I'd learned after my mom's death was that I was still able to breathe, even on the days it felt like I couldn't. I took another deep breath. "I miss him," I said.

Matt squeezed my hand. "I know."

We stood like that, staring at the busy street for a moment. The cars honking and tires squeaking had some-how become normal. Soothing even.

"You're shaking," Matt said. "I left my suit jacket in-side. I'll go grab it for you."

I reluctantly let go of his hand and sat down on the steps. The cement was cold on my stockinged thighs, send-ing another shiver down my spine.

"Did you mean what you said in your speech?"

I looked up. A man in a navy suit was standing a few steps down from me, staring at me. He had salt and pepper hair and the distinguished look of all the other students' parents inside the church. But I had no idea why he was talking to me.

"Excuse me?" I asked.

He pulled off his suit jacket. "You're shivering." He draped it over my shoulders. His jacket didn't feel any warmer than the cold autumn air. I shivered again. "What did you say about my speech?" I asked.

He smiled. But it didn't quite reach his eyes. "That last bit. About you no longer caring about meeting your father."

I pressed my lips together. "Yes, I meant it. My uncle was a wonderful person."

The man nodded. "I'm sure. And you were living with him, is that correct?"

I looked over my shoulder, hoping Matt would return. This had to be the weirdest funeral conversation ever. Other than someone making dead baby jokes. "Um…yes."

"Interesting. No other living relatives at all?"

Was he trying to rub it in? "No."

He nodded. "Just that ethnic guardian, then?"

The way he said *ethnic* made the hairs on the back of my neck rise. "Her name is Mrs. Alcaraz." I stood up. "I'm sorry, I have to get back inside."

"You know, I've heard a lot about you, Brooklyn."

I stopped. There was only one reason why this man would have heard about me. I only had two friends at Empire High. And this definitely wasn't Kennedy's dead father. "Are you Felix's dad?" Unlike his son…this man was not funny. If anything, he was socially inept.

He smiled again. It still failed to reach his eyes. "You really don't know who I am?"

I slowly shook my head. Was I supposed to?

"Have you ever picked up a paper?" he asked with a laugh.

I just stared at him. Thinking about the paper made me think of crossword puzzles. Which made my eyes tear up.

"No bother. I'd like you to come with me. I'll fill you in on the car ride." He gestured to the town car behind him.

"What? No."

He reached for my hand, but I stepped back.

"Right now, Brooklyn."

"I'm not going anywhere with you."

"You have ten seconds to get into the car by will." He glanced down at his watch. "Or I'll have you put into the car." He snapped his fingers and two large men stepped out of his town car.

"What?"

"Seven seconds, Brooklyn," the man said.

"Mr. Pruitt?" Matt asked.

I turned around.

Matt was standing there with his suit jacket in his hand. "What are you doing here?"

Mr. Pruitt? I looked back at the man standing on the front steps of the church. I saw the resemblance now. The fake smile for starters. He was Isabella's dad.

"None of your business, Matthew," Mr. Pruitt said. "Run along." He swished his hand through the air like Matt was a child that should go play ball or something.

"Isabella isn't here," Matt said as he joined me by my side. "She wasn't invited."

"Oh, I'm well aware," Mr. Pruitt said. "Two seconds, Brooklyn."

I felt like my heart was about to beat out of my chest. What did Isabella's father want with me? My stomach twisted into knots.

"Two seconds for what?" Matt asked.

"Matthew, if you'll please excuse us, this is a family matter. I'm here to retrieve my daughter from the slums. Times up, Brooklyn."

The two large men lumbered toward me.

Matt stepped in front of me. "And I told you Isabella isn't here. This is a funeral. Show some respect."

"I'm not the one making a scene. You're doing that all by yourself. And clearly I'm talking about my other daughter. This one. The illegitimate one. Her." He did that thing with his hand again, this time directed at me.

No. I pushed his suit jacket off my shoulders as I took another step back. There was no way this man with the fake smile was my father. There was no way in hell I was related to Isabella. "I'm not going anywhere with you."

"You are. You're only sixteen. I'm your father. And therefore your legal guardian. Now get in the car."

"No!" Mrs. Alcaraz yelled as she came running down the steps of the church. "Stay away from her!"

One of the large men grabbed my arm. I tried to move, but he had me locked in place.

"I'll be waiting in the car," Mr. Pruitt said and turned around.

"Jim left her in my care," Mrs. Alcaraz said as she caught up with Mr. Pruitt. "You can't. Por favor."

"And you expect me to let *you* raise my daughter? You can't even speak proper English."

"But I signed the papers. You can't take her. You can't." She followed him up to his car. "I promised Jim. You can't!"

"Well your poor excuse for a lawyer reached out to me. I'm her only living relative. And I'm not signing a damn thing. She's my daughter. Not yours."

The man pulled me down the steps.

"Let go of me!" I tried to squirm out of his grip, but the man was too strong. I looked at Matt for help, but the other bodyguard was holding him back.

"Get your hands off of her!" Matt yelled. The bodyguard smashed his elbow into Matt's back, knocking him down onto the cement steps.

Matt. I tried to get free of the large man's grip again, but it was useless. He shoved me into the back seat of the town car.

"I won't let him get away with it, mi amor!" Mrs. Alcaraz yelled as they slammed the door behind me. She put her hands against the glass. "Nunca!"

"Welcome to the family," Mr. Pruitt said. "You're welcome, by the way. What a hellhole that was." He pulled out his cell phone and started scrolling through his emails like this was a normal day for him. Like he hadn't just turned my life upside down.

I felt like I was going to throw up on the expensive leather seats. I was a Pruitt? *A Pruitt?*

No.

Never.

Nunca.

WHAT'S NEXT?

Elite (Empire High Book 2) is now available!

But before you read it…find out what Matt was thinking when he first met Brooklyn!

To get your free copy of Matt's point-of-view, go to:

www.ivysmoak.com/ehu-pb

A NOTE FROM IVY

Welcome to Empire High! I had so much fun going back to high school in this book. I hope you were able to relate to first loves, first heartaches, new friends, and loss. In a lot of ways I'm still that 16-year-old girl, just wanting to be accepted by my peers. Even though this story is fictional, every book I write has some of my own experiences throughout the pages. The truth - I had my fair share of mean girls at my high school. Didn't we all? Another truth - my uncle was indeed the janitor at my high school.

I've always felt like I didn't quite fit. Until I started writing. I dedicated this book to my Facebook group, The Ivy Smoaksters, because you guys make me feel accepted. It doesn't matter if I wear pajamas all day while I'm writing or high heels when I'm quarantined and have nowhere to go. You've read my books so you understand my heart. You support me despite my quirks and I support you too. I feel like our group is one big family! And I'm so grateful that you're on this journey with me.

I hope you're ready to stay at Empire High for a while. Because Brooklyn's story is far from over!

P.S. Screw Isabella. Am I right?

Ivy Smoak
Wilmington, DE
www.ivysmoak.com

ABOUT THE AUTHOR

Ivy Smoak is the USA Today and Wall Street Journal best-selling author of *The Hunted Series*. Her books have sold over 3 million copies worldwide.

When she's not writing, you can find Ivy binge watching too many TV shows, taking long walks, playing outside, and generally refusing to act like an adult. She lives with her husband in Delaware.

Facebook: IvySmoakAuthor
Instagram: @IvySmoakAuthor
Goodreads: IvySmoak

Recommend *Untouchables* for your next book club!

Book club questions available at:
www.ivysmoak.com/bookclub

Printed in Great Britain
by Amazon

80863931R00195